WHAT I NEVER EXPECTED

JENNIFER ARCHER

Editor: Archer Editing & Writing Services
http://archereditingandwriting.com

Cover Designed by Sarah Hansen, Okay Creations

Available in eBook & Paperback

eBook ISBN: 978-1-7358902-1-0
Paperback ISBN: 978-1-7358902-2-7

http://www.jenniferarcher.com

ACCOLADES

"Archer captures the voices and vulnerabilities of her characters with precision." - Publisher's Weekly

"Archer writes distinctive characters…" - Kirkus Reviews

"…a poignant novel that explores the issues and emotions associated with family, adoption, and love. I found this book to be quite a page-turner, and I did not want to put it down. Archer has a talent for developing interesting, "real" characters, and I was fully engrossed in this novel, which is nicely peppered with humorous anecdotes that add a light-hearted note to the serious topics. I highly recommend this book to fans of women's fiction."- Curled Up With A Good Book (Review of *What I Left Behind* under its previous title *The Me I Used To Be*.)

"...a warm, witty and poignant exploration of some of the most realistically complex, and appealing, characters I've encountered in a long time. Jennifer Archer's prose is lovely without a hint of pretension, never getting in the way of Allyson's narration of her own story. Characters are vulnerable, screwed up and courageous all at the same time, and I loved them for it. Fans of both women's fiction and romance will find a lot to make them happy here." - Karen Templeton, Author of the *Wed In The West Series*. (Review of *What I Left Behind* under its previous title *The Me I Used To Be*.)

"I predicted stardom for Jennifer Archer after reading her first book, and I haven't changed my mind. Every emotion rang true, and even though the novel is told only through the eyes of Ally, the main character, Archer does such a masterful job of showing the emotions of the other characters, you don't realize you're not inside their heads, because you absolutely know what they're thinking and feeling. Highly recommended." - Patricia Kay, USA Today Bestselling Author. (Review of *What I Left Behind* under its previous title *The Me I Used To Be*.)

"...a poignant tale of one woman's road to self-discovery. What she learns along the way is so touchingly emotional you can't put the book down." -- Candace Havens, Bestselling Author of the *Ainsley McGregor Series*. (Review of *What I Left Behind* under its previous title *The Me I Used To Be*.)

*. . . a little bird of the air shall carry the voice, and
that which hath wings shall tell the matter.*

Ecclesiastes, Chapter 10, Verse 20

CHAPTER ONE

*L*ike most children of my generation, I grew up eating balanced meals from the basic food groups. But in addition to the selections on the food pyramid chart, my grandmother, June Hester, spoon-fed me heaping helpings of her homegrown Texas legends – a colorful conglomeration of Bible verses (though she wasn't particularly religious), superstitious folklore (though she wasn't a flake), and her own vivid imagination (which she had in abundance). I called her Nanny, and because everyone else in Juniper did, I called my granddaddy Chick.

"Did you know I heard you before I ever laid eyes on your tiny pink face, Maggie Sue?"

I was only six years old when Nanny first told me the tale of my birth. It was a warm summer evening, and my grandparents and I were sitting on the front porch of our farmhouse. Beyond the pot-holed graveled road, darkness slowly swallowed an orange sun that clung to the edge of our neighbor's field.

"You was ten miles down the way," Nanny continued. "Out by Red Homer's place. Your mama pulled your uncle Ned's old truck into the ditch alongside Red's land when the pain got too much for her."

"That can't be." I cozied up close to her padded body in the rocking chair. Her blouse smelled like baked bread, her hands like Jergen's lotion. *"Ten miles is far. How could you hear me?"*

Ribbons of smoke curled out of Chick's brown cigarette. *"You came out screeching like a banshee, little girl,"* he said with a raspy chuckle.

Nanny's work-callused palm brushed hair from my forehead. *"You cried out to me, Sugarbee. Called for me to save you. Guess you sensed your mama wouldn't make it."* She glanced away, her eyes glossy with tears that she quickly blinked back.

"If I'd been bigger, I would've saved Mama," I said, patting her leg.

"I know you would'a tried," answered Nanny with a sniff, smiling as she faced me again.

"So you heard me crying and went running to find me?"

"Not 'til the blackbird came."

"The blackbird?"

"He flew by you and Leanne in that car and swallowed your wails."

I frowned and sat straighter. The rocking chair creaked. *"But—"*

"Chick was off workin', and I was on my knees digging radishes in the garden when that bird landed on the barbed wire. He opened his beak and out come your squallin'."

Even at six, I didn't quite believe her tall tale. *"My voice came out of a bird?"* I asked.

"So she says," Chick muttered with a lift of one bushy brow. Flicking ash from the tip of his cigarette, he added, *"Try as I might, I can't get her to share what she drinks to bring on them delusions."*

Scowling at him, Nanny said, *"Don't listen to that old fool. What I'm sayin's true. Birds are angels on earth, Sugarbee."*

I thought about that while tracing a fingertip across the raised blue veins lining the top of her hand. June bugs buzzed around the yellow porch light, and summer scents hung heavy in the air: the sweet, ripe aroma of peaches in the crate by the door, freshly mowed grass, the

WHAT I NEVER EXPECTED

tang of Chick's burning tobacco. Out by the road, fireflies flickered.
"Did Uncle Ned hear, too?" I asked.

"Ned was off fightin' the war then," Nanny said of her only son,
my mother's older brother.

"Over in 'Nam," Chick added, a ragged edge to his voice.

"Like my daddy?"

They glanced at each other. Nanny nodded.

"How did you know it was me crying?" I asked.

"Kinfolk know kinfolk, Maggie." My hand slid up Nanny's arm,
and beneath my touch, goosebumps erupted. Her sharp blue eyes met
mine and looked deep. "I heard your mama in your cries, heard my
own self, too. And my mama before me."

Summer 2013

I'm sitting in my office at Ascelpius Hospital, where I've worked
as Director of Nursing for the past six months, talking about a
difficult case with Buddy Meeks, my Labor and Delivery nurse
manager. We're wrapping up the conversation, and he mentions
his busy day ahead. Studying a file as he starts for the door,
Buddy ticks off a list of patient names, muttering quietly to
himself.

When he says "the Enlow baby" I sit straighter, and my gaze
darts to the photo of my son on the corner of my desk – Eliot in
his graduation cap and gown. "The Enlow baby?" I repeat.

Pausing at the door, he turns to me. "Yes. Born yesterday."

"What's the mother's name?"

Buddy glances down at the file. "Elizabeth."

3

My heart drops. I ask about the baby's health, and he explains that the boy has a minor respiratory issue.

After Buddy leaves, I pull up the mother's information on my computer, certain of what I'll find. The baby's mother, Elizabeth Enlow, is Eliot's Liza – the girl he broke up with seven months ago.

Five minutes later, I'm stepping off the elevator onto the third floor and heading toward the newborn viewing window when a baby's cry stops me short. The sound is familiar – the pitch, the tone. I tell myself I'm being silly. Yesterday Eliot had a birthday; he turned twenty-one. I'm a little sentimental today when it comes to babies; that's the only reason this one's cries unsettle me so much. That and Nanny's stories from my childhood. I loved and respected my grandmother, but I recognized her stories for what they were – superstition.

A giggling little girl who looks to be about three years old runs past me. "Whoa," I say and gently catch her arm. I glance up to see a young man approaching.

He eyes me warily, then shifts to the girl and hisses, "Macy! Slow down. I told you not to run." I let go of her arm, and the girl darts just as quickly back toward him. He scoops her up as they meet alongside me.

"Your daughter?" I ask, and the child's face draws into a wary frown.

"Yes, ma'am. I know she's not old enough to be up here. She was anxious to see her new sister. I—"

"The hospital has rules."

"It won't happen again."

"I'd appreciate it." He nods then turns and walks with his daughter back toward the elevators, but the image of the girl's guarded look stays with me, and I regret my sternness. Before they reach the elevator, I call out, "What's her name?"

Pausing, the young father faces me. "What's that?"

I lower my focus to his little girl. "Your baby sister ... what's her name, Macy?"

Macy places her index finger into her mouth and lifts her shoulders toward her ears. "Reese," she murmurs.

I smile. "That's a pretty name. I bet she's pretty, too. Just like her big sister."

"Nope." Macy wrinkles her nose. "She's baldheaded."

Her father and I both laugh. "Congratulations," I say to him, and they resume their trek toward the elevators.

A baby in the nursery howls again, returning my thoughts to the reason I'm here. I feel like I'm walking through water as I move forward toward the viewing window. Though the hospital is cool, a flash of heat spreads through me. *Maybe Liza's baby isn't Eliot's,* I tell myself. That's a possibility. A slim one, maybe, but I grasp onto it.

On the other side of the window, Alice Parker tends to an infant in an incubator. Despite the fact that I'm at least a decade younger than she is, Alice and I have been close friends for years. We met at Heritage Hospital, our prior employer. She left and came over to Asclepius a year before I did.

My breath catches when Alice shifts position and I glimpse the baby's flailing clenched fists, his scrunched-up red face. His shock of dark hair reminds me of Eliot's; they have identical little clefts in the center of their chins. Alice steps back so that I'm able to read the name *Enlow* printed on the blue card attached to the incubator's side.

As she leaves the nursery and exits into the hallway, she spots me and starts over. I gesture toward the man and girl standing out of earshot at the bank of elevators down the way. "Everybody needs to be stricter about following regulations regarding kids up here."

She follows my gaze and mutters, "Sorry, they must've slipped by."

"Sure they did, Miss Bleeding Heart," I murmur, my eyes on Liza's baby. "And I tap danced all the way to the hospital this morning."

"That'll be the day. You drove the speed limit and looked both ways twice at every intersection." After a pause, Alice adds, "Are you living here now? You, of all people, should know it's not healthy to work so much."

"I'm headed home, but I wanted to check on the Enlow baby first. How is he?"

"He's finally breathing on his own," she says.

"I hear that. Nothing wrong with those lungs now." Alice chuckles, and I ask, "What about the mother?"

"She's good. So young, though. Nineteen, but she looks sixteen, at most. She's a college student. And itching to get out of here."

"Patience never was Liza's strong suit."

"You know her?"

"Eliot used to date her." I don't tell Alice he broke up with Liza right before Thanksgiving.

She touches my arm, and when I look at her, I see realization in her expression. "You okay?"

"I'm fine. Just a little worn out."

"She's placing him for adoption," Alice says quietly.

"Liza's giving him up?"

She nods as the infant wails again, and irrational or not, I feel another tug of familiarity and hear Nanny's voice in my head saying, *"You cried out to me, Sugarbee. Called me to save you."*

"What room is Liza in?" I ask.

"She's in 333."

We walk together toward the nursing station, and on the way, the open door at room 333 draws my gaze. Pausing beside it, I glance inside, see that Liza is asleep.

"You going in?" Alice asks.

"Not yet."

Movement outside the window at the far side of the room catches my eye, something black fluttering. Like confetti. Or wings. We continue on as the Enlow baby's cry echoes through my mind, the call of a little boy who looks just like my son.

CHAPTER TWO

*A*fter returning to my office, I pull up Liza's medical information on my computer again. Then I head back to her room, pausing at the open door to make sure she's awake now before going inside.

Her blonde hair is shorter than when I last saw her. For a moment, I flash back to the memory of a cold November evening when I came home from work and found her curled up next to Eliot on my living room sofa, the two of them watching a sitcom. Tonight, though, her eyes are on the window instead of the television.

I knock on the doorframe and poke my head into her room. "Liza?"

She turns toward me. "Maggie?" Her brows draw together as she sits up in bed.

"May I come in?"

A long pause, then, "I guess."

"How are you feeling?"

"Tired." She shrugs. "I'm okay."

She doesn't look "okay." Her posture is rigid; tension rolls off of her body in waves. I sit in the recliner next to her bed, uncertain how to bring up the reason she's here – the reason I am.

"Do you work here?" she asks, sounding flustered. "I thought you worked over at Heritage." She doesn't say that's the reason she chose to deliver here – because she'd hoped to avoid me – but I see that truth in her eyes.

"Asclepius recruited me six months ago," I explain.

"Oh." She tilts her head to one side. "Do you have better hours now?"

"I wish." Smiling, I add, "If anything, the hours are longer."

"Too bad." She shrugs. "Eliot used to say you worked all the time." Liza looks down at her hands, her face as pale as the pillowcase behind her. "How is he?"

"Eliot's great. He graduated in May. He'll start med school in the Fall."

"I guess you're happy about *that*."

Her comment sounds like an accusation, but I try not to feel too defensive. We weren't close during the months she and Eliot dated, but we weren't enemies, either. Sometimes, though, I worried she distracted Eliot, tugged him off course. Liza was selfish about his time; she didn't seem to care that he needed to study.

The chair squeaks as I shift my weight. "I'm really proud of him. Not many kids earn their bachelors degree in three years." When she doesn't respond, I ask, "How about you, Liza? Are you in school?"

"Not this summer. I'll go back next semester."

"You'll be a senior?"

"A junior."

We both look away at the same time, and I realize she's as

uncomfortable as I am; she knows I'm dancing around the topic I really want to discuss. "I saw your baby," I say.

Liza's gaze flicks back to me. Tears fill her eyes.

The conflicted emotions I sense in her are no surprise to me. It's been a long time since I was in her situation – twenty-one years to be exact – but I haven't forgotten how it felt.

"The nurse told me you're placing him for adoption," I tell her.

"Yes."

"Don't you think you should tell Eliot?" It occurs to me that maybe she *has* told him. Maybe *he* just hasn't told *me*. "*Have* you told him?" I ask.

Her eyes narrow. "Why would I? If you're thinking the baby is his, you're wrong."

Stunned, I say, "The two of you broke up . . . what? Seven months ago?"

"That's right. Eliot dumped me. You got your wish."

"My *wish*? Is that what you think? Honey. . ." I shake my head. "I didn't have anything to do with it. I don't even know what caused you two to split up."

Liza stares at me, silent for an awkward few seconds. "After he dumped me," she finally says, her words emerging in a rush, "I met someone else. Right away. We didn't last long, and now I can't find him. I tried. . . because of the baby, the adoption. You know."

"Liza. . ." I lean in, place my hand on her forearm where it rests across her waist, but she pulls back. Standing, I back away from the bed to give her some space. "The baby's only four weeks early. Which means you and Eliot were still together when you conceived."

"So now you know why Eliot broke up with me. I met the baby's father while we were still together."

I suppose Liza could've cheated on Eliot and that her infidelity ended their relationship – but I don't believe her. Not after seeing that little boy in the nursery. "I wish I had Eliot's baby photos with me," I tell her. "If we put one next to your son, you'd swear they were the same infant."

"The baby isn't Eliot's." Her tone is defiant, final. I wonder if she's convinced herself she's telling the truth.

Silence stretches between us in the sterile room. A room with no flowers. No cards. No balloons. Nothing to celebrate a new life. Nothing to bring Liza comfort or let her know someone cares. I wonder about her family, her friends. Did she hide the pregnancy from them as well? It wouldn't be the first time a girl got away with such a secret. Liza doesn't have the face or body of a new mother. Her cheeks are gaunt, her stomach almost flat beneath the tightly-drawn sheet.

Despite her attitude toward me and the fact that I'm sure she's lying, compassion fills me. "You can talk to me, Liza. I only want what's best for everyone, including you. Believe it or not, I understand what you're going through. I've been in your—"

"I don't need to talk. I'm fine."

Trying not to feel stung, I return my thoughts to the baby down the hallway. Eliot's son. My grandson. I almost wish that I didn't know any of this. Ignorance would be preferable to the decisions facing me now. With a sigh, I ask, "Does Eliot know you were pregnant?"

"This baby has nothing to do with him."

"He cared for you, Liza. I know he still does. He'll be here for you when I tell him—"

"Don't." Her chin lifts.

"Why don't you want him to know?"

"Because he'll think the same thing you do. I don't want to deal with that. I told him I never wanted to see him again, and I meant it."

"I can't just walk out of here and never mention this to Eliot."

"My reason for being here is nobody's business but mine." Liza's voice rises. "It's private. Aren't there rules or something?"

Before I can answer or try to calm Liza down, Alice steps into the room. Frowning, she asks, "Is everything okay in here?"

"Miss Enlow and I were just catching up. Sorry if we got too loud."

I turn away from the bed and start for the door. Alice follows, and as we step into the hallway, I say, "I'm worried about her numbers."

"Her – how do you know about her numbers, Maggie?"

I avert my eyes from her startled expression and poke my head back into Liza's room. "Goodnight, Liza. Get some rest. I'll drop by tomorrow before you're released to see how you're doing."

"My doctor will check on me," she snaps. "I don't need you to."

"Maggie," Alice hisses, hurrying to keep pace with me. "I hope Buddy or one of the other nurses consulted with you about that girl. They didn't, did they? You tapped into her file. Is that why you went back to your office before you saw her?" When I don't answer, she adds, "Please tell me you chose her at random to audit."

"I can't. That wouldn't be true." I reach the end of the hallway, turn, continue on without looking at her.

"If you can't justify having a reason to look other than a

personal one–" She draws a quick breath. "Maggie . . . if something were to come up . . . "

Pausing in front of the elevators, I face her. "I know all of that, Alice."

"It isn't like you to do something like this," she says, her expression grim.

"I know that, too." The elevator dings and the doors slide apart. I step on. "Goodnight. I'll see you tomorrow."

Alice stares at me with worried eyes as the doors slowly close.

On my way out of the building, a balloon bouquet in the lobby gift store's window catches my attention, and I go inside. Liza's bare room haunts me, reminds me of another hospital room twenty-one years ago when I was the girl in the bed, alone and afraid.

"Deliver these to room 333, please," I tell the clerk.

"What would you like me to put on the card?"

"I'll write it."

The girl gives me a pen and a folded piece of yellow stationary. Lifting the flap, I scrawl, *Liza, If you need anything, please call me. All the best, Maggie Mahoney.*

On the drive home, I think about deception. Secrets. How easily they can weave their way through a life. How tightly they're woven through mine. At first they're seductive with their promise of protection and freedom. It's so easy to grab onto them, believing they're the golden twine that will hold your life together.

If Liza would listen, I would tell her that secrets quickly lose their luster, that they're only frayed threads in disguise. If you grab hold, you never stop worrying . . . wondering when they'll snap and your world will unravel.

But I doubt Liza would pay attention to my warnings anymore than I did Nanny's a long time ago.

"Where've you been?" Nanny asked one warm spring evening when I was fourteen.

Clutching my schoolbooks in one hand, my shoes in the other, I walked barefoot across the yard toward the small vegetable garden at the back of the house where she pulled weeds. Dandelion fluff hovered in the muggy dusk air like languid insects. Crickets chirped, singing of the summer to come, the end of the school term, blessed freedom from stuffy classrooms and boring lectures.

"Speak up, Maggie." My grandmother squinted at me when I paused beside her. "Where've you been?"

"At the library, Nanny." The lie slipped off my tongue as smoothly as Kyle Graham's jeans had slipped off his narrow hips a couple of hours earlier. Since I wasn't used to lying to my grandmother, the ease of it surprised me.

"Studyin' for that final exam tomorrow like you told me you would?"

"Yes, Ma'am."

She glanced back at the garden, coaxed a dandelion root free of the ground, then looked at me again, tilting her head to one side. "That how you got that sunburned nose and those apples in your cheeks?"

My gaze fell to my dusty toes, and my chest almost burst with the swirl of dazzling secrets I held inside; they were mine, why should I have to share them? Beneath my t-shirt and denim skirt, my damp bra and panties clung to my skin. Even if I wanted to, how could I tell my grandmother the truth? That I had walked with Kyle to Juniper Lake after the three o'clock bell rang. That he'd tried to coax me to skinny-

dip with him and I'd almost given in. That I'd experienced my first French kiss while we floated neck-deep in the water, him stark naked, me in my underwear. That his hands brushed across places no one except Doctor Wilburn had ever touched since I was a baby.

Standing, Nanny dropped the dandelion clump to the ground. She lifted her hat, revealing her short silver hair. "Fibbin's like a drug, Maggie. Once you start, it's hard to stop. In the end, it'll only hurt you and the ones you love."

I toed a rock. I knew she was right. How many times had Daddy told me he would pick me up, take me to dinner or a movie, then never showed? How many hours had I wasted waiting for him, my pride bruised and aching? How often had I wished he'd let me chase away the ghosts that I saw in his eyes?

My father lied more often than he told the truth. Because of the lie he told my mother – that they would marry after he got back from the war – she died broken-hearted at the side of the road the day I was born. Then Daddy lost job after job due to his drinking. And he lost me.

A judge gave Nanny and Chick custody of me right after I was born. I don't think Daddy fought too hard to keep me. He was too busy dulling his memory of the war at Hank White's bar. Daddy had lost an eye in Vietnam, and Nanny explained that the scar went deeper than anyone could see, that it had thickened all the way to his heart. But I didn't understand what war could do to a person. I only understood what Daddy's absence did to me. Wasn't I worth his time? His love? Wasn't I good enough?

"I'm sorry, Nanny," I murmured. "I went to the lake after school. It was just too pretty outside to study." I told myself that's all she needed to know. The lie was a small one compared to my father's.

Nodding, she pulled off her gardening glove and touched my cheek. "Always be straight with your kinfolk, Maggie."

I hugged her, then tensed and stepped back quickly when her fingers settled upon the damp band of elastic beneath my shirt.

Nanny's eyes narrowed. "Somebody go with you to the lake, Maggie Sue?"

"No, Ma'am." If she found out about Kyle and me, I knew she'd make it hard for us to keep meeting. I didn't want to give up Kyle. When Kyle touched me, I knew I was worth being loved.

My grandmother stared at me a long time, then said, "If you don't watch out, life can get cluttered up with so many weeds you can't see the beauty in it anymore, just like this garden. Don't let trouble take root, Maggie."

I brush aside memories and push the button on the garage door opener. The door lifts, and I see Eliot's old green Jeep parked inside. After pulling in, I turn off the engine and stare at the door that leads into the house. Liza's deception about the baby not belonging to Eliot stirs guilt in me about the lie I've let him believe all his life. She's denying Eliot his right to know the truth, but didn't I do the same thing? I had my reasons, *good* reasons. But Liza probably believes her reasons are good ones, too.

I fill my cheeks with air, let it seep out slowly. *God . . . my job*; I don't trust that girl. What was it she asked me? *Aren't there rules or something?* Liza's not stupid. She's a very sharp young woman. When she and Eliot were dating, I'd often hear her debating politics with him or arguing a cause. Nineteen or not, I wouldn't be surprised if she's aware of HIPAA and her rights regarding confidentiality. And she obviously has old issues with me. If I tell Eliot about the baby, I have a feeling she'll make it her mission to get me busted.

Still, Eliot is my son. How can I walk away from *his* son – my grandchild – and never acknowledge the boy's existence? How would I live with *that* secret?

I grip the steering wheel. Eliot is a father. How can that be?

With another push of a button, the garage door behind me descends, and a humorless laugh slips past my lips. How can Eliot be a father? Stupid question. About a year ago, I heard a noise out here in the middle of the night and came to check on things. When I flipped on the light, I saw Eliot and Liza in his Jeep, all over each other. I stepped out of sight as they scrambled to separate, and after my shock subsided, I wondered if what I had witnessed was only sex, or if they loved each other. I know how easy it can be to confuse the two.

The next day, despite Eliot's embarrassment, I talked to him about the responsibilities that go along with a serious relationship at any age, and the possible repercussions of one at this stage of his life.

Now I wonder . . . *Did* he love her? Did she love him? Obviously not, or they would still be together, wouldn't they? Couples in love stick together through thick and thin.

Or is that only a fantasy? A fairy tale I've always thought other people lived, but one that was out of my reach?

I gather my purse and satchel from the passenger seat, climb out of the car, close the door, lean against it. My heart pounds so hard and fast I'm dizzy. Too many thoughts collide in my mind. What will happen to my grandson? How will Eliot take this news? And what if Liza turns me in?

I haven't been at Asclepius long, but my record there is as spotless as my prior work history. Constance Bening, the hospital's Chief Operating Officer, knows I work harder than I have to, that I'm dedicated. Constance has hinted she plans to recommend me as her replacement when she retires in a couple of years. She would back me up, wouldn't she?

My head hurts and my feet feel heavy as I start for the door. I take a deep breath and go inside the house.

CHAPTER THREE

*E*liot doesn't hear me come in. He sits on the sofa in front of the television, his back to me. I stand beneath the doorway between the kitchen and den watching him, and out of nowhere, the memory of his first day of school flashes through my mind . . . walking him to his classroom, his uncertain expression when he turned at the door to look at me one last time.

"You'll come back?"

"I'll be right here waiting for you at the end of the day, honey."

A nod of his head, a lift of his pudgy hand, then, "Later, Tonto."

"Goodbye, Kemosabe."

That morning was the first time he'd ever said goodbye to me in that way, as if we were characters from the Lone Ranger videos I'd bought for him at a yard sale over the summer. I knew it was Eliot's way of letting me know that he trusted me.

When I walk into the living room, Eliot glances up and says, "Hey." He motions toward the open Chinese food containers on the coffee table. "You hungry? There's plenty left."

"No, thanks. I grabbed a snack earlier."

A cat mews on the other side of the back door. Eliot says, "The stray's back."

"I hear that."

"I tossed her out of the yard when I got home," he says. "Guess she found a way back in."

"Maybe we should just call animal control to pick her up."

"She's not bothering anybody. And she doesn't look like she's starving."

I suspect Eliot's been feeding the cat. He's always loved animals, but I've been allergic since I was a kid, especially to cats. He had a hard time accepting that when he was little and wanted a pet. *Just give it a chance*, he'd plead. *If you get sick, we'll find it another home.*

Eliot begins to gather up the mess on the coffee table.

"Don't worry about that now," I insist. "Let's talk."

He leans back, and his brows tug together. "Okay." Lifting the television remote control from the arm of the sofa, he lowers the television's volume as I settle into the chair facing him. "What's up?" he asks.

He wears athletic shorts, a blue t-shirt. His basketball shoes sit on the floor beside him. Dried sweat mats his hair to his head. In so many ways, Eliot still looks like a kid. It wasn't so long ago that his biggest worry was how long he'd have to wear braces on his teeth.

"Did you go to the gym after work?" I ask, putting off our conversation about Liza.

No matter what Eliot decides to do with it, the information about her and the baby will affect him. He'll change, maybe only subtly, maybe drastically, but his life will shift in some way. And I'll be breaking a patient's confidence, as well as the law, which goes against everything I stand for personally and professionally. But as much as I love my career, I love Eliot more.

"Yeah," he answers. "I shot baskets with some of the guys. I whipped Russ's ass, too."

"Good. Russ is too cocky." I force a laugh. "He could use a good dressing-down every once in a while."

Eliot's smile is subtle, and for an instant, his resemblance to Paul startles me. I had intended to ease into the revelation about Liza, ask him first about his work at the medical clinic today, make other small talk. But my throat closes as I look into his eyes – Paul's eyes – and I wish more than anything I could forget what I know so he could proceed with his carefully-planned life without disruption. But I can't do that.

Why, Eliot? Until now, he's managed not to follow the family tradition I continued – that of making stupid choices. He's always been mature beyond his years, always considered consequences before he acts. Or so I'd thought. I raised Eliot to be smarter than my mother and me. Smarter than Nanny when she was young. Stronger than his father, than *my* father. I raised him to have Chick's sense of what it means to be a man, of right and wrong, of responsibility.

"Is something wrong?" Eliot asks, and I realize I've been staring at him.

I sit still, my hands clasped in my lap. "I saw Liza today."

"Where?"

"The hospital."

He bolts upright. "Is she sick?"

"No, she's fine. . . Liza had a baby, Eliot."

"*What?*"

"She had a boy." I stand and cross to the sofa, sink down beside him.

"Did you talk to her?"

"Briefly."

"What did she say?"

"She said he's not yours, but I don't believe her. The baby's hair . . . his features . . . he looks just like you."

Eliot turns away, and for several moments, we sit in silence. Then he leans forward, swipes his keys off the coffee table, and stands.

"Where are you going?"

"To see her."

"Wait." I push to my feet. "Let's talk about this."

"Liza's the one I need to talk to." He starts toward the kitchen, taking long strides.

Following, I say, "Let me take you."

At the door leading into the garage, he stops and glances back at me. "I need to go alone."

I walk over and grasp hold of his arm. "Liza told me not to tell you. She doesn't want to see you. Please, Eliot, consider her feelings before you say anything."

His eyes flash. "Like she's considering mine?"

He opens the door, but I don't let go of him. "Talk to me. Liza implied that she cheated on you and that's why you broke up with her."

Uttering a sound of disbelief, Eliot says, "She's lying. If she cheated, I never knew it. And you said the baby looks like me. I'm not stupid."

"But why would she deny you're the father?"

"I don't know. She was pissed at me when we split." Pulling his arm from my grasp, he turns toward the door again.

"She's really vulnerable right now, Eliot. Storming in there and making a scene isn't going to solve anything."

He looks over his shoulder at me. "Whose side are you on, Mom?"

"This isn't a battle. Liza just had a baby. She's confused and emotional. We all need to pull together and work through this, not fight with each other."

He blinks at me, then turns and walks out.

I stare at the closed door, hear his Jeep's engine rumble to life, listen to the sound of it until it disappears, until the only noise that remains is the thud of my heartbeat. Should I follow him? Catch him before he confronts Liza? Try to calm him down?

I reach for the doorknob then lower my hand. Eliot is a grown man now, a father, as hard as that is for me to accept. I can't make this any easier for him. There is no *easier*.

I sit in the kitchen until my heartbeat slows then go into the den and clear away the Chinese food. Curling up on the couch, I prepare for a long wait. Questions spin through my mind. Will Eliot offer to marry Liza? Or at least say he'll be there to help if she really wants to keep the child? He wouldn't want her to feel forced into giving up the baby if that's not what she wants. But she *should* give him up. Everything in me insists that's the best solution for everyone.

The irony of that hits me as I stand and walk over to the window. Pushing aside the drapes, I stare into the darkness outside. I kept Eliot, despite all the rational reasons that insisted I shouldn't have.

Eliot.

While growing up, he was so eager to please that he rarely rebelled or complained about anything. The only time we ever butted heads was during my brief marriage ten years ago – and Eliot was right about that; Stephen was a mistake.

After the marriage ended and Eliot entered his teenage years, we bypassed the problems I heard other parents complain about. There were no battles of will over bad grades or missed curfews, no wild parties with drinking or drugs. Unlike me, he waited until he was older to start taking a real interest in the opposite sex. Or at least before doing anything about it. Eliot was almost eighteen the first time he brought a girl home, and twenty before he met Liza. She was the first one he saw more than a couple of times. When it ended, he was distraught, but he wouldn't talk to me about it. Watching him hurt, I remembered so clearly how it felt to be young and brokenhearted.

———

"Mope all you want to today, Maggie," Nanny said, "but tomorrow I expect you to pick yourself up and move on. Sixteen's too young to be tied down to a boy, anyhow. Besides that, I want a new dress for Bill Brennart's funeral, and I'll need your help pickin' it out. I can't take you shoppin' in such a state."

I pushed green peas into my mashed potatoes with a fork. I didn't look up.

"Bill chose a fine time to croak. My billfold's flatter 'n a flitter." Nanny sighed. "If we're goin' into debt, we might as well do it up right. We'll buy you somethin', too. Maybe that new pair of sandals you've been eyein' over at the Shoe Fair would put the perk back into your step."

I shrugged. The shoes didn't matter so much anymore. All that mattered was the fact that Bobby Allan, my boyfriend of the past seven months, had called this morning and broken up with me. He didn't even say why.

"Where's Chick?" I asked, wanting to change the subject, blinking my swollen eyes so the tears I felt gathering again wouldn't fall.

"Lord, if I know." Nanny glanced at the wall clock. "He should'a been home half an hour ago. Ray Allan got a shipment in and hired him on to help unload it. We could sure use the extra money around here."

Ray Allan, Bobby's father, owned half the stores in Juniper, Texas. At the mention of his name, the tears spilled over, despite my blinking.

"Now, here," Nanny said, handing me a napkin to wipe my eyes. "Go ahead and cry. But, if you ask me, it's for the best. You were spendin' too much time with that boy and headed for trouble because of it."

I blew my nose. By "trouble" I knew that Nanny meant sex. I could have told her she was worrying too late. Bobby and I had reached that destination months ago. He was my first, and I didn't regret it one bit. I loved Bobby, even if he didn't love me anymore.

Nanny sliced into her pork chop. "You may as well learn now as later that there's only a few things you can count on in this world . . . the sun . . . birds—"

"Birds?" I interrupted with a huff.

"Birds go away, but they always come back. And when you're down they can lift you up with just the sound of their singin' . . ." Her voice took on a wistful tone. "And the sight of 'em up in the sky . . . flyin so free . . . birds can save you, Sugar."

The front door slammed in the next room.

Nanny craned her head that direction. "That you, Chick?"

"Who else would it be?" Chick yelled back.

Nanny and I exchanged a frown. "Come eat. Your supper's gettin' cold," she called out to him.

The stairs leading to the bedrooms on the second floor creaked.

Nanny pushed back her chair and stood, leaving me alone in the kitchen. Seconds later I heard her say, "What happened to your nose?"

"It's busted," Chick snapped.

"I see that. How'd it get that way?"

My grandfather's voice dropped so low that I couldn't hear his next words. I got up and went into the entry hall. He stood on the stairway, pressing a bloodstained rag to his face. I gasped, and Chick stopped murmuring and shifted to look at me.

Nanny turned, her eyes ablaze with blue fire. "Go to your room, Maggie Sue."

"But—"

"I said go to your room."

Chick nodded. "Do what your grammaw says, little girl."

I pushed past them both and climbed the stairs. At the top, I turned right. But when I reached my room, I didn't go inside. I opened the door, closed it, crept back to the head of the stairs, staying just out of sight, straining to hear their conversation.

"You can't march in here, tell me Ray Allan called Maggie a slut, then expect me to leave it at that," Nanny hissed.

"You don't want to hear what else he said, June. All you need to know is that I knocked the hot air outta that foul-mouthed s.o.b."

"You hit him?"

"Damn right I did."

"Then why are you the one whose nose is bleedin'?"

"He hit me back!"

"Shhh! Settle down. Now, what's this all about?"

"Ray must'a forgot I was workin' in the back room when his boy came in."

"You mean Bobby?"

"Does he have another boy I don't know about, June?"

"Don't use that tone with me, Chick Hester."

The stair creaked again. Chick cursed quietly. "Ray asked the kid if he'd done what he told him to do, and Bobby said, yes, he'd ended things with Maggie."

My stomach turned over. I pressed my back against the wall. Bobby broke up with me because of his dad? He was almost eighteen. He could've stood up to his father if he'd wanted to, if he'd really loved me like he said he did in the beginning. He had to love me. When I was with Bobby, I felt beautiful, important, like he'd rather be with me than anywhere else in the world.

Outrage trembled in my grandfather's voice. "Then Ray said if he ever caught Bobby and that little slut with their pants down again, he'd have hell to pay."

"Maggie . . ." Nanny whispered.

The disappointment and worry I heard in her utterance of my name slapped me with shame. Last night, parked in Bobby's car at the lake beside the shack where the Allans kept their fishing boat, we'd heard a noise and fumbled back into our clothes. His dad, I now realized. That explained Bobby's sudden change of heart toward me.

"Ray said Shep's a yellow-bellied drunk," Chick continued. "Then he dragged the rest of our family through the dirt."

Chick hesitated, and Nanny murmured, "Go on."

"He called Ned a ravin' loony and . . ." My grandfather cleared his throat. "He said Maggie was her mother made over . . . that the apple doesn't fall far from the tree. That if Leanne had lived, she more'n'likely never would've amounted to nothin' more than a floor sweeper in one of his stores."

"Leanne worked hard for that man! How dare him put her down." Nanny's voice rose an octave. "And it's that damn war that made Ned how he is. Our boy's a hero. Ray Allan ought to be thankin' him, not callin' him names."

"That's what I told him before I busted him." On a roll, Chick

added, "But before I showed him what's what, I heard him tell Bobby he didn't want him gettin' a girl like Maggie pregnant and be stuck payin' child support, or worse."

"I know what this is about," Nanny said in a low growl. "Ray's mad on account of Shep owin' him money."

Sick inside, I slid down the wall and sat on the floor. Who didn't Shep Mahoney owe money? I'd heard the talk around town. That's why my dad had dropped out of sight a few months back, leaving me with nothing but a kitten in a crate and a note saying to take care of it; he'd be back.

I gave away the cat. What did Daddy think? That giving me a pet would keep me from being mad at him? That it could be his replacement? Every time I looked at that cat it reminded me of how mean Daddy was to me, how much he hurt me. I was happy to be rid of it, and rid of him. I had hoped, with my father gone, the rumors I'd heard all my life about Shep Mahoney would disappear, too. Rumors that he'd been a coward in Vietnam. I never asked him or my grandparents the details. I didn't want to know, didn't want to believe the whispers. Whenever anyone tried to taunt me with claims about his past, I walked away.

Right then, sitting in the hallway upstairs, eavesdropping on Nanny and Chick, I wanted to cry, but I refused to give in to that weakness. I told myself I should march right over to Bobby that instant and stand up for myself. Ask him if he agreed with his dad about my family and me.

When my grandparents' voices drifted into the kitchen, I pushed away from the wall, stood up, and started for my room. No, I wouldn't go see Bobby. Instead, I'd figure out how to make everyone see the truth about me, that I wasn't like my father. I would do it, too. No matter what it took.

I hear the stray cat *meow* outside as I let the drapes fall back into place. All these years . . . I worked so hard. I thought I had broken the family cycle through Eliot. I thought my son would be the first in three generations not to have to deal with the struggles and tough decisions those of us before him had faced. Me. My mother and Shep. Nanny and Chick. Even Paul.

CHAPTER FOUR

Sometime after two a.m., a door squeaks. I sit up on the sofa at the same time Eliot rounds the corner into the living room. "You're awake," he says. His hair is a wind-blown mess, and in the muted light from the end table lamp, his face looks strained.

"I've been worried."

He walks over and sits beside me, his legs apart, his forearms across them. Bent forward, he stares at his hands.

"What happened?"

He looks at me. "The baby is mine."

I hug him. "Why didn't Liza want you to know?"

"She said she was through with that part of her life. The *us* part." He breaks our embrace, leans back. "I guess I really hurt her when I broke up with her."

"Why *did* you break up"

"She wanted to get married after I graduated. Right after. Like this summer." He shakes his head. "I told her the timing was wrong, that med school was my first priority right now."

"And she couldn't understand and wait a while longer?"

"She said that was *you* talking, not me."

Stung, I say, "So that's what she meant when she told me I got my wish." Eliot looks puzzled, but I don't explain.

After a long pause, he says, "It doesn't matter. Even without med school, I wasn't ready to get married. *Jesus*, I'm only twenty-one. If Liza had said she'd wait, I would've had to tell her I didn't want to marry her. I mean, I cared for her, but . . ." His voice trails.

"So she's placing the baby for adoption?"

"Not anymore."

Everything in me shifts downward. "If you didn't want to marry Liza seven months ago . . . " I pause, choose my words carefully. "Raising a baby together isn't necessarily going to strengthen your relationship. In fact, it'll probably strain it even more. And it won't make med school any easier for you."

"We aren't getting married. Like I said, Liza's through with *us*, and this baby is definitely that."

"I think that's wise." Relief sweeps through me. "What did the two of you decide?"

"I've thought a lot about it." He clasps then unclasps his hands. "After we talked, I left her room and went to look at the baby. I just stood there at the window and—" Eliot's voice falters, and he falls silent.

"I know you and Liza are both confused. I know you both want to do what's best for everyone. Especially for the baby. Only you two can decide." I exhale a long breath. "Years ago, when you were little, I spent about a year working in an obstetrician's office. You can't imagine how many married couples we saw who wanted a baby so badly, but they couldn't conceive. Think about that, Eliot. You and Liza could give one of them such a gift, and you could give the baby a—"

I stop myself from saying more. Paul gave me this same sort of "encouragement" twenty-one years ago. I should understand better than anyone that bombarding Eliot with advice at a time like this is tantamount to torture. I do understand. And despite the difficulties I went through as a single mother at the age of twenty, I wouldn't go back and make a different choice. Keeping Eliot was right for me. Maybe keeping this baby is the right thing for Liza, too.

"I've thought about adoption," Eliot says. "It's just that I keep thinking about my own dad, how he didn't care enough about me to stick around."

I go still. "Oh, Eliot."

"I want the baby, Mom. I have to keep him. When my son grows up, I don't want him to feel about me the way I feel about my dad."

"So you and Liza are planning joint custody?"

He meets my gaze, his eyes shining with tears and determination. "Not Liza. I've decided to keep him by myself. I can't give him to some stranger, Mom. I can't."

Startled, I ask, "Do you know what you're saying?"

"I have a son, Mom. A *son*. When I saw him, when I heard him crying . . . "

Oh, Nanny. It isn't just the women in our family. I know what Eliot felt, what he's feeling now, and I'm proud of him for his sensitivity. But pride and understanding don't lessen my anxiety for him.

Eliot takes my hand in his. "Say you're behind me."

Behind him? I'm numb, in shock, my mind crowded with too many worries to process at once. He wants his son. *Really wants to raise him.* How can I insist he do otherwise?

His eyes narrow. "I won't abandon my kid like my dad did me."

Tears burn my throat. For the first time in his life, Eliot has verbalized the false belief I've silently nurtured. Hearing it now, spoken aloud and so bitterly, fills me with guilt and regret. Yet, I'm angry, too. And I don't know the source of that anger or where to direct it. At Eliot? Paul? Myself?

Myself.

My silence caused this, my willingness to allow him to believe something that isn't true. It doesn't matter that I wanted to protect him. I also wanted to make things easier for myself. Nanny warned me that secrets would come back to bite me in the butt. She warned me.

"Placing a baby for adoption isn't abandonment, Eliot," I say as calmly as I can. "In some situations, it's the most loving thing a parent can do."

"But not in my situation. I've given it a lot of thought."

"One hour?" My voice rises on the last word. I pull my hand from his. "How many guys your age do you know who are raising a baby alone?"

"What does that have to do with anything?"

"How many?"

"None." His face hardens. "So, what?"

"Maybe there's a reason for that. It's a big deal, Eliot. A very big deal. It's not like taking in a stray. This is your life we're talking about. That baby's life. Being a parent isn't easy. Everything changes. Everything. Especially at your age. You can't imagine the worry ahead of you if you do this. And you might as well kiss your friends goodbye. Forget about fun."

"Fun?" His eyes flash. "I don't care about that."

"You will. You'll be giving up your youth." I take a quick

breath. "You were an easy child, but I won't lie; raising you by myself was still tough. I hated making every decision alone. I hated having to be the one who always said no when you wanted something I couldn't give you. I worried non-stop about how I would support you."

"Maybe that's how you felt when I was a baby, but I'm not you."

Crushed by the wounded, defensive look on his face I say, "Don't misunderstand. I'm not sorry I kept you. I've never been sorry."

"I want him, Mom. I can take care of him."

"How?" I push to my feet. "You're twenty-one. Some of the most stressful years of your life are ahead of you in medical school."

"You were younger than me, and you hadn't finished school when I was born."

"Which is why I know what I'm talking about."

"That was different. My father turned his back on us. He should've at least sent money to help us out. Even Liza says she'll do that if she can."

"We didn't need his money."

"Only because you worked your ass off. You still do. He forced you to."

No. I did it because I was driven to prove something to Paul. To prove something to all the Ray Allans of the world. And to myself.

"I was my father's responsibility, and this baby is mine," Eliot continues. "I won't walk away like *he* did just to make my life easier. I want *my* son."

I consider admitting what really happened between his father and me; how can I stand back and allow him to make what might very well be the most serious decision of his life based on a misconception? But fear traps the words inside me. What will he think when he hears? What will happen to us? He'll never trust me again. And would knowing change his mind or only muddy the waters? Make things more confusing for him?

"What about Liza?" I steady my voice. "Did you tell her what you've decided?"

"Yes. She thinks I'm crazy, but she agrees it's my right."

"So what are you planning to do?"

"Liza's supposed to be released from the hospital tomorrow. The doctor stopped by while I was there. He says it might be another day or two before the baby can leave. Because of his respiratory problem, they want to make sure he's stabilized. He's getting better. Lots of babies born early have—"

"I know, Eliot. I'm a nurse." I hate the sarcastic tone of my voice. "Have you given any thought to tomorrow and the next day and the days and weeks after that?"

"Yes, I've thought about it. That's all I've done since I left here earlier. I'd *planned* to bring him home. I'd *hoped* you'd let us live here until I get on my feet. But that's fine." His chin snaps up. "I'll find us a place of our own."

"A place of your own?" My laugh is sharp. "How do you think you'll afford the rent? Do you know how much it costs to raise a kid?"

"I have a full-time job."

"For the summer. Isn't the plan for you to quit when med school starts?"

"Plans change." He shifts his gaze away from me.

"Don't tell me you're thinking about forgetting med school. You've worked too hard. Don't give up the scholarship you earned over this."

WHAT I NEVER EXPECTED

"Over *this*?" His eyes are cold. "*This* is a baby, Mom. *My* baby. My *son*. Do you know how much I wanted to know my dad growing up? I won't put my kid through that." He stands. "Why is it you think I'm weaker than you? You did it alone. You went to college when I was little."

"Nursing school isn't med school, but it was still tough. With a baby to raise, you'll need a lot of help to make it work. You'll have to want to be a doctor badly enough."

"Maybe I do, and maybe I don't. But I do want my son badly enough."

His implication slams into me. "You've wanted to be a surgeon for as long as I can remember. You've been talking about it since elementary school. Don't let this–" I catch myself. "Don't let becoming a father ruin your dreams."

"I'm starting to wonder if med school is my dream or yours. Why are you so gung-ho? I talked about being a fireman when I was a kid, too," he says derisively, squinting at me, his body visibly trembling. "I don't hear you telling me not to give up that idea. Does the thought of having a son who's a doctor boost your ego? Is that it?"

"It doesn't have anything to do with me."

He shoves a hand through his hair. "Tell me something, Mom. Did having *me* ruin *your* dreams?"

"No," I say quickly, shocked by the question. "Of course not." I touch his shoulder. "My situation wasn't the same."

"Why not?"

When he pulls away from my hand, I cross my arms. Every fiber in my body insists that Eliot raising this baby alone would be a mistake. At least I had nine months to adjust to the idea of becoming a parent, to ready myself before he was born. This is too sudden.

I step closer, ready to make him an offer, but the words won't come. *What am I about to do?* I tell myself that at least Liza is on board with his decision, so she has no reason to make trouble for me at work. Her plans haven't been upset. She's still giving up the baby; she can return to school and move on with her life.

But everything is about to change for Eliot. And for me if I tell him I'll help him raise this baby so he can go to medical school. I've already raised one child alone, and though I don't regret it, I swore I'd never do it again, never put myself or another kid in that difficult position. But with Eliot in med school, the weight of raising his son would fall on my shoulders.

I stare at the back of his head, his hunched shoulders. Now that he's grown, I had intended to devote all my energy to reaching the goals I set as a struggling young mother. Maybe I'm still trying to prove something, but I've pushed myself and now, finally, the reward is within my grasp. In less than two years, I might be promoted to Chief Operating Officer. I need to think things through, not make a rash decision about helping to raise this child.

"We're both upset," I say quietly, reaching out to Eliot again. His back stiffens, but this time he doesn't pull away. "Let's get some sleep and talk again in the morning."

"I'm not changing my mind."

"Let's get some sleep," I repeat.

Seconds tick by in silence. Then Eliot starts off toward his bedroom.

"I love you," I call after him.

He doesn't answer.

CHAPTER FIVE

*E*liot is dressed and at the table the next morning when I stumble, bleary-eyed, into the kitchen. "Is that coffee I smell?" I try to sound upbeat, though cheerful is the last thing I feel.

He's writing in a spiral notebook, and without glancing up, he says, "There's a full pot."

I take the largest cup I can find from the cupboard. "You're up and ready early."

"I want to run by the hospital before work. The doc said he'd be making rounds about seven."

No mention that he's changed his mind about keeping the baby. Gesturing toward the paper in front of Eliot, I ask, "What's that?"

"I'm writing down some things I need to do before the baby is released. I'm going to ask my boss if I can take off early today and take a four week leave of absence starting tomorrow. While I'm off, I'll look for a sitter and a place to live."

I pour coffee then cross the room and look over his shoulder at the list. *Buy toys* is at the top, which worries me some, but also makes me smile. Beneath that, he's written *a bed and stuff* then *baby food*, followed by *clothes* and *make appointment with pediatrician*.

A dull ache starts between my temples. "You forgot diapers," I say. It's easier to think about what we'll need then dwell on regrets.

"Oh, yeah." He scribbles the word at the bottom of the list.

I know I should butt out, let him handle the preparations; he could use a big dose of the same reality I'm feeling. Still, I ask, "Any of that I can help with?"

"Only if you want to." I catch a glimpse of uncertainty in his eyes when he glances up, but he covers it quickly.

"Tell you what . . ." I squeeze his shoulder. "If you don't mind me picking out the nursery furniture and the bedding, I'll shop for it on my lunch break. I'll buy a few clothes, too."

"Okay. Thanks." He returns his attention to the list.

I set my cup on the table beside him. "I think Diane Hager is working this morning's shift. She's one of my nurses, and she recently had a baby. Look her up. She could probably give you a few pointers on what else we might need."

He writes her name on the paper, then squints up at me. "We?"

I sit in the chair closest to him. "I have a proposition for you."

"Okay." His voice holds a note of caution.

"You and the baby can live here as long as you need to, and I'll help you however I can if you promise not to put off medical school. Even temporarily. You need to follow through on that for yourself as well as for your son."

Eliot lays down the pen. "Are you sure you're up for that?"

No, I think, then answer, "Yes."

After a long, assessing pause, he nods, and the tension drains from my body in a rush. Still, I know that in a couple of days, reality will hit both of us. And it will hit hard.

I stand again and motion toward his list. "As for those toys, you're the expert. You can pick them out on your own." When he chuckles, I worry even more that he doesn't have the vaguest idea what's in store for him, that he thinks this will be fun and games. "Just remember that bats and ball gloves are a few years down the road," I add.

"Give me some credit, Mom. I'm not clueless."

He's wrong about that. But he won't be clueless for long.

"Well, I'd better get going." Eliot pushes away from the table and stands, then surprises me with an impromptu hug. "Thanks for everything," he says in a choked voice. "I know you weren't expecting this."

"To say the least," I murmur, before I can stop the comment from slipping out.

He steps back, his eyes a little wounded. "Keep the receipts today. I'll reimburse you."

Realizing he thinks finances are my biggest worry, I bite my lip to keep from asking how he thinks he'll afford to pay me back.

As if he reads my mind, Eliot says, "I've been putting a little away out of my paycheck every month for a while, saving for another car. I'll pay you with that."

I flash back momentarily to my penny-pinching days. "No, keep saving."

"I don't need a new car that bad," Eliot says.

"But you do need a car *seat*." And money for sitters, too, for braces and glasses and bicycles. For his son's college tuition. I lift my coffee cup and sip, set it down again. "I'll look in on the baby when I get to work. Liza, too."

"She doesn't want to see anyone. Even me. They're supposed to release her around noon." Eliot shifts awkwardly, looks down at his shoes, then up at me. "I think it's going to be harder for her to leave him than she's pretending."

"What about her family? Will someone be there for her?"

"Just a friend; Joy's taking her home."

I nod. The girl's name is familiar from the time Eliot and Liza dated.

"Liza kept this whole thing from her family," Eliot explains. "They're all in California. The last time she saw them, her stomach wasn't big yet."

I ache for the girl. At least I didn't have to go through my entire pregnancy alone.

I drove to Juniper on a Saturday with my old LTD packed to the roof with all of my possessions. The trunk stuffed full, too. I'd left Oklahoma City and college behind. Now, there was only one thing left to do – tell my grandparents that I'd messed up, just like my mother. This was one secret I couldn't keep, though I'd considered trying. Then my gynecologist diagnosed me with pre-eclampsia, the same condition I suspected had claimed my mother's life, though Nanny never said. The doctor told me I'd have to stay off my feet the last two months of the pregnancy. There'd be no working, no cooking; I couldn't do much more than go to the bathroom and back. I needed my family.

With an odd mix of dread and longing, I watched the scenery pass. Old barns and rich red dirt, piercing blue sky and stretches of spring-green pasture. Each mile took me closer to Nanny's and Chick's disappointment, and to the warm acceptance and loving support I knew I'd find in spite of it. And there would be the town to face, Ray Allan and the rest of the holier-than-thou hypocrites who'd whisper to one another, "I told you so. Like mother, like daughter. The apple doesn't fall far from the tree."

I swore to myself that I didn't care anymore; let them whisper. But I did care. I had wanted so much to make Nanny and Chick proud, to show the world that they had raised me right. I wanted to lift my grandparents up like one of Nanny's birds might, save them from the struggles they'd faced all their lives in the only way I knew how. If I earned a degree and went on to a good career, I could give back some of what they had given me. Some of what they'd lost. I could help them out, allow them to retire with their heads held high and no worries. I'd worked hard to make that happen ever since high school. Since getting caught in Bobby Allan's backseat. Since Nanny and Chick had to endure hearing me called a "slut," their daughter labeled "worthless," and their son a "loony." Since my father proved that Juniper's tongue-waggers were right about him. He was a drunk, a thief, and a coward. He never came home to collect his cat and pay back the people he owed. Shep Mahoney disappeared without a word when I was sixteen. We hadn't heard from him since.

But I'd slipped up. One little slip, and now I was about to heap shame on my grandparents' shoulders again. For at least the thousandth time, I mentally kicked myself for not being more careful with birth control, for not making sure Paul was careful. But we'd been to a party and had too much to drink the night I conceived, and when Paul reached for me, birth control had not crossed my mind.

Nanny was in her garden at the side of the house when I drove up, and as I stepped from the car into the graveled drive, I heard her yell, "Chick! Chick! Get out here. Look who just pulled in." She took off running toward me, holding her straw hat atop her head.

It was a warm, breezy March afternoon, and I hadn't seen my grandparents since Christmas. I had suspected then that I was pregnant but was still in denial about it. There was no denying it now. I wasn't one of those girls who stayed thin enough to disguise such things.

One look at Nanny's face as she drew closer, and I knew there'd be no need to confess – my belly did that for me. I wouldn't have been surprised to see sparks flying off the heels of her sneakers she put on the brakes so fast.

"Oh, Maggie." She puffed up her cheeks and let the air out slowly in a hiss.

Behind her, the screen door squeaked, and when my grandfather stepped onto the porch, my dread over the conversation to come shifted to alarm for him. Chick had never carried much weight on his bones, but he was as skinny, bent, and stiff as a twig now, his skin dull and gray as tree bark.

"Nanny," I said in just above a whisper, my heart fluttering like a moth. "Why didn't you tell me?"

"He didn't want to worry you. You and me will talk about Chick later. He won't sit still for a fuss." She laid a hand on my stomach, then wrapped an arm around me. Together, we started for the house. "Looks like we have other fat to chew first, anyhow."

Chick hugged me before the three of us went inside. He felt so fragile I feared he'd snap in two if I squeezed too hard. As we made our way into the kitchen and Nanny poured iced tea, he asked me about everything except the subject on everyone's mind.

"How was the drive?"

"Long and uneventful."

"And the weather in Oklahoma City?"

"Humid already."

"Have you been keepin' up with the Sooners' basketball team?"

"I haven't had time."

Finally, "How's your schoolwork?"

I admitted I'd had to drop all my classes.

"Your job?"

"I quit."

Then the inevitable, "When's your baby due, little girl?"

"Three months. In June."

Chick nodded, set down his tea glass, pushed back his chair. "I'll leave you and your grammaw to talk." Excusing himself, he left the room.

Sadness and love filled me as I watched him walk away. I hated that I'd brought this new burden and stacked it on top of his health issues – whatever they were.

Nanny sat across the kitchen table from me, her tea untouched. I sipped from my glass. "The doctor said I'd have to be off my feet the last couple of months," I told her. I thought of Chick, how sick he looked. Nanny would have her hands full. "But if you're not up to taking care of me—"

"Who's the baby's daddy, Maggie?"

"His name is Paul Reeves." I cleared my throat. "He's a pre-law student. He'll graduate in May and start law school in the fall."

"You love him?"

"I thought I did." I lowered my gaze to my hands. "He never pretended to feel the same about me. I guess I just didn't want to believe he didn't love me back. We were more friends than anything, as far as he was concerned. We broke up before I knew I was pregnant."

"Hmph." She scowled. "Friends play cards together on Saturday nights, not—"

"I know, Nanny." Heat crept up the back of my neck.

"Does he know about this?"

"Yes."

"What does he plan to do about it?"

I shifted. Took another drink of tea. "Right after we split, he met someone else. They're engaged to be married in a few months, after Paul graduates." I cleared my throat again. "We decided it'd be best if I gave the baby up for adoption. He's paying all my medical bills."

"You both decided, or Paul Reeves did?"

I pressed my lips together, hesitant to answer her question.

She leaned back and crossed her arms. "If it was me, I'd wait 'til that little one's born, then I'd make up my own mind. But you listen to your gut and do what you think is right. It's not for me to decide."

I squirmed beneath her unflinching gaze. "I have to make arrangements, Nanny. It's the best option. For me and the baby."

"For Paul Reeves, you mean."

"For everybody. The baby will have two parents. I'll get to finish my degree. And Paul's not ready to be a father. Not financially or emotionally or in any other way. He was honest about that, too."

Huffing a humorless laugh, Nanny shook her head. "You think anybody's ever ready to be a parent? Oh, they may think so, but you got no idea what's in store until that baby's alive and kickin' and countin' on you. Then you just do what you got to do, ready or not."

I placed both palms against my stomach. "Don't you think this child deserves to grow up with both a mom and a dad?"

"You didn't have either and you did alright." She reached a hand across the table, and I grasped hold of her rough fingers. "Seems like you been searchin' for somebody to love and accept you since you was a girl. I don't know why. Chick and I love you to pieces just like you are. Don't you know that?"

"Of course, I do," I answered, my throat tight.

"You're a good girl, Maggie. Don't you think otherwise. Your granddaddy and me, we're proud of you."

"That's why I've done fine. I had you and Chick. You were my

parents. This baby won't have—" I couldn't finish the sentence; I didn't need to. My fear traveled between the two of us, unspoken. "Tell me, Nanny," I whispered. "What's wrong with Chick?"

I'd never seen her cry, and though she didn't now, I watched her struggle to hold her tears inside. "It's his lungs."

"His emphysema?" I asked, hoping that was all.

She shook her head. "Cancer."

I think I knew the moment I saw Chick step onto the porch. But hearing the dreaded word spoken made it real. "How long? Have the doctors said?"

"They said two months, at most. But I don't hold stock in their predictions. He'll go when he's ready, not before or after. The way he's been so down in the dumps these past days, I'm afraid he's thinkin' more along the lines of sooner than later." For the first time, I saw tears on my grandmother's cheeks. She swiped at her eyes then looked away from me. "I never thought he'd leave me. Not my Chick. Not so as he wouldn't come back."

"He wouldn't, Nanny. Not if he could help it." My voice sounded pinched. I reached across the table for her other hand and held it, too. "Maybe my being here will lift his spirits."

"And the baby," she said with a quiver. "Chick always did have a soft spot for little ones. I'm thinkin' he'll want to hang in there to see his first great-grandchild born. Don't tell him you're thinkin' of givin' it up."

"I won't, Nanny. I won't mention another word about it."

After I arrive at the hospital later in the morning, I walk by Liza's room on my way to the nursery and glance in as I pass. She's up and pacing. The balloons I sent are nowhere in sight.

As if an internal alarm warned her of my approach, she darts a look toward the door before I'm out of sight. Our eyes meet. I smile and lift my hand in greeting. She turns away.

When I reach the nursery, the baby is sleeping soundly on the other side of the window. I watch him from behind the glass.

Diane pauses beside me on her way down the hall. "Congratulations, Maggie," she says with some hesitation. "How does it feel to be a grandmother?"

"Surprising." I don't look at her.

"Eliot and I had a nice talk earlier. He's young, but he's going to do fine. He'll be a good father."

I'm suddenly alarmed I'll break down in front of one of my staff. I bite my lip.

"Wouldn't you like to go inside and see the baby?"

"No," I blurt too quickly. "I don't have time. I'm already running late for a meeting." That's true, but it isn't the real reason I'm avoiding my grandson. I'm not ready to fall in love with that tiny little boy. Not yet. And I know I will if I get too close to him. I'm still grasping onto the hope that Eliot will change his mind, though I know it isn't likely.

"He's doing better," Diane says. "I expect he'll go home in the morning."

I assumed they'd release the baby tomorrow, but hearing that possibility confirmed makes the future with him all too real, and me too panicky. "Thanks for talking to Eliot," I say to Diane, then head for my office without looking back.

I have meetings scheduled all morning. Throughout the first one, my thoughts continually drift to Liza. Despite our differences, I feel sorry for her. Leaving her child can't be easy. And we have more in common than she knows. I hope she's able to move on with her life; I wish her nothing but the best. After the meeting ends, I write a brief note and tell her so. And I say I hope she can forgive me for telling Eliot, but I didn't feel I had any other choice. Then I have my assistant, Tim, deliver the note to her room.

During meeting number two, thoughts of Eliot distract me. I know his feelings about his father are at the core of his decision to keep this baby. He thinks Paul abandoned us when I was pregnant. And that isn't true. I didn't actually tell Eliot that, but it's how he interpreted my vague answers to his questions about his father, as well as my refusal to divulge Paul's name. In the beginning, I thought I was doing the right thing. But after his outburst last night, I know I was wrong not to tell him about Paul years ago. I'm not sure I'm brave enough now. I'm afraid Eliot would never trust me again. And what would it accomplish?

Before lunch, I return to my office, sit at my desk, and stare out the window. What if I found Paul Reeves and told him I kept our son twenty-one years ago? Would he want to meet Eliot? Talk to him? If so, then I would definitely tell Eliot that Paul didn't abandon us, even if hearing it made him furious with me. I may be grasping at straws out of desperation, but if there's a chance Eliot would lose his bitterness toward his father, a chance Paul might reason with him about the wisdom of keeping a baby at his age and in his situation, a chance Eliot might listen to him, I'd be happy to withstand the worst of his anger.

I pick up my phone and immediately put it down again, afraid to follow through.

At the mall later, I shop in a trance, choosing a crib and bedding, a changing table and chest of drawers, a car seat. I schedule a furniture delivery for late in the afternoon, then move on to the clothing department. While selecting pastel gowns, feather-soft socks, and outfits with snaps in the crotch, I remember how Nanny hummed a happy tune while knitting baby blankets before Eliot's birth. How, despite Chick's illness and the toll it took on his energy, he built a cradle out of walnut. Their eyes would brighten with excitement when they talked about my baby's impending arrival.

I fall short of summoning the same enthusiasm about my own grandson's homecoming. And I feel guilty about my misgivings. Guilty, worried, and sad. Sad for all of us, but mostly for Eliot's child. He deserves happy humming, gifts given out of love, not duty, a woman's hands that itch to hold him. Family members other than his father waiting with eager eyes to welcome him home.

My grandson deserves a better grandmother than me.

By the time I return to my office later in the afternoon, my decision is made. I make a quick call to my lawyer and briefly explain the situation.

Doug Dowling says I could probably find Paul easily myself through an Internet search, but I can't bring myself to do it. So, he says he'll have his investigator start searching right away.

CHAPTER SIX

*A*fter the baby furniture arrives at the house, Eliot and I set up an impromptu nursery in the guest bedroom. The walls are tan instead of pastel blue or yellow, but Eliot doesn't mention it. I guess baby décor is something mothers and grandmothers notice, not fathers. Especially twenty-one-year-old fathers.

"You should pick out a wallpaper border." I tug the fitted sheet over the mattress. "Something little-boyish. You know, with animals or airplanes or trains on it."

Eliot shrugs. "Doesn't matter to me." He lays the padded cushion on the changing table. "I doubt it matters to the baby, either. The room's fine, as is."

I make a mental note to find something to turn the room into a little boy's. If not a border, then maybe some pictures to hang on the walls. Anything to make the space more cheerful. Maybe it would do the same for my mood.

Eliot motions toward the window. "There's that stray again." The cat is on the sill outside, looking in through the pane at us.

"Cats give me the creeps," I say.

"I like them."

I squint at him. "You're feeding him, aren't you?"

"Why do you think that?" Eliot avoids my gaze.

"Look at him, he's fat. And he keeps hanging around."

"Maybe we have a lot of mice. Or maybe he's lonely." Eliot shoots me smirk. "I don't think you're really allergic. That was just your excuse for saying 'no pets' when I was a kid."

"Oh, yeah? Just bring him in and watch me start sneezing." When he steps toward the door, I say, "I'm kidding. Don't bring that cat near me."

We continue to fold receiving blankets and tiny gowns, then tuck them into drawers. After Eliot hangs the mobile above the crib, he picks up a box and frowns. "What's this?"

I close a drawer and glance back at him. "A Diaper Genie®."

"Which is?"

"I don't have a clue. If such a thing existed when you were a baby, I didn't know it. But the lady at the store insisted it's a must."

"Then how'd *you* get by without one?"

"Good question."

"Now I know why I have this twitch." He winks one eye repeatedly. "You abused me. I was Genie deprived."

I toss a stuffed elephant at him and grin. It's good to know his sense of humor is still intact.

Ducking and laughing, Eliot catches the toy and sets it aside. He picks up a smaller box from the floor and lifts out a little rubber globe with a long cylinder tip. "And this is?"

"An aspirator."

"For?"

I touch my nose.

"Disgusting." After setting the box down, Eliot picks up another.

"That's a sling. You can carry the baby around hands-free with it. I haven't figured out how it straps on yet, though. It's different than the old one I used. I guess we should read the instructions."

His smile slowly deflates, and he pulls into himself as he puts the contraption away and stacks the box on top of the changing table with the others. I imagine if I listened hard enough, I would hear his nervousness vibrating through the room. The joking moments ago, his laughter, it was all a cover.

I smooth the soft blue comforter across the baby bed mattress then go to him. "If you're having second thoughts, it isn't too late to change your mind."

"I'm not."

"Then, don't worry. We'll figure all this stuff out. And if we don't, we'll raise your son the old-fashioned way." I catch his eye and raise a brow. "Except, I don't do cloth diapers."

To my relief, he smiles.

Determined to keep up my encouragement, although I'm queasy with fears of my own, I glance across at the crib. "There's something in the attic I need your help bringing down."

"What is it?"

"A gift for the baby from his great-great-grandfather."

Years ago, I covered the walnut cradle with an old quilt and wrapped it in plastic. With some maneuvering, we manage to carry it down the attic steps and into Eliot's bedroom.

After we unwrap it, Eliot says, "Wow." He drags a finger along the smooth walnut edge. "Chick made this?"

"Yes. For you. You slept in it in my room until you grew too big. I thought you might want the baby close by you at night for awhile, too."

Eliot stoops to inspect my grandfather's handiwork.

"Chick passed away before he could give it to you himself," I tell him. "He was so excited about meeting you." I smile, remembering how my grandfather's singing filled the barn while he worked on the crib. "You took his mind off being sick."

Standing, Eliot gives the cradle a push and it swings without so much as a squeak. "He did a great job."

"When my grandfather set out to do something, he did it right, or not at all."

Eliot stops the cradle when it swings our way again. In my mind, I see Chick doing the same thing, testing it, his hands touching the walnut as Eliot's are now.

I stroke a finger up a bar. "With a little polish, the wood will gleam." Sentimentality overcomes me. Before he can see, I turn away and start for the door.

"Mom?"

Pausing, I glance back.

"Thanks."

I nod. "Chick would've wanted you to give it to your son."

"I think I'd like to name the baby after him. William Chick Mahoney. I'll call him Will."

A shiver scatters up my spine; the good kind. For an instant, I sense my grandfather's presence so strongly I wouldn't be surprised to turn and find him standing behind me. "Chick would have loved that."

"I may not have known him, but I feel like I did," Eliot says, his voice thick. "He was all the things to you your dad should've been, and all my dad should've been to me."

I think of Paul and feel a twinge of regret.

A short while later, Eliot leaves for the hospital, and I close the door on the nursery and go to bed early. I haven't heard anything from my lawyer about the investigator's search for Paul. I don't expect to sleep much tonight.

———————

The next morning, I still haven't heard anything from Doug by the time I arrive at my office. After canceling my nine a.m. meeting, I close my door and watch the time. I can't concentrate on work; I don't even want to try. Eliot is on the third floor, where he's been since seven a.m., waiting for Will to be released so they can go home.

Since Eliot told me the name he chose for his son, I've been more torn than ever. A part of me wants to embrace the changes ahead of us, while another part still resists.

An hour later, Doug finally calls with news.

"I'm sorry to say it's not good," he says, then clears his throat. "Paul Reeves died eight months ago from kidney failure, Maggie. Apparently, they couldn't find a donor match because he had some kind of rare blood type."

"Oh, my God. That can't be true." I close my eyes, grief and guilt squeezing me so tightly I can barely breathe. Eliot has a rare blood type, too.

"I'm sorry," Doug says.

"Me, too." I lean back in my chair.

"He was living in Red Lake, Oklahoma."

"Paul grew up in Red Lake."

"He had a small private law practice there."

"What about his family?"

"He divorced twelve years ago."

I think of Kelly, how jealous I was of her, how I used to envy the smitten sound of Paul's voice whenever he spoke her name.

"He never remarried. He and his wife had one child."

"I knew that. The last time I saw them Kelly was expecting. Did they have a boy or a girl?"

"A daughter," Doug tells me. "Her name is Andrea. She's twenty and a student at O.U."

Eliot's half-sister. I pick up his framed photo and stare at it. When he was a toddler, I was jealous of her, too. Jealous and resentful, though I didn't even know that she *was* a she. I only thought of Paul's other baby as *Kelly's child.* But, after a while, I put away the jealousy, tucked Eliot's half-sibling into a place at the back of my mind. Sometimes, though, whenever he asked about his dad, or there'd be a father-son event at school, or I'd struggle to help him learn to dribble a basketball or swing a bat, *Kelly's child* would pop to the surface again to taunt me.

I set Eliot's photo down again, wondering if he and Andrea ever crossed paths on campus. They might've even met – brother and sister and unaware of that fact, thanks to me.

"Paul's mother Patricia is widowed. She still lives in Red Lake," Doug says. "So does his older brother, Mark. He's divorced. No kids. A building contractor. Owns his own outfit."

He rattles off Mark's and Patricia's phone numbers and addresses. "Thanks," I say as I write them down. I never met any of Paul's family during the short time we dated, but he talked about them. Especially his brother.

"You're welcome, Maggie. Like I said, I'm really sorry." After a short pause Doug adds, "I'm a good listener. If you need to talk, I'm here."

"I appreciate that."

We say goodbye, and I hang up.

I keep my gaze on Eliot's photo and think of Paul. His sandy hair. The serious eyes he passed on to our son, the glint of reserved humor that sometimes flashed in them. His laughter fills my mind, and for the first time, it occurs to me that Eliot isn't the only one I short-changed with my long-ago decision. I also wronged Paul. He didn't get the chance to know his son. If he had, Eliot might've been a kidney donor match. He might've saved Paul's life.

Eliot said he would call when he and Will were ready to leave so I can go home with them. I can't bear the waiting anymore. Pushing to my feet, I start for the door, pull it open, and come face-to-face with Tim.

"Constance just came by when you were on the phone. She wants you to come to her office right away."

"Would you let her know I'll call her in an hour or so? Explain the situation if you have to. Everyone in the hospital will know soon enough about the baby, anyway, if they don't already."

"Oh, believe me, they do. Constance said it's an emergency."

"Constance thinks everything is an emergency. Tell her—"

"I think she's serious, this time. She said you should cancel whatever else is on your schedule." Tim watches me closely from behind his little round glasses. He tilts his burred head and touches my shoulder. "Sweetie, you look terrible. If you faint on me, I'll never forgive you." When I don't answer, he adds, "You're right. Constance is probably making a production out of nothing. I'll call her and make an excuse."

"No." I sigh. "I'd better go and see what she wants."

Frustrated and impatient, I leave and start down the hallway toward Constance Bening's office, thinking of Paul and a day when I tried to tell him the truth, but didn't.

Most new mothers sleep after giving birth. Not me. I laid wide-awake in my hospital bed, staring out the window at the sunrise while my child's healthy cry echoed through my mind. I hadn't seen him yet. Until the delivery, I had intended not to see him at all, thinking that letting him go would be easier that way. I hadn't counted on his cry getting to me, like mine got to Nanny.

My son slept down the hall, only a short walk away. Nanny lay unconscious in the room below mine. She'd been admitted last night after suffering a massive stroke. My efforts to help her while waiting on the ambulance did her no good and threw me into labor. Things turned out fine for me, but the doctors said it didn't look good for Nanny. More than likely, she would not leave the hospital. The after-affects of the stroke would kill her, they said.

I knew better. Nanny might die without going home, but the cause of death would be a broken heart. Chick's lung cancer had taken him from us three weeks before, and when it did, I'd felt like grief and guilt would kill me, too. Maybe I could've saved him if I hadn't been bedridden. Maybe he would've rested more if he hadn't been preparing for the baby – building the cradle, helping with the nursery. Nanny could've focused all of her energy on him if I hadn't come home needing her attention.

My uncle, Ned, wandered off and disappeared in the middle of Chick's graveside funeral. It was only by chance that he'd been in town when Chick died. For years, my quiet, troubled uncle had floated from job-to-job, place-to-place, only getting in touch with his parents infrequently.

"What am I gonna do to help Ned?" Nanny asked me after the service ended and everyone had left. She rolled my wheelchair closer to the grave. "Before he got drafted, Ned was plannin' to make a doctor.

And your Mama, she'd set her sights on nursing. Nothin' worked out for them. They got cheated, both of 'em." She sighed. "I been hangin' on to my hopes that Ned'll pull hisself together. But without Chick, I don't know if he will." Nanny broke down, sobbing. "When your mama died, I never thought I'd hurt as bad again. Lord, I was wrong."

After that, she didn't shed another tear, at least not in my presence. Nanny erected a strong façade around her emotions. I knew she did so for me, because she knew I needed her to cook for me, do my laundry, drive me to doctor's appointments, and bolster my spirits. I tried to convince her to pause and grieve, to sit and cry with me, to reminisce about the man we'd both loved. She'd have none of it. So I sat back helplessly and watched my grandmother numb herself with chores and busy-work, watched the wall she'd built to hide her pain slowly chip away, bit by bit, until I could see that, behind it, she was crumbling, too.

That Saturday morning after Eliot's birth, as the sky came alive with light outside my window and the birds began their cheerful chatter, I felt more alone than I'd ever felt in my life. Before I could change my mind, I picked up the phone and punched in Paul's number in Oklahoma City. I held my breath through the rings. Through a friend still in school at O.U., I'd learned he and Kelly had married last month.

Paul seemed out of breath when he picked up.

"It's me," I said.

The sound of running water, the clink of dishes, "Maggie?" then silence.

"I thought you should know I had the baby this morning." More silence. Why wouldn't he say something? Had he hung up on me? "Paul?"

"I'm here."

"It's a boy. He's okay. He's healthy." I paused for a breath, to

61

prepare myself to tell him I'd changed my mind – I'd be keeping our son. But Paul spoke first.

"How are you?"

"I'm fine." My voice splintered on the last word.

"I know it's hard." Paul sounded strange, not like himself. Nervous and emotional. The words rushed out of him like the water I'd heard running from the tap across the line. "It's not easy for me, either, to realize I have a son I'll never know. But we're doing the right thing by giving him up. The right thing for him. He'll have a better life. Two parents. Things we could never give him apart."

"Paul, I—"

"Think of your own childhood, Maggie. You told me once it was tough not having both your parents. You said it was a struggle for your grandparents and a struggle for you."

I had told him that when we were together. But maybe all kids struggle with something. Maybe in that way, I was no different than anyone else. On the other hand, without a mom and dad, I might've missed out on wonderful things I couldn't even imagine. Could I risk my son missing out on them, too?

"Adoption is the right thing for him, Maggie," Paul assured me again. "When you raise a kid, don't you want to be able to give him all he deserves? The best life possible? I know I do. If I can't give him a hundred percent, then he should have a father who can."

I'd heard this all before from Paul. But was he right? Was I being selfish? Only thinking of my needs? I hung up and, for hours, debated with myself, certain one minute, uncertain the next.

I'd keep my son.

I wouldn't.

He needed me, his real mother.

He needed both a mom and a dad who could give him more than I could, the best of everything.

My love would be enough, as Nanny's and Chick's love had been enough for me.

It wouldn't be enough – he'd blame me for every difficulty in his life, the same way I'd often blamed my dad. He'd resent not having a full-time father. I couldn't count the times I had thought I would've rather not known Daddy instead of the rotten relationship we had.

Late that afternoon, I pushed myself from the bed, put on my slippers, my robe. The nurses had told me to walk as soon as I felt able. Moving slowly, one hand against the wall, I made my way to the elevators, turning my gaze away when I passed by the nursery window.

When I slipped quietly into Nanny's room, her face was as pale as the bed sheet. Even her lips were colorless.

Careful not to disturb monitors, the I.V. bag, I sat at the edge of her bed, touched her cool, slack cheek, pulled the blanket up higher over her sagging breasts. "What should I do, Nanny?" I whispered, knowing all along what she'd answer if she could. I watched her closed eyes, my own misting over. I eased my hand beneath her palm where it rested on the sheet. "I need you. Please don't leave me. I'll be alone."

I wouldn't be alone if I trusted my gut, did what it told me to do – that's the message she'd send if she could. "Trust your gut." One of the many mottos by which Nanny lived. My grandmother knew me better than I knew myself. She knew what I wanted, no matter how much I denied it.

I stroked her wispy hair. "You have a great-grandson. A healthy little boy. Seven pounds, eight ounces. Right after the birth, I decided I'd keep him. But I was reacting on emotion, not good sense. I've had time to think about it now. I have to do what's best for him, Nanny. I've decided that's adoption."

Her words came back to me. "You decided, or Paul Reeves did?

If it were me, I'd wait 'til that little one's born, then I'd make up my own mind. Trust your gut."

A thump sounded at the window. A blackbird perched on the sill, wings fluttering like my pulse. I stared at the bird. It stared back. Slowly, calm certainty wrapped around me like a hug, and all my confusion evaporated.

Leaning down, I kissed my grandmother's forehead. "Thank-you, Nanny," I whispered. "I think I'll go see my son, now."

I didn't have to search for 'Mahoney' on the bassinet or scan the row of tiny bundles to find a face that seemed familiar. I was drawn to him at once by a current too strong to resist. And when I saw him, an undertow sucked the floor from beneath my feet, as if the tiles were made of sand. For the first time in my life, I knew the true meaning of "falling in love."

A nurse passed by. "Miss Mahoney?" Her brow furrowed. "I thought you didn't want to see him?"

Trust your gut. "Is it time for a feeding?"

"Yes."

"Bring him to me, would you? I want to do it this time."

"But—"

"Bring him to me."

I told myself I'd call Paul in the morning. Tonight was for my son and I to get to know one another. To learn each other's scent and touch and voice. I would tell him about the good life we'd share, all the things I'd teach him, the places we'd go. I decided to call him Eliot – Paul's middle name.

Later, after the nurse took Eliot back to the nursery, I slept, but only for a few hours. At nine that night, I woke up excited and making plans. I wasn't able to save my mother or save my father from himself. I couldn't save Chick, either, but I would save Nanny. Tomorrow, after I told Paul I'd changed my mind, I would take Eliot down to her room.

She would hear him and wake up, and when she saw him, she'd find her desire to live again and get better. The doctors didn't know how stubborn my grandmother was; when Nanny put her mind to doing something, nothing stopped her.

I wouldn't go back to school yet. Eliot and I would live at Nanny's; I'd take care of them both. I'd get a job in Juniper, even if I had to ask Ray Allan for one. I didn't need to prove anything to him or anyone else now. Paul would understand when I explained. We'd be apart, but we'd be the best parents we could.

Happier than I'd ever been, I climbed out of bed to go take a peek at Eliot again. But as I stepped from the room and glanced toward the nursery, the sight of Paul stopped me short. He stood at the viewing window, and though I only saw him in profile, and he didn't see me, I recognized tension and uncertainty in his posture. It was a three-hour drive from Oklahoma City across the Texas state line to Juniper, and he'd driven it to have one look at our son.

In that moment, I thought maybe he had changed his mind, too. That when I told him what I'd decided, he'd be relieved. Though we would never be husband and wife, he could be a father to Eliot.

I took one step toward him, then Kelly turned the corner at the opposite end of the hallway. She held two steaming foam cups. We looked at each other, and her eyes held a clear message: Back off. I wanted to march over and tell Kelly this wasn't about her; she should back off, not me. Paul and I had our son's future to discuss. Eliot was more important than her jealousy and possessiveness.

As if he sensed her beside him, Paul turned to Kelly, took one of the cups, kissed her.

Every ounce of self-confidence drained out of me with that kiss. Kelly was beautiful, polished, smart. Her father was a partner in one of the biggest law firms in Dallas. Paul loved her. Or maybe he only loved what she represented. Either way, he'd listen to Kelly, not me. I doubted he'd go against her wishes; he wouldn't want to risk losing her.

And so I did what I'd always done when I felt betrayed; I didn't stand up for myself. Before Paul could see me, I returned to my room.

Nanny died the next morning. As it turned out, I couldn't save her, either.

CHAPTER SEVEN

*A*lice stops me outside my office, out of breath from hurrying down the hall. "I was hoping I'd catch you. Do you have a second?"

"I'm on my way to see Constance. Supposedly it's an emergency."

"I know." A few feet away, the elevator dings, and Alice glances toward it with an anxious expression. She waits for the occupants to pass, then in a lowered voice says, "I just left Constance. She called me in, too. I didn't volunteer any information, Maggie. She asked about you accessing the medical information on the baby's mother, and I said you were doing an audit."

"Alice . . ." Baffled, I step closer to her. "What's this about?"

"You don't know?"

I shake my head. "What is it?"

"The Enlow girl filed a grievance against you."

Surprise jolts me, then dread. I've known from the beginning that this might happen, but I allowed myself to believe that Liza would let go of her anger toward me now that Eliot is taking responsibility for Will.

"Constance has already talked to everyone who was working on the floor that evening you found out about the baby," Alice explains, talking in a rush. "Buddy, me, all of us. A few others who weren't there, too. Like Diane."

Probably because Diane talked to Eliot. I sent him to her. How stupid could I be? "Thanks for telling me, Alice."

She places her hand on my arm. "We're all behind you."

"I appreciate that, but no one should lie for me. I wasn't doing an audit of Liza Enlow's medical information. You and I both know that."

"You could've been," she says, sounding stubborn.

"But I wasn't. I wanted to find out about her case because of Eliot." I force a smile. "I knew what I was doing. I decided it was worth the risk."

"I'm sorry, Maggie."

"Don't be. I don't have any regrets. You're a mother. A grandmother, too. What would you have done in my place?"

"The same thing. In a heartbeat."

I smile again and glance down the hall. "I'd better go face the music."

"Good luck."

"I have a feeling I'll need it."

Moments later, I enter Constance's office and discover she isn't alone. Derek Piedmont, the hospital's Director of Corporate Compliance, sits stiff as a pencil in a chair across from her desk, next to the empty chair Constance motions me toward.

"Good morning, Maggie," she says, and Derek nods.

"'Morning, Constance. Mr. Piedmont." I make my way to the chair.

Derek is known around the hospital for his overbearingly sweet cologne, the severe comb-over he uses to cover a growing bald spot, and his perpetual power hard-on. As I sit beside him, I notice he's wearing all three.

Constance relays what I already know – Liza Enlow filed a formal complaint that I broke HIPAA regulations by my unwarranted reading of her medical information and telling Eliot about her and the baby.

"This is your chance to state your side of the story," Derek says. "Alice Parker indicated that your *random choice* of Miss Enlow's information to audit was pure coincidence."

His compassionless stare penetrates my resolve to be stoical about all this; I can't hide the fact that I'm shaking.

Constance sits forward and adds, "I don't doubt Alice for a minute, Maggie. I've told Derek that your previous work record is crystal clear, both here and at your prior position."

I take a breath. "Alice told *you* what I told *her*. She thought it was true. I told her that I had randomly chosen Miss Enlow's records to audit." This is the only false statement I intend to utter to these people who hold my professional future in their hands. And I'm only telling it to protect Alice, since she was trying to protect me. "I lied to her," I add.

"I see." Derek taps his foot. "Surely you knew your online activity could be traced. What were you thinking? You've jeopardized this hospital's reputation. I hope you know your career is seriously compromised."

"Eliot is my son. That baby is my grandson. I knew I was breaking HIPAA, but I didn't see any other choice. I couldn't face him every day knowing what I knew and never telling him.

As a father, he has rights, too. Or he should." I think of Paul and feel like a hypocrite.

While I speak, Derek sits back in his chair, one forearm across his middle, the opposite elbow propped on it, his hand covering his mouth. Suddenly, he lowers the hand, his brows rising simultaneously. "Your son's rights aren't at issue here. Elizabeth Enlow's are."

"I realize that."

After a short silence, Constance says, "I'll be conducting an investigation over the next two weeks."

Her voice is all business, but her uncomfortable expression betrays her concern for me and the awkwardness she feels. When I first came to work here, she and I clicked immediately. Not as friends, necessarily, but as business associates. Constance, who is fast approaching sixty-five, said I reminded her of herself at forty. By the book. Driven and ambitious. Passionate, not only about patient care, but about rising through the ranks.

Why bother to investigate? I've already admitted my sin. But I know the hospital has protocol to follow, a flawless, professional appearance to uphold. An investigation will look good, even if it serves no other purpose. Bracing for the worst, I ask, "Is Elizabeth Enlow suing the hospital?"

"No talk of that yet." Constance shifts her gaze to Derek, then back to me. "She has to be able to show harm first, that she was damaged in some way by what you did."

Derek scowls. "No talk of it? Come on, Constance, let's be realistic. Her brother is an attorney. He flew in from California to be with her when she filed the grievance. The threat of a lawsuit was implied simply by his presence."

Constance picks up a stack of papers and straightens it. "The hospital has a policy, Maggie. You–"

"Best case scenario," Derek interrupts, "you'll be counseled with the understanding that if any further problems arise in your work, you'll be fired. Worst case, you'll lose your job right away. It all depends on what the investigation reveals."

He's not fooling me. It all depends on the outside pressure the hospital receives, on whether or not Liza files suit.

"The fact that you had your assistant take the girl a note explaining why you did what you did isn't going to help you any."

"Of course, your prior work history will be taken into account," Constance hastens to add.

Derek adjusts his tie, smooths his comb-over, uncrosses his legs, and with that, I'm cued that this meeting is adjourned. "Until the investigation is over, you're on paid mandatory leave of absence, effective immediately." He stands. "We'll be in touch."

After he exits the office, Constance mutters under her breath, "Arrogant asshole." She looks at me. "Don't quote me on that. One way or another, this will all be over in two weeks, Maggie. I'll do what I can for you, you know that. But, first and foremost, I have to consider the hospital's reputation. It's my job."

"Do what you have to do. I would in your position."

She sighs. "The investigation is a must, I'm afraid. We can't just let you go back to work with a simple reprimand and a slap on the wrist. I'm sorry."

"Really, I understand." I rise and start for the door.

Behind me, Constance sniffs, as if the stress has gotten to her, too. Despite her professionalism, she's one of the easiest criers I've ever met. Still, I wouldn't want to face her in a deposition. "I understand, too, Maggie," she says. "If it were my son, I might've done the same."

Pausing, I look over my shoulder.

"I sympathize," she says. "I only wish that were enough."

Tim meets me in the hallway outside my office, ushers me into the reception area where his desk is located, then closes the door and locks it behind us. Before I can speak, he embraces me. "Shit, Maggie. I'm sorry. I'd feign stomach-flu, take off early, and get you snockered, but Eliot just called. He said you weren't answering your cell."

"It's on mute."

"He's waiting on you." Tim steps back, and the genuine concern in his eyes makes me want to hug him again.

My assistant is a demonstrative guy. I'm used to it. During the six months we've worked together, we've become more than boss and employee; we've become good friends. I sniff back the tears I feel gathering. First the news about Paul, then this grievance. It's all too much. But I haven't cried in years, since Eliot was a baby, as a matter of fact. I'm not about to start now.

"Wow," I say. "News travels fast."

"Like housewives to a Tupperware party."

"How would you know about that?"

Tim looks smug. "I was raised on Tupperware. My mother owns every sealable, stackable, burpable container on the market." He rounds his desk, lifts a note from beside his phone. "By the way, Constance called, too."

Scowling, I say, "She must have picked up the phone the second I left her office. What now?"

"She called for me, not you. While you're away, I'm doomed to help out her assistant on some project. Lord, hurry back. I can't bear that whiny witch."

"Constance?"

"No." He smirks at me. "Her 'yes girl' Melanie."

"Melanie's nice."

"Okay, so she's not a witch." He winks. "I only said that for the sake of alliteration. But you can't deny that her voice screeches like an exposed nerve-ending."

"Well, hopefully I won't be gone long. Constance said two weeks, tops. I'll either be back at work by then or off permanently." To my horror, I feel my lower lip quiver.

"Oh, shit. I'm sorry. Here I am babbling while you're having a crisis." He rounds the desk and crushes me against him again.

"Tim," I gasp. "I can't breathe."

"I've never seen you cry."

"That's because I don't."

"And now those monsters . . . look what they've done to you. You're a blubbering mess." He lets go of me and steps back, his eyes narrowed and angry. "It just isn't *fair*."

"I'm not blubbering." I straighten my blouse. "I'll be fine. The baby will keep me so busy I won't have a second to worry about all this."

"Just promise me if they axe you, you'll take me along to your next job."

"I would, but I don't think burger flippers require an assistant."

He tilts his head to one side. "Don't talk like that."

"With this on my record, do you really think any other hospital would hire me?"

"In a second. Haven't you heard? There's a shortage of nursing administrators." Despite his assurances, Tim looks as deflated as I feel.

I pat his arm. "Thanks for the positive thoughts. I guess I'd better get out of here." I start into my office. "Would you call Eliot and tell him I'm on my way?"

"Sure."

"Don't mention the trouble I'm in. If he hasn't already heard, I'd rather not burden him with it yet. Eliot has enough to face right now."

"Won't he wonder why you're not working?"

"I'll tell him I took off a little longer than I'd originally intended. You know, to help with Will."

"To be a granny, you mean." Tim snickers.

I glare at him over my shoulder. "What's so funny?"

"I just had a flash of you rocking and knitting."

"There's not going to be any knitting, I can promise you that. I'm no good at it."

After gathering some personal items, I take what I'm afraid might be a final look around my office, then head for the third floor. Maybe it's only my imagination, but I sense the staff watching me and whispering, some with sympathy, others relishing the drama. Scandal junkies, getting high off my misfortune.

Down the way, Eliot paces in front of the nursery window. I pause to watch him, recalling the day I took *him* home from the hospital. I was alone and terrified, grieving for Nanny and wondering how Eliot and I would ever manage without her.

"Hey," I call out, smiling when he catches sight of me. "Ready to go?"

Something about his nod, his body language, screams his uncertainty.

I won't tell him about his father. Not yet. Maybe not ever. Paul is gone. What purpose would it serve? I want Will's homecoming to be a joyous day for Eliot, one he'll think back on in the future with a smile, not heartache.

Once released from the hospital after Eliot's birth, I called a cab to take us home to the farmhouse; I had no one else to call. After we arrived, I held him close and walked through each room, every one of them filled to the brim with echos of meals and music, laughter and arguments, praising and scolding. Love.

Still, despite those memories, the house seemed empty to me, the life drained out of it.

Crying and cradling my son, I stopped in the living room alongside the easy chair where Nanny last sat while knitting before the stroke hit her. The buttercup yellow baby blanket, three quarters finished, lay in a heap on the floor where it fell from her fingers, the knitting needles atop it, a skein of yarn. For an instant, I saw myself bent over her, giving her mouth-to-mouth. Then the image vanished, and I scooped up everything with one hand while holding Eliot with the other. I pressed my face into the down-soft square and breathed deeply, trying to summon my grandmother's scent.

A floorboard creaked. Lowering the blanket, I opened my eyes, looked up. Mary Nell Cleveland, the pastor's wife, stood above me, her cheeks wet with tears.

"The door was left open," she said, then held up a large grocery

sack. "I brought food. I thought, if you'd let me, I'd like to take care of you and your baby 'til you're on your feet and settled in. And, well, I know it's a bad time, so difficult for you to think about with the baby and all, but have you made arrangements for June's—" Her voice cracked. "For your grandmother's service?"

"No." Still holding the blanket, I stood. The needles and skein of yarn dangled to my knees. "I haven't done anything." Moving to the couch, I sat, numb inside.

"What about your uncle?"

"I contacted the sheriff in Mead where we last heard he was working. He found Ned and had him call me. I told him about Nanny. I haven't heard from him since."

"I could take care of everything for you if you want. I'd be happy to do it. You shouldn't have to fret with the details. All you should be doin' is lovin' that little one." She lowered her gaze to Eliot.

Mrs. Cleveland's kindness confused me, and my mind travelled back to my infrequent visits to Grace Baptist Church growing up. Until I was thirteen, Nanny hauled my butt there at least once a month. She did so for the sake of appearances more than anything. Not that Nanny cared what people thought of her.

"I don't give a whit if they think I'm a heathen. This town's full of self-righteous hypocrites who ain't half the human being I am," she often told me. "I don't got time for their phony folderol."

But Nanny cared what people thought about me; she wanted to do right by her only grandchild. And so, when the Baptist guilt instilled in her by her parents at a young age stuck in her craw and wouldn't budge, we put on our best dresses, and ignoring my protests, she and I drove in Chick's truck to Grace Baptist.

We sat in back, placed money in an envelope, signed it, then dropped it in the plate when one of the faithful brought it by our pew. The instant services ended, Nanny would whisper, "Let's hightail it *outta here," then we'd cut out fast to escape greeting Pastor Cleve Cleveland and Mary Nell. For the longest time, I couldn't figure out what Nanny had against them; they seemed nice enough.*

It was obvious that my grandmother avoided the preacher's wife most. Whenever the tiny, prim woman caught sight of us in the congregation, Mrs. Cleveland's eyelids twitched, and she'd jut out her chin. Nanny would pretend not to see, lifting the hymnal to cover her face.

Then, one Sunday morning when I was in eighth grade, Mary Nell caught up to us before we could push through the throng of Juniper's worshipers gathered at the church door. Nanny fussed quietly as the other woman led her behind the pulpit, away from the crowd. I knew it was only because of my presence that my grandmother didn't make a scene. I followed them, standing back while they whispered and glared at each other.

I only caught two sentences of the conversation, both uttered by Mary Nell. "It's ancient history, June. When will you ever forgive me?"

After that day, we stayed home with Chick on Sunday mornings and gave thanks for our blessings by enjoying each other and life's simple joys: Nanny's buttermilk pancakes slathered with syrup and peanut butter; Chick's guitar music and his beautiful, baritone voice; sunshine on our faces in the summer, the changing colors of autumn leaves, a warm, crackling fire in winter, the sweet smell of rain in the spring. As far as I was concerned, that way of giving thanks was a hundred times more inspiring than Pastor Cleveland's nasal sermons and an off-key choir singing "Bringing in the Sheaves."

Soon, I forgot all about the mystery surrounding Mary Nell Cleveland and my grandmother. In fact, I didn't think of it again until that day when the pastor's prim wife stood across from me in my grandparent's house, eying my newborn son.

"Why are you doing this?" I asked. "Being so nice to me? We barely know each other."

"I'm sorry about that. I've always been sorry we aren't close." She lowered the grocery sack to the coffee table, gestured toward the opposite end of the sofa. "Do you mind?"

I shrugged. "Go ahead."

Mary Nell moved to the empty space and settled herself. When Eliot hiccuped and squirmed against my breast, she smiled. "Could I see him?"

Lowering him to my lap, I unwrapped the blanket and she scooted closer.

"Ohhh. He's beautiful." Her fingers brushed the blanket's edge. "Couldn't you just kiss blisters on him?"

It was the same thing Nanny used to say whenever she saw a pretty baby, a cute puppy or kitten. "I could kiss blisters on that sweet little thing."

Mary Nell's fingers stilled, and she fell silent. Eliot made sucking noises. The old mantel clock ticked as she lifted her gaze to mine. "June and I were joined at the hip as girls. Closer than sisters. I loved her like family, and she loved me."

Stunned, I asked, "What happened?"

"We fell head over heels for the same young man."

"Chick?" It had to be him. I couldn't imagine Nanny in love with the weak-chinned pastor.

"No, Sugar. This was before Chick. His name was J.D., and he was a sight to behold." For a moment, Mary Nell looked wistful, almost young again. "Unfortunately, he knew it, and he played June and me against one another like pawns in a chess game. He'd court me, then her, then me again, back and forth, making us both so pea-green jealous we couldn't see what he was up to." Her eyelids twitched, like *they always had in church whenever she'd spot Nanny. "J.D. finally chose, though. He married your grandmother."*

She might as well have shoved me face-first into a wall. Nanny married to someone before Chick?

"They tied the knot on a whim one night, quick, before they could think twice about it. That's what J.D. told me two months later when I finally managed to run into him accidentally on purpose. June was shopping in the fabric store when I cornered J.D. outside Allan Hardware. We stepped to the side of the building to talk, out of sight of the street. He told me then that he loved June. Really loved her. My heart broke, but I loved June, too, so I let him go that day." Mary Nell's eyes darted away from mine, and she blushed like a teenage girl. "J.D. kissed me. Oh, it didn't mean a thing, mind you. Just goodbye. But someone saw us and told your grandmother."

The pieces fell into place. No wonder Nanny wouldn't give this woman the time of day. But, after so many years, wouldn't she have gotten over it? Obviously Nanny divorced this J.D. person. She had Chick, my mother, Uncle Ned. Me.

Mary Nell sat straighter, folded her hands in her lap, looked down at them. "The rumor was that, on the way home, they fought about it. J.D. dropped her off at this very house and said he'd be at the bar drinkin'. He never came back."

"Where did he go?"

She sighed. "No one knows. The man just disappeared off the face of the earth. June blamed me. She wouldn't listen when I tried to tell her that kiss meant nothing to J.D. Or to me, for that matter." Mary Nell looked at me. "Eight months later, your Uncle Ned was born, and June married Chick about a year after that."

My chin jerked up. "What? You mean Chick's not—"

"He's not Ned's daddy. Not by blood, anyhow." Mary Nell patted

my hand. "But in every way that mattered, Sugar, your granddaddy was Ned's father."

I sat quietly for a minute, trying to take it all in. So, Nanny had kept secrets of her own. I wondered if they haunted her. Is that why she always lectured me about them? "Why didn't she tell me?" I asked Mary Nell when I found my voice.

"Maybe she didn't think it mattered. Of course, she might've been ashamed. Times were different for women back then. Maybe she just wanted to wipe that memory right out of her mind. She and little Ned had it rough before she married Chick. Those were hard times, you know. I tried to help her – her folks were gone by then, but she wouldn't talk to me. Your grandmother was always stubborn as a mule. Tough as one, too. She made her own way with that baby. She would've made it even if Chick hadn't come along when he did. I'm sure of it."

"How did they meet?"

"He was a crop-duster from out of town, here doing work for the Allan's since we didn't have any folks who did that kind of thing in Juniper then. His plane crashed in one of their fields and that was that. He couldn't afford another one."

"He mentioned once that he used to fly." My gaze drifted to the window and the field beyond it. His field. "I never knew he dusted crops for a living."

"He didn't after the crash. June hired him on to help her around the farm. She was seven or eight months pregnant by then and money was scarce. Word around town was that Chick worked in exchange for meals and a bed in the barn. After a while, he quit and left town. But he came back in little more than a week. I guess one thing led to another, because he never left again."

"Does Ned know all this?"

"Who can say? I think most folks forgot he and Chick weren't *father and son. Those two were like peas in a pod before Ned became a soldier. He came home from Vietnam a different boy than the happy-go-lucky one who left Juniper, that's for certain. It was a sad thing to behold."*

"I never saw him like that. Happy-go-lucky, I mean." *I'd grown up knowing an odd, reclusive uncle who disappeared for months at a time. Even when he did come home, I'd almost forget he was around because he was so withdrawn.* "Did Nanny love my grandfather?" *I asked.*

Mary Nell's face softened. "I think you know the answer to that. Your grandpa was something, even then. June wouldn't have married Chick if she didn't love him. She would've relied on herself to survive, not some man she didn't give a whit about."

Didn't give a whit. *This woman had been close to my grandmother.*

"June gave your granddaddy his nickname, did you know that?"

"You mean the name Chick?"

Mary Nell nodded. "She's the one who started calling him that. A mutual friend of ours told me June said he was her guardian angel come to earth. Of course, June didn't tell me that. She wouldn't talk to me." *Mary Nell sighed.* "So many wasted years. I always wondered why she chose Chick for his name instead of Gabriel, or something like that, since he was her angel. Our friend Sue asked her once, and you know what June said?"

I shook my head.

"She said 'cause he didn't like Goose." *Mary Nell made a scoffing sound.* "As if that explained anything! Why, it doesn't even make sense."

My heart lifted, and I laughed out loud. Mary Nell blinked baffled eyes at me, but I didn't share the reason I thought Nanny might've chosen Chick for my grandfather's name; chicks are earthbound birds, and Nanny had told me many times that birds are angels on earth.

I doubted Mary Nell would understand.

On that day, sitting next to Nanny's oldest friend and biggest rival, I made a promise to myself. I would be as steadfast and tough as my grandmother. With or without Paul's help, without Nanny and Chick, Eliot and I would make it just fine. We didn't need anyone else. My grandparents had already given me all I required to survive – their strength. It streamed through my veins.

CHAPTER EIGHT

*W*e take Will home and spend the afternoon getting to know him. Late in the evening, I enter the living room carrying a soft drink for Eliot. The television is on low, tuned to a baseball game. He sits in the leather chair, his feet propped up on the ottoman and Will draped across one arm. As far as I can tell, he hasn't moved in the last half-hour. A bottle of baby formula sits on the table at his elbow and when Will hiccups and twitches, Eliot jumps and reaches for it. He touches the nipple to the baby's lips.

"I doubt he's hungry," I say. "He'll let you know if he is." He returns the bottle to the end table, and I set the can I carry on a coaster beside it.

Eliot frowns. "How can holding something so small make a person's arm so sore?"

I sit on the ottoman when he lowers his feet. "Relax a little. Will won't break if you loosen up. Why don't you lay him in your lap for a while? Like this." I take the baby from his arms, place Will lengthwise between Eliot's legs, with his head at Eliot's knees. "Let me take another look at my grandson."

Shifting my position, I add, "I think I could sit and stare at him all night." I peel back the blanket. Will wears a long receiving gown over his diaper, socks on his feet. I lift the gown to expose his skinny, pink-mottled knees.

"Don't worry, Will," Eliot says in a mock-teasing tone. "I'll get rid of these sissy clothes Mom bought you and find you something to wear that's not so embarrassing."

"All babies wear gowns," I protest. "Girls and boys." I stroke a fingertip up Will's calf and realize that, until today, I had forgotten the true definition of softness. *Softness* is a baby's earlobe, Will's earlobe, the soles of his feet, his powdered bottom, his silky head. I had lost touch with the meaning of *precious*. Will's fragile weight is the physical embodiment of that word, the cooing sounds he makes, his tiny, yawning mouth. It's been years, decades, since I experienced a flood of new love so overpowering it terrified me. But it all comes back when I look at Will. And in Eliot's eyes, I see exactly what *I'm* feeling – love and terror in equal measure.

He's been quiet throughout the day, awkward in his new role of father, maybe even embarrassed. Eliot's hands can dribble a basketball, tinker with a car engine, deftly pick out a tune on a guitar, but when it comes to tending to Will, they may as well be attached to his wrists by his thumbs. Throughout the day, as his fingers fumbled to care for his child, they also tugged at my heart. He's always been so self-assured in the face of a challenge. In this challenge, though, it's clear he feels he's met his match.

I pull off one of Will's socks. "Look at these long, narrow feet." Cradling one in my palm, I say, "Where'd you get these, big guy? Your daddy's are wide as boxcars."

"Liza's feet are narrow. It's weird. He has her feet, my chin and hair, Liza's mouth."

Melancholy tinges Eliot's voice. Or maybe I only imagine it. I wonder if he misses Liza? I remember missing Paul when I discovered every crease and curve and bump on Eliot's infant body. I wished him with me to *oooh* and *ahhh* over what we'd created together, a combination of Paul and myself more perfect than either of us alone. Since coming home, I've tried my best not to become too smitten too soon with my grandson. Now, I admit that I've failed.

"I love him already, Eliot," I murmur, without looking up.

"Me, too."

"Will might sleep better with a bath before bedtime."

Eliot's head jerks toward me. "A bath?"

"I'll show you how." I pick Will up, place him over my shoulder, and stand. He smells sweet and pure, like baby powder and formula. His fine, dark hair feels like a feather against my palm. "Until he's too big, we can bathe him in the bathroom sink."

"On that big sponge you bought?"

I nod. "It will keep him from slipping and sliding around."

Eliot follows me to the bathroom located between his bedroom and Will's. While he was feeding Will earlier, I set out everything: the sponge, a soft hooded towel, a washcloth.

"It's like a sauna in here," Eliot says.

"I turned on the heat light a minute ago. We don't want him to catch a chill."

Eliot draws the water. "Is this too hot?"

I dip a finger into the sink. "That feels about right. We don't need much. Just enough to get him wet. You don't want to submerge him."

He turns off the tap.

The sponge sits beside the sink on the countertop. I gently

85

place Will on it, face up. "Here," I say to Eliot. "You undress him now." When his gaze darts to mine, I smile my encouragement. "You have to learn sometime." Keeping one hand on Will's stomach, I step back, and Eliot takes my place.

Overcome with conflicting emotions, I watch his long, wide fingers worry with the delicate drawstring at the gown's hem then struggle some more while maneuvering Will's tiny, clenched fists through the snug long, narrow sleeves. Eliot blows out a noisy, frustrated breath.

"It'll get easier with time," I assure him.

Last Friday evening, he was at the lake water-skiing with friends, cooking out, sunburned and carefree, enjoying the summer break from school. One week later, he's learning to be a father. I push the thought from my mind as Eliot removes Will's diaper. Earlier, I promised myself I'd only think happy thoughts after bringing Will home today. No worries. No regrets. No *what-ifs*.

"Careful not to bump his umbilical chord," I warn. "And try to keep it dry."

"That thing's gross." He hands me the diaper. "How long before it drops off?"

"Two or three weeks." I set the diaper aside.

"Doesn't it need to be cleaned, too?"

"Doctors used to tell moms—" I catch myself. "The consensus used to be that you swabbed the cord with a gauze pad and alcohol after a bath, then let it dry. But the new advice seems to be that if you let it dry naturally, it'll fall off sooner."

"I'm all for that." Eliot lifts Will, holding him away from his body like a Thanksgiving turkey on a platter. "Now what?"

I transfer the sponge into the sink. "Put him in."

As Eliot places Will onto the damp sponge, the baby's body

goes rigid, his face reddens and screws up, and his cries emerge in furious shrill bursts.

Eliot panics and starts to take him out. "The water's too hot!"

"No, it's okay." I ease his hand back, soak the washcloth with water, squeeze it over Will, crooning soothing words until he slowly relaxes. "You're just not used to taking a bath yet, are you Will? Doesn't that warm water feel nice?" I run my wet hand gently over his head. "You're no bigger than a wink." And that's how quickly he appeared in my life. In the time it takes to blink an eye.

Once, when I was a girl, a friend at school asked me why Nanny always called me Sugarbee. I didn't know, so when I went home, I posed the question to her.

"Because when I first laid eyes on you, I thought you was sweet as sugar," she said. "And you stung my heart."

That's how I feel now – as if Will's stung my heart and it's swelling with love for him, despite my resistance.

"Your turn," I say, and Eliot and I change places.

With one palm on Will's head, he lifts the cloth, and when the warm water drizzles over the baby's thighs, a stream of pee shoots Eliot in the face.

Startled, we both shriek, and Will begins to cry again.

Eliot turns to me, his nose wrinkled, his face wet. I burst out laughing, and after a moment, his expression shifts, and he laughs, too.

"Sweetie, you've either just been initiated into parenthood or baptized, I'm not sure which."

He wipes at his forehead. "At least his aim is good."

"Go wash your face. I'll finish up here."

After Eliot leaves, I get busy washing Will, and as I'm wiping the damp cloth over his scalp, a phone rings in another room.

The noise stops abruptly, and I hear Eliot say, "Yeah, we're home. You should see the kid. He's a little stud, just like his old man." He laughs, then after a long pause, says, "I can't, Russ. No, I'm putting him to bed. I know we bought the tickets two weeks ago, but a lot's happened since then." Another pause, then, "He's a baby, there's no guarantee he'll sleep through the night." His voice lowers, "No, I won't ask her. It's Will's first night home. Give me a break, dude."

Seconds later, Eliot returns to the bathroom as I'm drying Will off. "I'll take him and put him to bed," he says. I pass Will over, and he drapes the towel's hood over the baby's head. I push hair behind my ear and study him. "You okay?"

"I'm fine. My friends will just have to get over it. Things are different for me now."

I remember the moment I had the same realization after Eliot was born – that although something precious had come into my life, in order to keep him, I would lose other wonderful things I'd always taken for granted. Spontaneity with my friends. Carefree fun. Freedom.

As Eliot starts toward the door, I call his name, and he pauses to look over his shoulder. "I'm proud of you," I tell him. "It takes guts to do what you're doing."

Pressing his lips together, he shrugs, then leaves the room.

I'm awakened in the middle of the night by Will's cries. Rolling over, I look at the clock. *A quarter past midnight.* Yawning, I push from bed and pad down the hallway toward Eliot's room where I see a glow of light beneath the door. I knock, and he mutters, "Come in."

The first thing I notice is Will in the center of Eliot's double bed with Eliot sitting next to him, tugging at the tape on his diaper. The second thing that catches my eye are the posters hanging on the walls around them, a couple with pictures of rock bands, another displaying a giant peace sign, one scantily dressed, pouting brunette in a semi-erotic pose. It isn't as if I haven't seen these before, although I'm rarely in Eliot's room. But the incongruity of them in the same setting with the cradle and other baby paraphernalia strikes me now. "Need some help?" I ask.

I'm taken aback by the weary, helpless look on his face. "I don't have a clean diaper," he says with an edge to his voice. "They're in the nursery."

"Just a second. I'll get one." I leave and come back with a stack of them, a box of wet wipes, the talcum powder. Then I sit beside him on the bed.

Will moves his head from side-to-side and mouths his fist as Eliot removes the wet diaper. I hand him a dry one. "It's stupid for him to be sleeping in here when everything's in the other room," he says, in the same grumpy tone.

"If you want him to sleep in the nursery, that's fine. I just liked having you closer to me when you were a newborn and getting up all the time, so I kept your diapers and things in my room for the first two or three months. I was afraid I wouldn't wake up and hear you crying."

"I don't think that's going to be a problem," Eliot mumbles, the words so low that I barely hear him over Will's shrieks. He places the clean diaper underneath Will then sprinkles on some powder before securing it. "How often did I wake up?"

"Three times, maybe? Twice on a good night."

Eliot stares at me blankly a moment before pulling Will's

gown down around his feet. He cleans his hands with a wipe, tosses it across the room into a trash can, picks Will up. The crying ceases. Making cooing noises, Will turns his mouth toward Eliot's chest and continues moving his head from side-to-side, as if searching for a breast. Realization dawns in Eliot's face, and he shifts Will up to his shoulder.

"I'll go fix a bottle," I say.

"I fed him not more than two hours ago."

"He's right on schedule, then. Every two or three hours is pretty standard for a newborn. Try giving him his pacifier until I come back."

While warming the bottle in the kitchen, my earlier self-made promise of positive thoughts only – no worries, no what-ifs – disappears like a dream. After only one day and night of having Will home, I feel as if I've set myself up for disaster. The past fourteen or so hours have confirmed how ill-prepared Eliot is for fatherhood and reminded me how much time and attention a baby requires. Eliot's first semester isn't far off. Studying will consume most of his time for the next several years. He'll be exhausted. I'll be on my own. More a mother to Will than a grandmother. A single mother. Again.

I test the formula's temperature on my wrist, assuring myself it won't be as difficult this time. I have prior experience now. And I won't really be flying solo. It isn't as if Eliot won't be around. He won't be occupied every second of every day. We'll share the burden of caring for Will.

The burden.

The thought fills me with shame.

Pulling the bottle from the pan of warm water, I tighten the cap, turn off the stove, and silently scold myself. I need to quit fretting and start making plans. We could use a live-in caregiver, a woman who would become part of the family. Someone who'd shop for groceries, clean, and cook meals.

Nice fantasy.

I start toward Eliot's room. I make a good living, but not enough to pay full-time wages to an employee.

Eliot and Will aren't in his bedroom. I hear a quiet, deep voice drifting from the nursery and head that way. Before I reach the door, I stop to listen.

"Sorry about the bad mood, Will," Eliot murmurs. "It's not you. I'll try to get used to the middle of the night stuff, I promise."

The mix of weary apprehension and gruff affection in Eliot's voice gets to me. Composing myself, I step into the room. They're in the rocking chair, and Will is sucking on the tip of Eliot's forefinger. I hand over the bottle, and when Eliot offers it to Will, he takes it eagerly.

"You need anything else?" I ask.

"I'm fine." He keeps his focus on the baby.

"If you do, come get me. I'll take the next shift, okay?"

Eliot nods, but doesn't answer.

Back in my room, I sit on the side of my bed and stare into space, twisting the edge of the sheet between my hands, as conflicted as I've ever been in my life. They need me, both of them. And I want to be here for them, but I can't be the sort of grandmother Nanny was to me. I have a career to think about, three people to support now. I don't have the energy or inclination to juggle a full-time job and mothering an infant, as I did with Eliot. Yet here I am with a baby to care for, a son to help through school. I might not have to worry about the career soon, thanks to Liza's grievance. Which brings up an entire new set of problems.

I consider calling Liza in the morning, but I know it's not a good idea. If she complained to the hospital, it could be considered harassment on my part and would be another strike against me. I don't want to harass the girl. I wouldn't even try to change her mind. I only want to ask why she's doing this.

Not a good idea, I repeat to myself.

I fluff my pillow, lie down, and turn off the lamp. Two weeks. How will I survive the wait? I should be doing something to save my ass at work. But, what?

I sit up again, turn the light back on. My work satchel is on the floor, propped against the nightstand beside me. I decide to write down my perspective of the sequence of events that led to Liza filing the grievance against me. If a hearing is held, I don't want to forget any details that might swing a decision in my favor. While rummaging for a legal pad inside the satchel, I find the piece of paper where I wrote the information about Paul's brother and mother.

Paul. I can't believe he's dead. He's the only man I've ever really loved. I was fond of Stephen Simms, the man I married when Eliot was eleven, but there was no real passion between us.

I trace the numerals in Mark Reeves' phone number with my fingertip. Did Paul ever tell his family he fathered a child during college? Did he mention me? Voice regrets? All these years I've told myself I didn't care, but for reasons I can't understand, I care now.

I lay the paper aside, wondering if Mark Reeves would talk to me and answer my questions. Maybe if I knew more about what happened to Paul in the years since I last spoke with him, I could stop blaming myself. I made the only decision I could that afternoon that I drove to Oklahoma City when Eliot was five months old. It seemed clear to me how Paul felt about our son – about me. I can't believe I was wrong about that.

I didn't return to school the fall semester after Eliot's birth. I stayed at the farm and worked full-time as a waitress at Riley's Cafe. The tips weren't great, but at least Ray Allan didn't own the place.

Mary Nell kept Eliot during my shifts. We had become close, thanks to her persistence. At first, I resisted her camaraderie, afraid I would betray Nanny's memory by returning Mary Nell's friendship. But the truth was, I needed her. And I liked Mary Nell. She boosted my spirits and made me laugh with stories about her and Nanny when they were kids.

I thought, after New Year's, Eliot and I would move back to Oklahoma City, and I would resume school the spring semester. But as Halloween came and went and the wind blew colder, the prospect of returning to college seemed more and more unlikely. Eliot had grown accustomed to Mary Nell. How would I find anyone in the city to keep him who was as loving and trustworthy? Someone affordable? I would be forced to put him in daycare, and I felt uneasy about that. Good places might exist, but they couldn't give him the attention Mary Nell did. There would be too many babies competing for someone to hold them. Besides, daycare was expensive. I'd have to work full-time to pay for it, as well as for rent and groceries, tuition, and everything else we'd need. How would I manage a job, a baby, and school all at once? Just thinking about it overwhelmed me.

"I don't know how Nanny did it," I told Mary Nell one Saturday when she dropped by to check on Eliot and me. I sat on the living room floor surrounded by piles of dry laundry while Eliot fretted nearby in his baby swing.

"Did what, Sugar?" Mary Nell surprised me by plopping onto the floor too, despite the fact she wore her usual attire – crisp blouse, long skirt, and pantyhose.

"How did she stay so strong when she was raising Uncle Ned by herself?" I folded a pair of jeans and avoided her eyes. "Sometimes I catch myself resenting Nanny's strength. I'm not proud of that. She deserves better from me than resentment."

Mary Nell patted my knee. "I know you loved your grandmother, and she knew it, too. You're just feeling pressured, that's all." She reached for a t-shirt and proceeded to help me fold clothes.

"This is harder than I thought it would be. I bet Nanny never wished J. D. would come back and help her, but that's what I keep wishing about Paul." I also doubted my grandmother had ached for the man who'd left her behind. But I couldn't say that to Mary Nell. I couldn't admit that, late at night, lying in bed alone, Paul was all I thought about. The sound of his voice. His eyes and hands. His mouth.

"You're only human, Maggie," Mary Nell said with sympathy.

"You think Nanny ever wanted to live somewhere besides Juniper? Or maybe do something other than work at the grocery store and take care of the farm?" That's what Mary Nell had told me my grandmother did before marrying Chick.

"When we were young, she talked some about becoming a teacher." Mary Nell sighed. "Life has a way of changing plans."

But did that have to be true for me? I had been serious about becoming a nurse since high school. Even before then, I'd thought about it. When I was small, Nanny told me my mother had wanted to be a nurse. As a little girl, I fantasized about time-traveling back to the day my mother died, the day of my birth. I'd arrive wearing a starched white uniform, and I'd save my mother's life in Ned's car on the side of the road. After that miraculous feat, I would time-travel to Vietnam and use my medical skills to save my daddy's eye. He would come home a strong, happy man, a father who adored me. He'd keep his promise to marry Mama, and we'd be a family.

Did Nanny have similar dreams? Did she always regret not becoming a teacher? I never asked her if she pushed aside any plans to stay home and raise children, and I regretted my lapse. No matter what she might've said, though, I wouldn't give up my *dream. But I had come to the conclusion I needed Paul's help in order to achieve it. If Paul knew I'd kept our son, I was convinced he would want to be involved in Eliot's life.*

"Why don't you call the boy's father?" Mary Nell said to me, placing a folded towel on top of a stack of others. "Tell him everything. Ask him to give you a hand. You're not the only one responsible for your son, you know." She glanced toward the swing where Eliot kicked and gurgled. "It takes two to tango." Mary Nell winked, surprising me.

After she left, I called Jan Isabel, a friend from school whose boyfriend, Tom, hung out with Paul. We made small talk, and I could tell she was carefully avoiding the subject of the adoption. Everyone at school believed what Paul had told them – that I'd given up the baby.

"Have you seen Paul lately?" I asked Jan outright.

"No, Maggie. I haven't," she answered slowly, as if she was afraid I'd burst into tears. "Tom keeps up with him, though." She hesitated again before adding, "He's married."

"I knew that." I tried to sound nonchalant. "Do you know if he's started law school?"

"He did. And he's working, too. That's why we don't see him much. Everyone's just so busy, you know?"

I thought of my life since becoming a mother. I could've told her she didn't have a clue about "busy."

"I wonder where he's working?" I asked.

"At a law firm. I can't remember which one, Keys and something, I think. You know, one of those firms that has three names."

I laughed. "Don't they all?"

After we hung up, I dialed Information and asked them to look up a business listing for a firm starting with the name 'Keys.' They gave me a number for Keys, Turner, and Smyth. I called, and the receptionist informed me that Paul was off but would be in at one o'clock the following afternoon.

The next morning was typical November-blustery. I called in sick at Riley's, bundled Eliot up, and buckled him into his car seat. Then we drove to Oklahoma City. At a quarter to one, I pulled my rattling Ford LTD into the parking lot of Keys, Turner, and Smyth and let the engine idle. I climbed into the backseat to change Eliot's diaper, mentally rehearsing what I would say to his father.

"What do you think about this, Eliot?" He stopped sucking on his bottle long enough to smile up at me. "Now, listen. This is serious business." I pulled the diaper off, cleared my throat, and said, "Paul, I kept our son. I thought you'd want to know."

Eliot farted.

I laughed. "Okay, I get the message. I'll try again." I put the dry diaper on him, snapped his pant legs around it. "How about this?" I lifted my chin. "Paul, when I saw our baby and heard him cry, I couldn't let him go. I love him. I know you will, too."

Pulling the bottle from his mouth and throwing it to the floorboard, Eliot whimpered.

"Well, geez. You're a tough one to please today, aren't you?" I lifted him to my shoulder and patted his back while he twisted my hair. "What if I said, this?" In a haughty voice, I recited, "Paul, you don't owe me anything, but you owe Eliot. He's your son."

A loud burp sounded in my ear.

I held Eliot away from me and looked into his eyes. "If you don't like this next one, then I guess I'm up shit creek, as Chick used to say." Placing my hands beneath his armpits, I let him stand on my knees.

"Here goes." I cleared my throat again and made a stern face. "Grow up, Paul. Stand up to that rich bitch you married and act like a father to your child." Eliot shrieked a laugh and pumped his legs up and down, making me laugh, too. I hugged him. "Okay, then. You want me to get tough with your old man? Then that's what I'll do."

The LTD's heater didn't work great with the car in idle; my teeth started chattering as I put Eliot's coat on him. We'd wait for Paul inside the law firm lobby.

A second after I opened the car door, a second before my boot touched the parking lot pavement, I spotted Paul and Kelly walking arm-in-arm toward the building's entrance, laughing together. I had never seen Paul in a suit. He looked handsome, older than I remembered. More polished. Like the quintessential lawyer. While Kelly, in her dark slacks and knee-length wool poncho, hair shining like a magazine model's, still looked like the trust fund daughter she was rumored to be.

They paused at the building's entrance, and Kelly turned toward the parking lot, lifted onto her toes, and kissed him. When they parted, Paul stepped aside to reach for the door. The wind caught Kelly's poncho and blew it open in front, exposing her round, pregnant belly.

At that moment, the truth slid through me, landing like a rock in the pit of my stomach. Paul had lied when he said he wasn't ready to be a father; he simply wasn't ready to be a father to my child.

I returned Eliot to his car seat, wiped the wetness from my cheeks with the back of my hand, and climbed behind the wheel of the car again. No more tears. Not ever. They would only drag me down.

Eliot and I pulled out of the parking lot. I never looked back.

CHAPTER NINE

I pull a load of laundry from the washing machine, worried that I haven't heard a word from Constance about the investigation. Will lies in his baby carrier on the floor at my feet. Wide awake, he mouths his fist. I talk to him as I toss wet baby clothes, receiving blankets, and hooded towels into the dryer.

"I'm hungry, too, Wink. I wonder what's taking your dad so long?" I glance at my watch and try to tamp down my irritation. I need to take a shower before my dentist appointment at one o'clock. I had planned to stop cleaning out closets for awhile and go to the pharmacy for a few things then pick up some lunch. But Eliot clearly needed a break, so I asked if he'd like to run the errands for me.

He was up quite a lot during the night. The night before, too. After Will's first day home, I've let him handle the middle of the night feedings alone, like Mary Nell did me. She spent one night with me at the farm before the pastor insisted she sleep at home. I was on my own. I learned from doing, and Eliot should too.

I throw in the last of the clothes and shut the dryer door as

Will starts to cry, and when my cell phone rings, he startles and cries louder. I lift him from the carrier and slide my phone from my pocket to answer the call.

"Sounds like I caught you at a bad time," Alice says.

"You might say that. Eliot left over an hour ago to run an errand that should've taken twenty minutes. Then Will messed up his clothes for what seems like the tenth time today, and he only had one dry outfit left to put on. All this trying to do five things at once reminds me of when I was going to school and raising Eliot alone. I'm mad at Paul right now, isn't that crazy? The man's dead. And even if he wasn't, all this chaos has nothing to do with him."

"I'm sorry, Maggie. You want me to call later when you don't have your hands so full?"

"No, it's okay. I didn't mean to vent on you." Sitting in a kitchen chair, I hold the phone to my ear with an upraised shoulder and pat Will's bottom to calm him. "What's up?"

"I thought I'd fill you in on the hospital gossip."

"There's gossip?"

"Isn't there always?"

Will continues to shriek, stretching my nerves tighter. "Let me put him down. Just a sec, okay?"

Returning to the utility room, I drag Will's carrier into the kitchen, put him in it, then go after a bottle. This morning I rocked him while Eliot took a shower. When he finished, he said he'd make up a new supply, but there aren't any bottles in the refrigerator. I find Will's clean pacifier, put it in his mouth, and he quiets.

"Just let me finish this call," I say to him. "Then I'll feed you."

When I return to the phone, Alice asks, "How's the little guy doing?"

"Good." I take canned formula from the pantry then go to the sink and wash my hands. "As you heard, his lungs are working."

She chuckles. "How is Eliot?"

"After two nights with no sleep, I think reality has finally crashed down on him. He's exhausted. He and Will are both a little grumpy today."

"Sounds like they aren't the only ones."

"Am I that obvious?" I ask, pouring formula into a clean bottle.

"'Fraid so, but don't worry about it. Who wouldn't be frazzled in your situation?"

"Thanks. I needed to hear that."

"Other than exhaustion and short tempers, how are you all holding up? Honestly."

"I don't know; I'm confused. This morning Will woke up inconsolable, and when I went in to check on them, Eliot looked like he was about to burst into tears, too. He was so confident about all this before Will came home, but now he seems to be doubting himself."

"Bless his heart. Yours too, Maggie."

"I don't know whether to shake the kid or hug him. Just when I start feeling sorry for myself and get upset with him, he turns around and makes me so proud I could bust. You should see them together sometimes. Eliot loves Will so much it hurts."

I pick up Will and sit at the table again with a bottle this time. "Sorry I got off track. So, what's the talk at the hospital?"

"I hate to be the bearer of more bad news, but Sheila Barnhill has supposedly been talking to the bigwigs about your job."

Sheila is one of my nurses – the only one I wouldn't be

disappointed to see quit. "About what? She wasn't even working the day I found out about Liza, was she?"

"A lot of folks seem to think she's after your position."

"Is that rumor or fact?"

"I wish I knew. I can't talk long; I just didn't want you to be caught off guard."

We say goodbye and break the connection as Eliot walks in from the garage.

"Where have you been?"

He places two sacks on the counter and frowns. "Wasn't I supposed to get lunch?"

"It doesn't take an hour and a half to pick up sandwiches."

"I went to the pharmacy, too, like you asked. And it hasn't been an hour and a half."

"Close."

"The line was long, and I ran into Trevor Banks. We talked for a second."

"A second? When you were a newborn, I didn't have help making bottles, and nobody was at my beck and call to babysit so I could socialize."

"*I wasn't socializing. Jesus.*" Shoving the sack across the counter, Eliot strides over and stops in front of me. "I'll take him." He lifts Will from my arms and sits at the table.

I turn my back on them and take deep breaths. When my nerves steady, I face him again. "I'm sorry, Eliot. I'm upset about something going on at the hospital, and I took it out on you."

"What's wrong?"

"Liza filed a grievance against me for telling you about Will. I'm on paid mandatory leave until they make a decision."

"That's crazy!" His face flushes crimson. "I'll call her."

"No, don't. I could get into worse trouble if we try to contact her. And don't blame yourself. That evening when I first saw her at the hospital, before I ever brought up telling you, she seemed to have some kind of issue with me."

Eliot's lack of response is telling.

"Whatever it is with her, I won't get my feelings hurt. I need to know what's motivating her to do this to me."

After a long pause, he says, "Liza thinks you pressured me to break up with her."

"I didn't."

"I told her that. She always said you were a control freak. That you were always reminding me I needed to study whenever we had plans to do something together."

"Is that what you think, too?"

"Sometimes you did remind me."

"So, I'm a control freak?"

"*She* said that, not *me*." He curses under his breath. "What are you going to do? Have you called a lawyer?"

"I thought I'd wait out the couple of weeks and see what happens. But maybe I should talk to Doug."

"Who is Doug?"

"He's the attorney who helped me with the insurance company when I had that fender bender last year. And after that he updated my will. Maybe he can tell me what would constitute harm in a case like this."

"Harm?"

"Constance said Liza would have to show I'd harmed her before any attorney would be willing to file a lawsuit against the hospital."

"You think they'll decide about your job based on whether or not she sues?"

"I doubt they'd admit that, but they'll never convince me it's not what's delaying their decision. They're waiting to see how far she'll take this."

———

Doug Dowling has a cancellation in his schedule and sees me at four. I drive to his office after my dentist appointment.

I sit across a dusty, mahogany desk from him, studying the assortment of degrees and certificates, framed in black, that decorate the walls. The first time I came here, those documents were the only reason I gave his competence the benefit of the doubt. Then, as now, Doug wore shaggy long hair, a scruffy beard, and wrinkled clothes. He hasn't changed in that regard. But Doug proved himself to be sharp and thorough; I trust him.

When he mentions statutory and punitive damages, I ask, "Are you talking about money? I didn't cause Liza to incur any expenses."

"She might sue for mental anguish, invasion of privacy. They'd assign a dollar amount to those."

"Mental anguish? All I did was talk to her and ask a few questions. As for invasion of privacy, Eliot knowing about the baby hasn't seemed to cause so much as a blip in her gameplan. She relinquished her rights to Will just like she would've in an adoption." I set my water bottle on his desk. "I can't imagine any sane lawyer would take on her case."

"You'd be surprised." He drums his fingers on the messy desk, leaving prints in the dust. "You say her brother is handling this for her?"

"That's what I was told."

"It's not unusual for a lawyer to take on a case they wouldn't touch otherwise for a family member." He watches me for a moment, scratching his chin. "What do you think she's after? Money or revenge?"

"Revenge, I guess. She thinks I'm responsible for Eliot breaking up with her."

"That's at the core of this? A boyfriend problem?"

"As far as I can tell. And the crazy thing is, I didn't have anything to do with their breakup. Eliot made up his own mind about that."

"Are you sure there wasn't something else?"

"Believe me, I've been trying to remember what horrible thing I ever did to her. We never had an argument or even a harsh word that I can recall."

Doug's chair squeaks as he leans back. "Maybe it's baby hormones," he mutters.

My cell phone rings. I pull the phone from my purse and look at the display. "It's Eliot. Do you mind if I take it?"

"No. Go ahead."

The instant I connect, I'm hit with the sound Will's screams. "Hello? Eliot?"

"Mom? Something's wrong with Will."

The urgency in his tone shoots alarm up my spine. "What's the matter?"

"I don't know. He started screaming about half an hour ago, and he hasn't stopped. I've tried everything."

"Does he have a fever?"

"I don't think so. He isn't that hot."

"You haven't taken his temp?"

"I don't know where the thermometer is."

"I *showed* you where I put it, Eliot." *Patience*, I remind myself, and take a deep breath. "It's in the medicine cabinet in your bathroom," I say more calmly.

The screaming intensifies. "*Geez*. Listen to him. I'm going crazy. It sounds like he's in pain. I must be doing something wrong."

"Calm down."

I slide a glance at Doug and find him still leaned back in his chair, arms crossed, watching me over the top of his crooked reading glasses. When our eyes meet, his dart to a stack of papers on his desk, and he begins sorting through them.

"Will's probably just a little colicky," I say to Eliot. "But let's rule out anything else first. Take off his clothes and make sure nothing's poking him. Then take his temp like I showed you. If it's normal and he keeps crying, put him in a warm bath. That might soothe him."

"Can't you come home?"

"I'm on my way."

"How long?"

"I'll be there as soon as I can. If Will's temp is high, call me back."

"Okay," he says, and I end the call.

"Sorry about that," I tell Doug.

"No problem." He shoves the stack of papers aside, his smile sympathetic.

I lift my purse from my lap. "I guess I'd better head home."

"New father jitters?"

"Something like that. I hope that's all it is."

We both stand, and Doug follows me into the office reception area. "My hat's off to him, Maggie. You, too. It's no small thing you're dealing with here."

At the bank of elevators, I push the *down* button then turn to him. "Six pounds three ounces. That's fairly small, I'd say."

He pulls off his glasses, tilts his head to one side, and smiles.

"You know what I meant. I raised two kids. I remember the baby days. I wouldn't want to go through it again. Not at our age."

"And just what makes you think I'm as old as you?" He laughs at my scowl, and I add, "Seriously, Eliot and I are doing fine. We'll make it."

"Of course, you will." After a pause, he adds, "Let me know when you hear from the hospital. And try not to worry too much. If that girl really wants to move on like she says, maybe she'll drop all this when she's had some space away from it."

The elevator dings. The doors open. After stepping through them, I turn and say, "I hope you're right. 'Bye, Doug. And thanks." The doors glide together.

Five minutes later, after merging into traffic on the highway, I call Eliot on my cell, but he doesn't pick up. A dozen scenarios flash through my mind – none of them good. I should have told him to call our neighbor, Lillian Peyton, a seventy-ish widow who raised three sons and a daughter. She could've been across the street and at the house in less than a minute.

I pass an eighteen-wheeler, pull back into the right lane, regretting our earlier argument and how short I've been with him lately. We're both on edge from too much stress and too little sleep. And, as much as I hate to admit it, something more is at the core of my short temper. Resentment. I should be at work today, having my weekly dinner with some friends tonight – a date I cancelled thinking Eliot wasn't ready for an entire evening alone with Will. I had also planned to attend a conference in San Antonio week after next, where I'd catch up with a former classmate, also attending. I'm sure I'll have to cancel it, too.

Hitting *redial* on my phone, I let it ring ten times before I hang up. Then I press on the accelerator and break the speed limit the rest of the way to the house.

An old Nova and a black Mustang sit side-by-side in my driveway, so I park at the curb. The Nova belongs to Russ, Eliot's best friend, a kid who has been in and out of our house so much over the years he's like a second son. As I'm exiting the car, a small group of people come out of the house and into the yard – Eliot, Russ, and his girlfriend, Gigi, Aaron Ambrose, and two other girls. One of them, a redhead, holds Will.

"Hey, Miss M." Russ waves me over. "Sorry we blocked the drive. I thought you'd still be at work."

"I'm taking a short leave." I hurry to Eliot's side. "How's Will?"

"Okay. I found the thermometer, and he doesn't have a fever. I guess he was just in a pissy mood."

Eliot's rigid body language and the gruffness of his voice tell me that Will isn't the only one suffering from a foul temper.

Russ hugs me. "So you're home on granny duty, huh?" He steps back, grinning.

I grin back at him, thinking of Tim's similar comment and wondering what men find so amusing about the granny label. "That's *grandmother* to you, wise guy," I say. I glance between him and Aaron. "I haven't seen you two in a while."

They both look down at their shoes. "Yeah, well . . ." Russ says, and tugs at his ear. "You've met Gigi, haven't you?" he asks, indicating the girl at his side.

We greet each other, then Aaron introduces me to the blonde beside him, whose name is Clare. Throughout the exchange, the red-haired girl holding Will watches Eliot, as if waiting for him to introduce her, too. But he only jams his hands into his pockets, his tired eyes shifty.

She steps toward me, Will nestled in one arm. "I'm Anne Williams."

I recognize her name. She's called the house a time or two. Eliot took her to a movie last week. "Are you the one responsible for finally calming our little guy down?"

She looks at Will sleeping peacefully in her arms then at Eliot, and her brows tug together. "I just have good timing. He was ready to stop crying by the time we got here."

Eliot huffs. "He was screaming his head off with no end in sight. The second I handed him to you, he shut up."

Scanning the group, I ask, "So what are you all out doing today?"

"For once we had the same afternoon off, so we decided to drop by and meet the kid," Russ answers.

"We brought a baby gift," Gigi adds. "It's inside."

Anne faces Eliot and says hesitantly, "We weren't sure what to get. My older sister just had a baby, and she said you can never have too many diapers, so that's what we brought. I'm sorry it isn't more."

"It's fine," Eliot snaps.

"Your sister is right, Anne," I say, wary of his angry tone. "You can't have too many diapers with a baby in the house."

Silence and tension descend upon us like twin dark clouds. Claire coughs. Aaron whistles under his breath. A plane soars overhead. Nobody looks at anyone else.

Finally, Russ says, "We're headed out for a beer. It's happy hour." He tugs at his ear again.

"We thought you might want to go, Eliot," Aaron adds. "We wouldn't have to be gone long."

"Will's a little young to start hanging out at bars." Eliot takes the baby from Anne's arms, and Will sputters and stiffens as they make the exchange.

When Gigi turns a pleading look on me, I say, "Go ahead, Eliot." Maybe I have been too hard on him. Mary Nell showed up to give *me* breaks in the first days after Eliot came home. "I'll watch Will for a couple of hours."

"If you're going to watch him, I'd rather take a nap."

"A nap!" Russ elbows Eliot. "Don't tell me you're gonna turn into an old man just because you're a dad now." He laughs, but cuts it short when no one else joins in.

"*Russ*," Gigi hisses.

Will starts to cry, and without so much as a goodbye, Eliot starts for the house with him, his face ablaze.

Russ utters a quiet curse.

Moving closer to him, I touch his shoulder. "It's okay. Give him some time. This is all so new right now."

"Sorry, Miss M. I guess we'll go."

Everyone starts toward the cars except Anne. She stares at the house, her face pale and stricken. When Claire calls out to her, Anne turns toward the driveway and starts off without meeting my gaze. Car doors slam.

Russ rolls down his window. "'Bye," he says to me.

"Goodbye, Russ." Our eyes lock, and I swallow past the hard lump of emotion in my throat. "You're Eliot's best friend. He needs you right now. Don't forget about him, okay?"

"You know me better than that." He starts the Nova, then adds, "I'm not gonna forget about him."

I know Russ believes that. I'm not sure I do.

CHAPTER TEN

*E*liot sleeps the rest of the day until I wake him for dinner at seven. Constance calls while we're clearing away the dishes. She asks me to come to her office at eight tomorrow morning, her tone more brisk than usual. I wait for a reason why, but she doesn't give one. When I ask, she says we'll talk about it tomorrow then assures me there's nothing to worry about yet.

Yet.

It isn't like Constance to be so vague.

At ten, Eliot goes to bed again when Will does. An hour later, I turn out my bedroom light, too, thinking about our altercation at lunch, plagued with guilty feelings one minute, defensiveness the next. The last thing I want to do is alienate him, make him doubt his parenting abilities even more than he already does. Adjusting to fatherhood is as difficult for him as I thought it would be. But I had no time to get used to the idea of a baby in the house, either. Eliot got himself into this situation, yet I'm dealing with the consequences as much as he is. I've come too far to be back where I started.

I promise myself I'll do better tomorrow. We both will.

At three a.m., I'm awakened by Will's cries. I listen for signs of Eliot stirring, and when he doesn't, I'm irritated with him all over again. Tonight, of all nights, I need my rest. I want to be fresh when I face Constance and Derek in five hours. I stare at the illuminated face of the clock on my nightstand for thirty more seconds before climbing out of bed.

Will's cries drift from the nursery rather than Eliot's bedroom. I go in and switch the lamp on low. "Shhh, little Wink." He stops crying when I lift him from the bed.

As I turn to carry him to the changing table, I catch a glimpse of Eliot in the shadows beyond the doorway. He ducks out of sight, unaware I've seen him. I catch up to him before he enters his room. "Eliot?" He turns, but I can't see his features in the darkness. "Didn't you hear Will crying?"

"No, I–"

"You must have. You're up, aren't you?"

"I thought he'd go back to sleep."

"Not likely. He's soaking wet and hungry." Eliot doesn't move, doesn't apologize. "You were going to let me take care of it, is that it? You know I have an important meeting in the morning. Don't you care?"

"Yes, I care."

"Then where were you going just now?"

He turns and walks into his bedroom, flips on the overhead light.

Following him, I say, "You made the decision to keep Will, Eliot, not me. I can't just drop everything and become his mother. I have a career to worry about. If I lose my job, how do you think we're going to get by?"

He jerks open his closet door, tugs a t-shirt off a hanger. "You said you'd help."

"I will, but I can't do it all."

Eliot pulls the t-shirt over his head then grabs a pair of crumpled jeans off the floor beside the bed. "Why don't you just say it?"

"Say what, Eliot?"

He steps into the jeans. "You were right. I can't do this. It's too hard."

"I never said you couldn't—"

"Today, while you were gone, nothing I tried calmed him down. I can't do anything right with him."

"That's not true. You're learning. You're doing fine."

"I hate my dad for walking out on us, but I guess I'm a loser just like him."

"He wasn't a loser," I blurt, and I'm as startled by the statement as Eliot looks. His hand pauses on his zipper. Our gazes lock.

I hold my breath, certain all the clocks in the house have stopped ticking. I know the time is right to tell him the truth about Paul, but I find myself hoping that he won't ask me the questions I see in his eyes. I'm not ready to deal with them. I'm not sure I'll ever be ready. `

Eliot breaks our gaze, zips his jeans, and the clocks start ticking again.

"I can't do this," he repeats, then lifts his shoes from the floor, his car keys off the dresser. "Liza was right. Will would be better off with two parents instead of with me."

I call after him as he pushes past me, but he's through the living room and into the kitchen before I can stop him.

The door leading into the garage slams when I round the

corner. With Will crying in my arms, I fling it open, see the garage door rising behind Eliot's Jeep. The engine rumbles to life, and he backs out.

Returning to my bedroom, I pick up my phone and punch in his cell number, hear it ringing in *his* bedroom. I take Will back to the nursery, change his diaper, feed him, put him back in his crib.

At six a.m., exhausted and worried, I call Russ.

"I haven't heard from him, Miss M."

"You think he could be with Anne?"

A long pause, then, "Maybe. You want me to call her?"

"Would you, Russ? I'd really appreciate it."

"Sure."

"You'll call me if he's there, won't you? Even if he says not to? I'm really worried about him."

"I'll call you. I promise."

I break the connection, agonizing over whether or not I should get in touch with Liza. Ten minutes later, desperation has me finding her number in my cell phone contacts and making the call.

"Liza, it's Maggie Mahoney." She doesn't respond. Afraid she might hang up, I talk fast. "I'm sorry if I woke you. It's just – I'm looking for Eliot. Have you heard from him? Sometime last night or this morning?"

"No, I haven't. Is something wrong?"

"I just need to reach him. He had to leave last night, and he left his cell phone here at the house. If he comes by there or contacts you, would you ask him to call me?"

"I doubt I hear from him, but if I do, sure, I'll tell him."

"Thanks, Liza." I break the connection, and when Will's cries start up again in the nursery, it takes everything in me not to cry too.

———

After two prior tries with no answer, my neighbor Lillian Peyton finally picks up the phone at seven. Often, on my drives into work at sunup, I see her walking her dachshund. I guess that's where she's been this morning.

"Lillian?"

"Yes?"

"This is Maggie Mahoney from across the street."

"Yes! How are you, Maggie?"

She sounds surprised. I can't blame her; we aren't close. Since moving into this house ten years ago after Stephen and I married, I've had little time for neighborly visits. I'm usually out the door by seven a.m., and not home again until ten or more hours later. Lillian and I have done little more than exchange pleasantries from the curb.

"I have a huge favor to ask," I say to her.

"I'll help if I can."

"Eliot was called in early to work this morning, and I have an eight o'clock meeting that I can't miss. I was wondering . . ." I wince, and suddenly I'm angry with Eliot for doing this to me, furious and worried at once. "I know it's a lot to ask, but could you watch my grandson for a couple of hours?"

"I didn't know you had a grandchild, Maggie."

"He's something of a surprise to me, too. He's Eliot's son, and he's less than a week old. Eliot is raising him alone." I clear my throat and add, "Well, with some help from me, that is."

After a short silence, she says, "Oh, my dear, what an adjustment for you. My sister raised her grandchild. It wasn't easy, but the girl turned out to be the biggest blessing of her life."

The sympathetic encouragement in the older woman's tone brings sudden tears to my eyes. "His name is Will." My voice quivers.

"Will. That was my husband's name." She sounds wistful and delighted at once. "I can't wait to meet the sweetheart, and I wish I could watch him, but I have to see my doctor this morning."

Disappointment threads through me. "Not for anything serious, I hope."

"No. A little inner ear problem. A change in my medicine will do the trick, most likely. I'd postpone the appointment, but it takes forever to get in these days."

"Don't even consider it. I'll find someone."

"Please call me to babysit again. I'd love to, Maggie."

We say our goodbyes then I head for the kitchen where I grab a bottle. On my way to the nursery, I rack my brain for a name of someone who doesn't work and realize with a pang of surprise and regret that my social circle has a very small circumference. I switch my mind to Eliot's friends. A few come to mind, but I wouldn't leave an infant with any of them on such short notice, if at all.

Resigned to the fact that my only choice is to take Will with me, I enter the nursery and walk to the bed. "It's A Small World" tinkles from the mobile that hangs above Will. He peers up at the twirling shapes above him, stars and a moon with a cow jumping over it. I wonder if he sees them yet, or if only the music draws his attention.

"Up and at 'em, Wink."

There's no time to change his clothes. I scramble to fill his diaper bag, tossing in the bottle, a few diapers, his pacifier, a blanket. All the while, my anger at Eliot grows, does battle with my apprehension that something bad might've happened to him. After he left last night, I didn't go back to sleep. Instead of worrying away the hours, I should've prepared to take Will with me this morning, just in case. But I was so sure Eliot would come home. He wouldn't leave me in a lurch. It isn't like him.

"No time to play this morning," I say to Will.

Yawning, I pick him up and pat his bottom, thankful the car seat is in my vehicle rather than Eliot's Jeep. Grabbing the diaper bag, I head for my bedroom to get my purse, setting down the bag while I search for it with Will in tow. I finally find it and sling the strap over my shoulder, snatching up the diaper bag again on my way out of the room, juggling everything as I head for the door.

Russ calls while I'm in route to the hospital. "Anne said Eliot stayed with her last night, but he's already left. She didn't know where he went. Sorry, Miss M."

"Thanks, Russ. If you hear from him, please ask him to call me."

At the hospital, I stop by Constance's office first, thinking Tim will be there since he's working for her while I'm on leave. My hands are too full to knock, so I tap on the door with the toe of my shoe. Soon, Constance's assistant, Melanie, opens up. "Hi," I whisper. "Is Tim here?"

"He's at your office," Melanie whispers back. She nods at the bundle in my arms. "Can I see?"

I motion her out into the hallway, and she closes the door. "I don't want Constance to know I'm here yet," I say. "Take a quick peek. I'm late."

"I know. They're waiting." She lifts the edge of Will's blanket. "Ohhh, he's so cute!"

"So, Derek Piedmont's here already?"

"Unfortunately. Constance will be in a bad mood the rest of the day. He always does that to her."

"She isn't alone."

Melanie grazes her palm across Will's head. "Want me to watch him for you?"

"I'd better let Tim. If Will starts crying, I don't want him close by. I doubt a crying baby would be appreciated by the powers that be."

"Right. Lord knows we don't want to disturb Mr. Piedmont."

"Back in a sec," I say over my shoulder as I hurry away. A couple of minutes later, I burst into the lobby of my own office. "Tim! Thank goodness, you're here. And hard at work, I see."

He lowers his feet from the desk. "Hi, Maggie. I needed a break from Mel's whiny-ass voice. What are you doing here?"

"I'm late for a meeting with Constance and Derek Piedmont. Here." I thrust Will at him and drop the bag to the floor. "Everything you might need is in here."

He holds Will at arms-length. "But—"

"I shouldn't be long. Wish me luck."

"I've never – babies aren't–"

Closing the door on his protests, I walk as quickly as possible down the hallway. By the time I reach Melanie again, I'm out of breath. I straighten my jacket and run a quick hand over my hair. "How do I look?"

She points at my shoulder and winces. "Oops."

I zero-in on the smear of spit-up baby formula on my lapel at the same instant Constance's office door opens.

Derek looks out. "You're late." The censure in his tone slices like a knife.

"I'm sorry. I had—"

"Never mind. Come in. Let's get started."

When I pause in front of her desk, Constance's gaze lowers to the burp on my lapel. "Hi, Maggie."

"I'm sorry I was late. Traffic was horrible." Her compassionate expression tells me she knows the real reason I'm running behind.

"Have a seat." Derek motions to the chair beside him. "I don't have all day to devote to this. Liza Enlow's brother called yesterday. He's a lawyer."

My stomach drops as I sink into the chair, and the scent of soured milk on my jacket suddenly overwhelms me. "You mentioned that before."

"He was tossing around dates to depose you and some of the rest of the staff."

"So, Liza filed suit?"

"Not yet. But the fact that they want depositions doesn't look promising. It can't hurt for us to go over your story again. Don't be surprised if the girl sues you individually. In situations like this, that's often the plaintiff's course of action."

He sounds so matter of fact, so completely unconcerned about me. I meet Constance's stare briefly before her eyes lower to the desk.

Derek opens a file. "Let's see . . . what would be the best way for you to approach this?"

"You're not suggesting I lie, are you?"

He looks up. "I would never encourage a staff member to lie, Miss Mahoney."

"But you wouldn't discourage it, is that it?"

He blinks at me. "Refresh my memory. You randomly chose Miss Enlow's case to audit without realizing you knew her, correct?" Glancing down at the notes in his lap, he adds, "Alice Parker backs that up."

"I explained to you last time we met that Alice was misinformed."

"I see. So was it the floor's nurse manager who chose the case for you to audit?" He scans the page in front of him. "Here we go. Buddy Meeks."

"Wait a minute. Please." I take a steadying breath. I know what he's attempting; Derek is trying to cover the hospital's proverbial ass. Without actually speaking the words, he's coaching me, reciting the testimony he'd like me to state in the deposition. For a second, I consider going along with his ploy. I have a lot at stake. But I can't lie about this. Lies have cost me too much already. "Buddy didn't choose anything for me," I say. "I told you exactly how it happened the last time we met."

He leans back and thumps the legal pad. "You might want to hire an attorney."

"So, the hospital will sue me if I don't change my story?" I ask, my heart hammering.

"I didn't say that. The hospital *could* sue you, though. And no matter what Ms. Enlow decides to do, you won't escape the HIPAA fine now that the grievance has been filed." I stare at him, and he adds, "You should also be aware that if the hospital decides to terminate you based on yours and Miss Enlow's testimony, there's nothing Ms. Bening or I can do."

"Don't you mean if I don't call Elizabeth Enlow a liar while making up my own lie?"

Derek leans toward me. "Don't put words in my mouth, Miss Mahoney."

I gather my things. "Don't put words in mine." A knock sounds on the door as I stand.

"Excuse me," Constance murmurs – the first words I've heard out of her since she greeted me. "Come in," she calls.

The instant the door opens, I hear Will's quiet, persistent sobs and distress and frustration compete for a place in my chest.

Melanie pokes her head into the room. "I'm sorry to interrupt but—"

"Help," Tim squeaks, his head appearing in the narrow space beside hers.

I glance at Derek, at Constance. Right now, I hardly care what either of them thinks. I'm disgusted with him and disappointed in her for not speaking her mind. "Sounds as if my grandson needs a diaper change." I turn to Tim. "There are diapers in Will's bag. Wipes, too."

The door opens wider, and I see Will squirming in the crook of Tim's left arm. He winces. "This one?" With his free hand, Tim lifts my work satchel.

Heat sweeps up my neck as I realize I must've grabbed the wrong bag at home when I was in such a rush to leave.

"Well . . ." Derek sounds inconvenienced and smug. "I guess that's the end of that. We're through here." He tightens his tie. "I'll be calling you."

I can't leave the building fast enough. Avoiding eye contact with every person I pass, I move through the hallways with Will in one arm, my satchel in the other, my purse slung over my shoulder. When I reach the hospital lobby, I push on toward the exit, focused on the sliding doors.

Outside, the sun seems too bright. Heading across the parking lot toward my car, I suck in huge gulps of air. Will fusses while I strap him into the car seat. As I'm closing the back door, I hear my name called and turn.

Tim crosses the lot in long strides. He stops in front of me, panting, his face flushed. "I'm sorry, Maggie. I don't know what I was thinking when I brought the baby to you. I *wasn't* thinking. I panicked. Babies are as foreign to me as football."

For a split second, I want to blame him. Not only for disrupting the meeting and embarrassing me, for everything wrong in my life. I want to lash out at someone. Tim, Eliot, Paul. Make my misfortune their fault. But it isn't, and I know it. I planted the seed for this blooming disaster a long time ago. Back when I decided to keep a secret from Paul and chose to mislead Eliot. What was it he said last night? *"I hate my father for walking out on us, but I guess I'm a loser just like him."*

"You didn't do anything wrong, Tim. I did. Babysitting isn't in your job description. I took advantage of you. I'm the one who's sorry." I open my car door, and Will's fussing noises drift out.

Tim sighs. "Before I so rudely interrupted, how was the meeting going?"

"Don't ask."

He scrapes his fingers across his buzzed head. "Are you going to be okay?"

I laugh a little. "To tell you the truth, I'm not sure."

"What can I do?"

"Nothing, but thanks. No one other than Liza can make a difference in any of my problems." The shattering words Eliot uttered last night come back to me again, and I shrug. "And me.

I can make a difference. It's time I did that." No more putting it off. Eliot will come home eventually.

A few minutes later, when I turn onto my street, I see Eliot's Jeep parked in the driveway in front of our house. I pull in beside it and sit for a moment to pull myself together. Too soon, I gather my purse and satchel, take Will from the backseat.

Holding him close, I slowly start up the walk toward the house, asking myself how everything went so wrong. On that winter day in when Eliot and I left Paul and Kelly in the law firm parking lot without looking back, I was certain I was headed the right direction. I never dreamed my decision would lead me here.

———

I tracked down Uncle Ned through Mary Nell's husband. Pastor Cleveland had recently visited the nearby town of Colley for a funeral, and he'd spotted Ned outside an employment office with a group of day laborers. Mary Nell kept Eliot while I drove the sixty miles, and there was my uncle, right where Pastor Cleve had last seen him, huddled against the building's crumbling brick wall amidst a cluster of downtrodden men with centuries-old eyes just like his.

"Uncle Ned?" He didn't act the least bit surprised to see me. Any bystander would've thought we talked every day.

"Hey there, Maggie." His gaze darted away from me.

"How are you?"

Shoving his hands into the pockets of an old coat he had worn for years, he mumbled, "I'm good."

"I missed you at Nanny's funeral."

"I couldn't come."

A surge of something between anger and annoyance shot through me. "She was *your* mother."

His mouth moved silently, as if the words he wanted to say were stuck in his throat and he was trying to work them free. Pulling a pack of cigarettes from his pocket, a matchbook, he fumbled to light up with a trembling hand.

Watching him, I suddenly realized that by "couldn't" he meant it would've been too difficult for him to see his mother buried so soon after Chick. I grasped his forearm to steady his hand, wondering if I had ever touched him before. "It's okay. She would've understood. Nanny loved you so much, Uncle Ned."

The sickly-sweet scent of alcohol seeped from his pores. He eased his arm away and lit the cigarette without my help. Then he looked at me with his ancient eyes, and I realized that he had seen difficult things I couldn't even imagine. Horrible things. His throat shifted hard. His face remained blank.

Tobacco smoke swirled around me, reminding me of summer evenings at the farm, sitting on the porch swing beside Nanny while, a few feet away, Chick strummed his guitar, a cigarette hanging from one corner of his mouth. I'd been forced to say goodbye to my grandparents; how could I say goodbye to my home, too? But I didn't see that I had any other choice, so before I could change my mind, I blurted, "I had my baby, Uncle Ned. A boy. He's five months old."

My uncle showed no signs of surprise or disappointment that when I had contacted him to let him know Nanny died, I didn't mention Eliot's birth.

"I want to go back to school, and I really need some money," I explained. "If you don't want the farm, I was thinking I'd sell it."

"Okay."

"You sure?"

"I won't be goin' back there."

"Whatever price I get for it, I'll split it with you."

"Use it all for yourself and your boy. I got plenty."

I glanced behind him at the restless group of men waiting for someone to drive by and hire them to do odd jobs for the day. My uncle was lying, but I didn't argue with him. I doubted it would do any good. "Why don't you come home for a while? Stay with me? You could see the farm one last time before it sells and meet your great-nephew."

"Wish I could." He drew on the cigarette. "I got business to tend to. You know how it is."

The smoke drifted above him, twisting like the ache in my chest. I managed a smile, though I felt a core-deep sadness. "I know, Uncle Ned." I stepped back. "Well, I'll be seeing you. Keep in touch, okay? Let me know how you're doing and where you are. When I move, I want to give you my new address and my phone number, so I need to know how to find you."

"I expect I'll be here for awhile."

"Okay. Goodbye, then."

I'd made it halfway across the street when I heard him call out to me. I turned around, and Uncle Ned said, "Your boy. What's his name?"

"Eliot."

A hint of a smile crossed his face. "Eliot." He flicked ash onto the sidewalk. "That's a fine name."

Minutes later, I drove away with one eye on my uncle in the rearview mirror – a loner, like my father. Nanny had told me more than once that they lived within the walls they'd built around themselves during the war, a war long over, but one they still fought inside themselves. The truth of that finally registered as I watched Uncle Ned and the group of men he stood with become smaller and smaller behind me.

For the first time since my father disappeared, I wished that I could see him again, that I could force him to talk to me, to answer my questions, to give me a reason to try and understand all the heartless things he'd done to my mother and me.

When I arrived home, I called Ray Allan and asked him if he still wanted to buy the farm; he had been after my grandparents to sell it to him for years. Mr. Allan jumped at the chance. Then I contacted a small college in the Texas Panhandle about applying for their nursing program as a transfer student.

What Mary Nell said was true; even if Chick had not come along, Nanny would have survived, made a good life for herself and her child. No more feeling sorry for myself; I would follow my grandmother's example. Eliot would have no less a life than Paul's other child – Kelly's child. He would rise above our family legacy of poor choices and struggle. I would see to that on my own.

CHAPTER ELEVEN

*E*liot sits at the kitchen table, hunched over, his head in his hands. He looks up when I enter. "Hi," I say to him. The clothes he wears are the same ones he wore last night. They look as if he slept in them, but I know he didn't sleep. Beard stubble covers his chin and cheeks, and his eyes are a red roadmap. They flick to Will, who rests in my arms.

Eliot stands as I move further into the kitchen. I lower my satchel to the floor then slip my purse off my shoulder.

Reaching for Will, he says, "Here, I'll take him."

I hand the baby to him, and Eliot brings him to his shoulder, tilts his face to the top of Will's head, and begins to weep. "I'm sorry, Will."

Watching him, my throat aches.

After a minute, Eliot looks across at me, his face twisted with emotion. "I'm sorry."

I wrap my arms around him and Will, and Eliot's shoulders shake as he silently cries. "It's okay. You're under a lot of stress. We both are. I'm sorry, too. I said things I shouldn't have. Things that weren't really meant for you."

He pulls back to look at me. "I was wrong to leave."

"You're here now. That's what counts."

I step back, a stillness gathering inside me; the calm before the storm. "Will had a busy morning. Why don't you give him a bottle then put him down for his nap while I fix us something to eat."

He nods, then prepares a bottle in silence while I search the pantry with blind eyes.

After he leaves the room with Will, I close the pantry, take off my jacket, fold it over the back of a chair. Then I walk to the window that overlooks the backyard.

Eliot was eleven when Stephen and I bought this house. He quickly made friends with Russ, who lived a couple of streets over, and the two of them set to work building the treehouse that's still perched in the silver oak. They earned money by throwing papers that summer, then spent it on scrap lumber and other supplies. For two weeks, the boys sawed and hammered and nailed non-stop. When I came home from work each day, Eliot's sitter would widen her eyes and say, "Go take a look," or "You won't believe what they did today." The progress they'd made always amazed me, their creative solutions to whatever problems cropped up.

When they finished, Eliot asked me to climb up and take a look inside, but after that, I wasn't invited. I understood. It was a boy's club, a place for them to escape a mother's eyes and ears, to talk about whatever eleven-year-old boys talk about.

But Stephen wasn't invited, either. Not even for a look. I *didn't* understand that, though Stephen seemed less bothered than me by the snub. I had imagined my child and my new husband bonding, having fun together. Father and son. That never happened.

Eliot acted uncomfortable around Stephen and me whenever we were together. He was explosive at times, too quiet at others. Anger and resentment simmered within his long silences. I felt the heat. It flowed as slowly as lava toward Stephen, but it raced like wildfire toward me. During my one year of marriage, I was miserable more often than not. I'd gained a husband but lost a son. It wouldn't have mattered who the man was; what Eliot felt was not about Stephen. He thought I had betrayed him by marrying. He'd been the man of the house for too long.

I press my fingers against the windowpane, feel the sun's warmth on the glass. Eliot is going to think I've betrayed him again. This time, maybe I did.

"Mom?"

I turn, find him watching me. "I know you're tired and hungry, but could we sit down and talk for a minute?"

He eyes me warily, shrugs. "Sure."

"Let's go into the den." When I walk past him, Eliot follows. We sit at opposite ends of the sofa. "There's something I need to tell you." I clasp my hands together; they're ice cold. "I should have told you a long time ago."

"What is it?"

"It's about your father."

He frowns. "Okay."

"I've misled you. At first, I thought I was doing the right thing for you, but now that Will's come into our lives, I know I was wrong."

Eliot's knee bounces up and down. "You're freaking me out."

I take a breath. "I know you believe your father turned his back on us. That he left us. But that's not what happened."

"What are you talking about?"

"He thought I placed you for adoption. That's what we agreed to do. It's what I'd planned to do. We were young. He was about to start law school. We weren't married. Adoption seemed like the right thing for everyone. For you, most of all."

"He—?" I watch Eliot's confusion turn into an emotion I've seen often in him – bitterness toward the father he never knew. "Did he even *offer* to marry you?"

"Paul and I broke up before either of us knew I was pregnant."

"Paul?"

"Yes. Paul Reeves. That was his name." I take another breath and continue, "So we decided to place you for adoption. Paul was honest with me. He said he wasn't ready to raise a child. He was putting himself through law school, Eliot. He was already engaged to another girl. I was still in college. Neither of us had any money."

I wait for him to speak, to nod, to take my hand . . . something, but Eliot only stares at me.

"As much as I wanted to keep you," I continue, "I didn't know how I could do it alone. I loved Paul, but he loved someone else. There was no chance we were ever going to be together. So I agreed with him that we should let a couple adopt you who could give you all the things we couldn't, all the things you deserved. But then you came. I saw you, and I couldn't do it."

"Why didn't you tell him?"

The chill in his voice sends a shiver up my spine. I explain the rest, every detail. Paul at the nursery window; the warning in Kelly's eyes when she spotted me; the time when Eliot was five months old and I drove to Paul's workplace to tell him, then found out Kelly was pregnant. "When I saw her, all I could think was that he'd lied to me about not being ready to be a father. I thought he just didn't want *my* baby."

"But you said it yourself, they were *married*." His voice rises, and now the bitterness is directed at me. "You don't give a baby up when you're married."

"I realize now that his situation with Kelly was different than ours. I guess I should have realized it then, too, but you have to understand how young and confused I was. Seeing him with Kelly, the two of them so happy, it hurt me."

"Didn't it cross your mind that he might've felt different if he knew you'd kept me? If he knew I didn't *have* a father? He thought I was living in some happy little two-parent home." I flinch as Eliot pushes to his feet. "He had a right to know what really happened to me. He had a right to decide whether or not he wanted to be a part of my life."

"You're right." I stand, too, reach out to him.

Eliot yanks his arm away from my grasp. "You did the same thing to him that Liza tried to do to me."

"That's not true. She didn't even tell you she was pregnant. If I hadn't seen her at the hospital, she wouldn't have told you about Will."

Eliot walks to the window and stands with his back to me.

"Say something, Eliot."

"There's nothing to say."

"I wanted to protect you."

"Protect me?" He whirls around. "From what?"

"Please try to understand. I've never told you much about my relationship with my own dad, but it wasn't good. I can count on two hands the times we spent together. He didn't care enough to keep his promises to me, to show up when he said he would, to be there for my birthdays or—"

The words stick in my throat, and tears I've held in for years burn the backs of my eyes. "I took second place to everything else with that man. So, when I found out Kelly was pregnant, I promised myself you would never feel like you took second place with Paul. I knew how it felt to have a neglectful father, and I wanted to spare you that pain. By the time the wrongness of what I'd done really hit me, I was afraid to change things."

He shakes his head. "What were you so afraid of?"

"Everything. I was afraid he'd either shun you and hurt you more, or that he'd be so furious with me that he'd go to the opposite extreme and try to take you away from me. He was a lawyer. He would've had every advantage. He would've known how to use the system, while I—"

"Where is he?" Eliot asks, impatience in his tone.

A second wave of dread knocks the air from my lungs. "When you told me you'd decided to keep Will, I started looking for Paul. I thought it would help you make the right decision about Will if you finally knew the truth. If you—"

"Did you find him, or not?"

I sit on the couch again. "He's been living in Red Lake all these years."

Pulling his cell phone from his pocket, Eliot starts toward the hallway.

"Wait," I say, following him.

"I've waited twenty-one years. Don't you think that's long enough?"

I catch his arm, and he pauses to look back at me, the anger on his face filling me with shame. "Your father got sick."

"Sick? What do you mean? What's wrong with him?"

"Paul died, Eliot." The room falls so silent, all I hear is sound of blood rushing in my ears. "He had kidney failure. He needed a donor, and they couldn't find a match because . . ." I bite my lip.

"Because *why?*"

"He had a rare blood type. Apparently, no one else in his family had it."

"Except *me*. I have it." Eliot looks stricken.

"I'm so sorry," I say in a choked voice. "His brother, Mark Reeves, your uncle, he still lives in Red Lake. His mom does, too. Paul and Kelly were divorced. Their daughter is a student at OU."

"I had a sister. I had a *family*. I could've saved my dad's life."

Jerking his arm from my grasp, Eliot walks into the hallway then into his bedroom. The door slams.

He could've saved his dad's life. I lean against the wall. *He had a family.* More than only me. How could I have kept them apart all these years? I know how much family means. And I know what it means not to have it.

Uncle Ned didn't call me before I sold the farm. A few days prior to my leaving for the Texas Panhandle, where I'd be going to school, I made one final drive to Colley, but I didn't find him there. Thinking we'd seen the last of each other, I pushed him again to the back of my mind, where he'd been all my life.

But once I was alone in a strange place with a baby to raise, I missed Nanny and Chick with a longing so sharp it pierced every waking moment. I missed being a part of something bigger than myself. I missed the noise and mess, the comfort and security of family. I wanted that again, not only for myself, but also for my son. Who would Eliot have if something ever happened to me?

I started thinking a lot about Uncle Ned, worrying about him, wondering what had happened to make him such an introverted loner. Nanny and Chick never said much about his mental state, but small comments they had made over the years led me to believe the war had messed up his mind. Mary Nell had supported that theory, but she'd also added to it. I couldn't help wondering if my uncle knew he wasn't Chick's son by blood. If so, had he grown up knowing? Or had he found out later?

Mary Nell had insisted that Chick was Ned's daddy in every way that mattered, but she was looking in on their lives from the outside. Chick would not have been mean to Ned, it wasn't in him. But when he looked at Nanny's son, did he always see her first husband? And did Ned sense that? Did Ned ever wonder about biological father?

During my second year away at nursing school, I began making phone calls. I called employment offices in all the places I knew Ned had worked at one time or another. Mead, Colley; I even called Juniper. One lead led to another, and I finally learned he was living in the small town of Chile, New Mexico, not far from where I lived.

One Saturday morning, I took off work, packed Eliot up, and we drove to see Uncle Ned. I didn't let him know we were coming.

As I traveled the long straight highway, past flat farmland and cattle grazing in fields, one of Nanny's stories came back to me. One about the odd bald spot the size and shape of a quarter on my uncle's left temple. He'd had it since birth, Nanny said.

"When I was carryin' Ned, I marked him with that spot," she told me, her hands shelling the black-eyed peas she planned to cook for dinner. "I was about due to deliver at the time, and one morning, I was feedin' the chickens out in the yard when Chick pulled to the edge of the field closest to the house in his tractor. I lifted my hand to wave at your granddaddy when a hen startled up right beside me. She flapped up into my face and started squawkin.'"

Chick hooted and blew out a ribbon of gray smoke. "Scared the pee-waddlin-poo out her."

Nanny gave him a look, half-grin, half-scowl. "I screamed to kingdom come, jumped backward, and slapped my hand up against the side of my head, smack dab on the left temple, the same place where Ned's got his bald spot. That's when I spotted the rattlesnake. I would'a stepped right on him if not for that hen."

I pulled into Chile, laughing aloud over that long-forgotten story and Nanny's bird fetish. A blackbird alerted her of my birth. A hen marked Ned and saved her from a snake. She named my grandfather Chick. Though Nanny and Chick didn't say so when they relayed the story, thanks to Mary Nell, I knew they weren't married at the time it took place. Chick was Nanny's hired hand, working for her on the farm from time-to-time in exchange for three square meals and a place to sleep in the barn. All while keeping one eye on the pretty pregnant deserted divorcee, I guessed.

After locating Uncle Ned's apartment, I took Eliot from the car and went to knock on his door. When Ned found us on his porch, he didn't seem any more surprised than he had when I showed up at the employment office in Colley. He let us in, and as I looked around, it occurred to me that if the hen scare was true, that bird might've marked my uncle's mind as well as his temple. The hen, the war, the knowledge that he wasn't Chick's son. Maybe, together, it had all been too much for him to take.

The one room efficiency contained a small kitchen table, a single kitchen chair, a television with one thread-bare recliner in front of it. There was a twin bed with no comforter. The window shades were down, blocking all outside light from the room except the slivers that slipped in on the sides. No pictures hung on the dingy white walls, no rugs covered the scuffed linoleum floor. He didn't have a phone.

"How are you, Uncle Ned?" I asked, knowing I'd made a mistake to think that I might find the family I'd lost within this broken man.

"I'm good," he answered.

"I've been worried about you. Why haven't you called me?"

"I got nothin' to say."

I studied him, his nervous shifty eyes, his thin bent shoulders, the tight mouth that barely opened when he spoke. Catching his gaze, I said, "I've missed you."

His brows tugged together before he looked away, and right then I thought of how little attention I'd paid him all of my life.

Shame crept into me like the light around the window shades crept into the room. While I was growing up, he had simply been a holiday fixture, no different from the reindeer salt and pepper shakers that appeared at our table each Christmas, then disappeared afterward. Being with him now, alone with my little boy and without my grandparents present, made me uneasy. I thought of Nanny, how she had always drawn inside of herself for awhile after seeing Ned. I'd always dismissed it. She was tired from the company, I thought, if he'd been at the farm. Or tired from the trip if she'd been to see him.

Eliot squirmed in my arms, and I shifted him on my hip. "This is my son," I told Uncle Ned.

Squealing and giggling, Eliot reached out a hand and wiggled his fingers. "Hi!"

Uncle Ned looked at him and cracked a stiff smile that I suspected felt as foreign on his face as a beard would on mine.

"Eliot's almost two now," I told him.

"You're a big boy." His eyes darted quickly away from my child.

I set Eliot down, and he ran around the room, his arms spread wide like an airplane's wings. "Slow down, honey," I called, and he skidded to a quick stop and tried to stand on his head.

Uncle Ned surprised me with a quiet chuckle.

"Are you working?" I asked him, crossing my arms.

"I'm assistant janitor over at the school."

"That's good." I glanced at my watch. "It's almost lunchtime. Why don't we grab a bite to eat somewhere? I'll buy."

"No, thanks, Maggie. I ate already."

I sighed, then told him that Ray Allan bought the farm.

He nodded.

I gave him my phone number and address.

He wrote the information on a napkin.

I picked Eliot up, and we left as quickly as we'd come.

After that short, tense visit, I called Uncle Ned once a month at the school where he worked to check on him. I always invited him to share holidays with us, then held my breath, hoping he'd decline. My wish was always granted, and I'd feel relieved, guilty, and sad all at once. I guess he grew tired of drifting because he stayed in Chile and kept his job as janitor until he died ten years ago.

The ten thousand dollars bequeathed to me in his will was a surprise that left me tearful and speechless; I deposited the money in Eliot's college account. But the Bronze Star medal he left to Eliot, one awarded "for heroic achievement while engaged in action against an enemy of the United States" stunned me more than the money. If Nanny and Chick had known their son was a decorated war hero, they would've told me. They would've told everyone.

I don't know how Eliot found out Mark Reeves' phone number since I didn't give it to him. But I hear him talking in a low voice to the uncle he never knew, and I think again of my own uncle.

After that one visit to Ned's apartment, I convinced myself that Eliot and I were a complete family in and of ourselves. As my grandparents had brought my mother to life for me, I promised myself I would bring Nanny and Chick alive for my son. It would have to suffice, and for me, it did. Often, though, when I thought about Paul and guilt got the better of me, I worried that our family of two was not enough for Eliot. But when Eliot rejected Stephen, I decided he was content with what we had.

I know now that I was wrong.

I pour my second cup of coffee the next morning, wondering if Eliot will ever leave his room, if he will ever talk to me, tell me about his conversation with Mark Reeves. I wonder how Paul's brother reacted when Eliot introduced himself. With shock? Happiness? Disbelief?

After they talked yesterday, Eliot closed himself in the nursery with Will and didn't come out again until I went to the grocery store. I only know he did then because a bottle was missing from the refrigerator, and Eliot and Will had moved from the nursery to Eliot's bedroom. That door remained closed, as well, and I heard Eliot's television playing on low.

More than once, I considered knocking to ask if he was hungry, if they needed anything. If he would forgive me. But as afternoon slid into evening, my guilty conscience went on the defensive. Eliot doesn't understand what I went through after his birth, how alone and overwhelmed I was. I made mistakes, but I did the best I could. How can he fault me for that? How can he judge me?

Now, as I pour cereal into a bowl, spoon blueberries on top

of it, I waver again. One minute I want to apologize to him, the next minute I want to defend myself.

I'm sitting down to eat, the newspaper spread on the table in front of me, when the landline phone rings; I'm startled, since it rarely does. I've only kept it for backup reasons. Reaching across the counter, I pick up. "Hello?"

"Hi – um – this is Andrea Reeves. I'm calling for Eliot Mahoney? I tried his cell, but I guess it's turned off."

My heart lurches. "Yes, Andrea. Just a minute. I'll get him for you." Laying the cordless down, I head for Eliot's bedroom, my heart thumping hard as I knock on his door.

"Come in," he says after a short hesitation.

I open the door, look in. The television is tuned to the morning news. Eliot sits propped up against pillows in bed. Will lies, stomach down, on Eliot's bare chest. "The phone's for you. The landline. It's Andrea Reeves."

His chin lifts, his eyes flash apprehension. "I'll pick up in here." As I close the door again, I hear him say, "Hello? Yeah. Hi, Andrea."

I don't taste my cereal, and I re-read a newspaper article twice, but the words still don't register. When I look up and find Eliot standing in the doorway, I startle and drop my spoon. Without speaking, he crosses to the counter and takes a mug from the cabinet.

I clear my throat. "You know, I was thinking about calling Diane to ask if she knows any sitters that might be good possibilities for keeping Will after we both go back to work."

He pours coffee into the mug but doesn't respond or look my way.

"We should probably get on that. We want to take our time, find the right person."

Eliot walks to the counter and faces me. "Will and I are going to Red Lake." He sets down his cup.

"When?"

"Today. As soon as I can throw some things together."

"I'll help you." I move to get up. "It's about a four-hour drive, isn't it? You'd better leave soon so you'll have a few hours to visit before you have to start back."

"We're not coming back today."

"Oh?" I sit again. "How long will you be gone?"

"I'm not sure. A week, maybe."

"A week? Where will you stay?"

"Mark Reeves said Will and I can stay with him, so I won't be out the money for a motel."

"Honey . . . are you sure that's smart? You don't even know these people."

"That's why I want to spend more than a few hours there. So I can *get* to know them. *These people* are my family. My uncle and my sister. My grandmother. We have a lot of years to catch up on."

I look down at my bowl. He's trying to make me feel guilty and doing a good job of it. "What about work?"

"I took next week off." He rounds the counter to leave the kitchen, the coffee mug in his hand.

"Why don't I go with you? I'm not working. We can get a hotel. I can help take care of Will."

Eliot pauses to look back at me. "I want to go alone. Just Will and me."

I stand and cross to him. "I love you, Eliot. I love Will, too. I know you're mad at me, and I deserve it, but don't *stay* mad at me. Please."

"I'm not mad at you."

"Okay, you're upset with me. What can I do to make things right between us again?"

"I don't know."

Turning, he starts for his room. Seconds later, I hear the door close again.

CHAPTER TWELVE

*A*fter arriving in Red Lake, Eliot called to tell me they made it. That was seven days ago. I haven't heard from him since. I've picked up the phone at least a dozen times, but never followed through on calling him. *Give him time.* My new mantra.

My neighbors must think I've morphed into a different person; since I've nothing else to do, I've been gardening. Some of my flowerbeds actually contain flowers for the first time since I've lived here.

Most days, with my fingers dug deep into the cool, damp soil, and the sun on my back, I escape all my troubles for awhile. This morning, though, faced with a weed-infested patch of ground on the side of the house, my troubles don't seem so easy to evade. I decide to ignore my mantra and call Eliot. I go inside, and I'm about to punch in his number, but the phone rings before I start.

"Hi, Maggie," Constance says, when I answer.

I start into the living room. "I was afraid it was you."

"Gee, thanks."

"You know what I meant." I sit down on the sofa."Any news?"

"Yes."

The following silence tells me everything I need to know. Sinking onto the couch, I say, "Let me make this easier on you. Should I start looking for a new job tomorrow?"

"I'm sorry. The Enlow girl is going through with a lawsuit against the hospital. It's official. When we found out, the powers that be–" She sighs. "I fought for you, Maggie. Unfortunately, I was outnumbered."

"I appreciate that."

"I'm happy to give you a good reference. I don't think you'll have any trouble finding another job."

"You mean you won't have to rat on me to prospective employers?" I don't even try to hide the sarcasm in my voice. "I wouldn't want you to get into trouble with the powers-that-be."

"Screw 'em. I don't care anymore. I'm close to retiring. We'll keep this under wraps. It's not much of an issue, anyway, since we usually only say whether or not we'd rehire."

"Besides, revealing more about my situation would reflect poorly on the hospital, wouldn't it?" When she doesn't respond after several moments, I feel ashamed of myself for lashing out at her. "I don't mean to sound so cynical, Constance. None of this is your fault."

"It's okay. I understand."

"Do you mind if I ask Tim to pack up my things and bring them to me?"

"You have to come in, Maggie, I'm sorry."

"What? *Why?*"

"It's hospital policy. You have to officially turn in your badge so that — God, I hate this."

"Just say it."

"They'll want to make sure you can't access off-limits parts of the building. Also, be prepared to be escorted out."

"You've got to be kidding. By whom?"

"Security. It's so that—"

"Stop, Constance. Don't feed me any bullshit. Not you. It's so they can humiliate me and make an example of me."

"I'm sorry."

"So you've said." A dull ache throbs behind my eyes. "Thanks for telling me instead of having Derek do it."

"You're welcome." She sniffs, and I smile a little. Constance is tough as beef jerky on the outside, a marshmallow inside. "I've loved working with you, my friend," she says. "It's been a pleasure."

"For me, too. Most of it, anyway." Until this. Until Liza.

"I hope I was a part of that 'most'."

"You definitely were. When should I come up there?"

"You decide."

"How about now? I'd just as soon get it over with."

"Sure. Come by my office and let me know you're here."

"I'll be there in an hour."

I break the connection, return to the kitchen, and stare out the kitchen window at Eliot's old treehouse. I'd thought that time in our lives when he was building it and hiding away from Stephen and me was about as difficult a time as I'd ever face again. Little did I know. Now, I have no son, no grandson, no job.

Needing to hear his voice, I punch in Eliot's number and count the rings.

"Hey, Mom."

"Hi." Emotion rises inside me. "I haven't heard from you."

"I've been pretty tied up."

When I'm confident I can speak without crying, I say, "I understand. You've had a lot to deal with the past week. How's Will?"

"He's good."

"No more colic?"

A pause then, "Some. Nothing I can't handle."

"We need to buy Will an automatic swing. Sometimes motion helps. I'll—"

"Patricia already bought one for him. And a white noise machine. That's helped more than anything."

Patricia. Paul's mother. Eliot's grandmother. "That's nice of her," I say, hurt by the fact that another woman is doing my job, and that Eliot is leaning on her instead of me. "I can't wait to see you and Will. I'll make a special dinner for tomorrow night. How about shrimp creole?" Eliot's favorite dish.

"That's fine. Don't go to any trouble."

His curtness stings. "It's no trouble. I want to do it. What time do you think you'll be home?"

"Around five."

"Okay. Oh, and I think I've found the perfect lady to keep Will. Diane recommended her. She raised five kids of her own. I could ask her to stop by day after tomorrow so you can see what you think."

He clears his throat. "I've decided to move here."

I grip the phone tighter. "You're moving to Red Lake?"

"Mark offered me a job with his company."

I look down at my hand where it rests in my lap. Each fingernail has a line of dirt beneath it, a smudge so dark my chipped and faded rose-colored polish can't hide it. I'm overcome with an urge to drop the phone and run back out to that patch of weedy soil. To the sun, the breeze, and my own denial.

"When will you move?" I ask.

"I'll pack up our things and drive back here a couple of days later.

I sink into a chair.

"Mark has a garage apartment out back of his house. It's empty, and he said Will and I can live there."

"I see." *I see.*

"I won't have to pay any rent," he continues, talking fast. "He said I can live there free until I can afford to pay a little something."

I take a deep breath, release it slowly. "Is Mark Reeves . . .? What's he like? I mean, he's a stranger, really. You can't know much about him after only a week, and you're going to move into his place and go to work for him? You're giving the man a lot of power over you, Eliot. You have Will's best interest to think about, not just your own."

"Mark's a good guy. Don't worry about it."

Don't worry? "What about school?"

I hear a noise like a chair leg scraping the floor. "I'm postponing it."

"Postponing, or quitting?"

"I don't know . . . maybe quitting."

"Oh, Eliot." I close my eyes. "What's the man doing? Filling your head with big ideas about taking over the family business?" I can see how such treatment from Mark Reeves might entice Eliot to take a detour away from his plans. Mark is his link to Paul. Eliot wants to please the man, to be close to him.

"No, Mom, he isn't doing that at all. But what if he was? Mark is my uncle. He's divorced, and he doesn't have kids. If he wants me to take over the family business someday, why would you have a problem with that?"

"Because you had your own plans. And now you meet your uncle, and you're willing to just forget what you've worked so hard for? You're willing to give it up? You've been accepted to *medical school*. You have a scholarship you worked your ass off to get that will help pay your way. I doubt they'll hold the money in account for you while you take a time out."

"Maybe this isn't just a time out. Maybe I've changed my mind."

"Just like that? *Why* have you changed your mind?"

"For a lot of reasons."

"I'll help you with Will while you go to school. I want to. If you move, I'll miss you both so much I don't think I could stand it. And I'll worry about you. I know we've had a rocky start, Eliot. It's been a tough adjustment for me, I admit that. But I'm okay now. We're going to be fine. The three of us." When he doesn't respond, I add, "Please don't do this to punish me for not telling you about your dad."

"This has nothing to do with punishing you."

"I regret what I did. I wish I could tell you how much. I wish I could go back in time and make a different choice, but I can't. Don't leave everything behind – school, your friends, your home – just because you're upset with me."

"It's not about *you*. It's about *Will and me*. About what I want to do for us. Plans change, Mom. I gave this a lot of thought."

"Eliot—"

"Let's talk about this later, okay? Or not. There's nothing else to say. My mind's made up."

I press my palm over my mouth.

"I'll see you tomorrow, Mom."

Lowering my hand, I say, "Drive carefully, okay?"

"I will."

I end the call and slam the phone down hard on the table. I can handle losing my job, but I can't lose Eliot. He's the reason I've worked so hard for so long, why I've pushed myself to succeed, why my career was so damn important to me. Eliot's life. My dreams for him. His dreams for himself.

———

"Mr. Reeves?"

"Yes?"

I listen for a resemblance to Paul in the deep voice on the phone. "This is Maggie Mahoney. Eliot's mother."

A pause, then, "I'm glad you called. I've enjoyed getting to know Eliot this past week. He's a great kid."

"Yes, he is."

"I'm looking forward to working with him."

I nibble my lip.

"Will's been a lot of fun, too."

"I hope he hasn't kept you up nights."

Mark laughs. "He's woke me up a time or two. Eliot's good with him, though. I would've been a lousy parent at his age. 'Course, Andrea and Mom have jumped at every chance to help out. They're spoiling the kid rotten. Will, not Eliot," he adds with a chuckle.

A twinge of something — jealously, or maybe resentment — increases the steady thump of my heartbeat. "Do you have some time free today? I'd really like to talk to you. I could drive to Red Lake."

"Matter of fact, I'm headed your way now to take care of

some business. I should finish up in time for a late lunch. Could you meet me at, say, 1:30?"

"Perfect." That leaves plenty of time for hospital security to kick me out of the building. "Where do you want to eat?" He tells me the location of his meeting and suggests a nearby diner. "That works. It's close to the hospital, and I'll be leaving from there. I'll try to be a little early so I can find a quiet table."

"How will I know you?" Mark asks. "Does Eliot look like his mom?"

"I've always thought he looked like Paul, don't you?" My question is greeted by silence, and I wonder if I've crossed a line. "My hair is light brown," I tell him. "Shoulder length. And I'm wearing a blue shirt."

"I'll find you. I'm looking forward to it, Maggie. Paul talked a lot about you."

The statement surprises me so much that I can't think of a response, so I simply tell him how sorry I am about Paul's death.

"Thanks," he says. "Me, too."

Constance's office door is ajar. I tap on it and peek in. "I'm here. Call security so they can issue a red alert."

She slides off her reading glasses. "Hi, Maggie." Her voice oozes pity with a sprinkle of guilt.

I cross to her desk. "I'm not mad at you. I'm only taking shots at you because you're in my line of fire."

She stands. "Go ahead. You deserve to, and I have thick skin."

"You aren't the one I want to hurt right now." I motion behind me at the door. "Give me half an hour to clean out my desk, and I'll be ready to go."

Nodding, she says, "I'll come down and say goodbye."

Minutes later, outside my own office, I pause, recalling my first day at Asclepius not so long ago. Walking through this door for the first time had been my reward for years of sacrifice. Now I've lost that reward. I push the door open and go inside.

Tim stands in front his desk, dumping the contents of a drawer into a large box.

"What are you doing?"

He glances up, and the fury in his eyes almost blinds me. "Melanie called and told me what happened. If you go, I go."

I close the door. "No way, Tim. I won't let you quit over this."

"Just try and stop me." His chin juts out as he pulls another drawer free of the desk.

"Your support means a lot to me, but this is my problem, not yours. If you walk out now, tomorrow morning you'll wake up and wonder what in the hell you were thinking."

Shoving the box aside with an elbow, Tim sets the drawer down on the desk with a thud. He sinks into his chair. "How can I keep working for these narrow-minded—"

"I broke the rules. They're just doing their job."

"Those bastards," he snarls. "So what will you do now?"

I start past him toward my inner office. "Clean out my desk, turn in my badge, then go to lunch."

Standing he follows me. "I meant for the rest of your life. But, for now, lunch sounds good. I'll take you. We'll have a martini."

"People only drink martinis at lunch in the movies. Anyway, I can't go. I have a date."

Tim grabs my arm. "*Really?*"

"Not a date date. An appointment date." I pull away from

him and round the desk. "Go put your things back in your desk and bring that box to me, would you?"

As he returns to the reception area, I start clearing out my things, and when Tim comes back, he brings the box I asked for and two others. He sets them at my feet then goes to work alongside me, pulling files and books, packages of chewing gum, and tissue boxes from my desk drawers. Other than telling him what's mine and what to set aside, we disseminate my business life in silence.

"Maybe you *should* have a date date," Tim finally says without looking at me. "More than one, as a matter of fact."

"That's just what I need. More drama on top of everything else I'm dealing with."

"Who said anything about drama?"

"In my experience, it goes along with dating."

"In your experience?" He smirks. "Please. When have you ever dated?"

"You forget that I have a son."

"Okay. You had at least one date back in college. Eliot is grown now. You're a grandmother, for crying out loud. You don't have time to waste. I could introduce you to—"

"No, thanks." I point a finger at him. "I mean it. Don't be giving out my number, okay? Let me get through this first. Then I *might* consider it, but not under pressure from you. Besides, you're talking like I'm at death's door. I'm barely in my forties. There's plenty of time if I decide I want to date."

He takes a box of tampons from a bottom drawer, tosses it into the box. In a huffy voice, he mutters, "Spoil sport. Heaven forbid you actually have a little fun every once in awhile. You might short-circuit, blow smoke out your ears." Jerking spasmodically, he squeals, "Danger, danger! I'm laughing and dancing. Danger! I'm having sex. Danger! I'm—"

"*Tim.*" I glare at him before putting a lid on the final box. "Not now. Please. Not only have I lost my job, Eliot and the baby are moving."

"Out of the house?" He frowns.

"Out of town. To Red Lake."

His jaw drops. "Oh, sweetie . . . Why?"

"It's a long story. Come over some time, and I'll tell you. I could use the company."

"You don't deserve any of this shit." He squeezes my arm.

I toss a paperback book into the box, and we're about to finish up when Constance walks in with the head of security at her side and Derek Piedmont behind her. Tim crosses his arms and glares at the threesome from behind his glasses. I reach in my jacket pocket, pull out my badge, and hand it to the officer. "Here you go."

The burly man tips his gray head. "Thanks, Miss Mahoney."

"Don't forget to check inside those boxes, Bob," Derek tells him. Looking at me, he adds, "Hospital policy."

"Of course." Though I'm seething inside, I smile at him. Then, returning my attention to Bob, I sweep a hand toward the boxes. "Knock yourself out."

He pulls off each lid and makes a cursory scan of the contents. "These look fine," he says in a curt voice to Derek.

"I'll need some help getting them to the car, if you don't mind."

Bob stoops to pick one up while I lift the second one. Constance glances over her shoulder at Derek. When he doesn't budge, she picks up the third.

I can tell that Tim wants to hug me, but he restrains himself.

I'm glad; I'd lose it if he touched me, and my last shred of dignity would shrivel and turn to dust if I broke down in front of Derek Piedmont.

"I'll call you, Maggie," Tim says.

"I'm counting on it."

My escorts start out. I follow, pausing briefly to look back at Tim before I cross the threshold. He winks, lifts his chin and gives me a thumbs up. Then he rotates his hand and flips off Derek and Constance behind their backs.

Thankful for Tim's ability to lighten even my darkest moment, I turn and exit my office. Once we're out in the hall, Derek leads the way, while Constance walks on my left side and Bob on my right.

"I thought you might want an ally," Constance says quietly, "but if you'd rather I leave – "

"No, stay." I glance at her. "Thanks."

As we walk, I look straight ahead at Derek's bald spot, trying not to let the stares and whispers of people we pass affect me. Still, I feel naked and vulnerable. For a moment, I'm back at the farmhouse, hiding in the upstairs hallway, hearing Chick tell Nanny that Ray Allan called me a slut and said I would never amount to anything.

A few familiar hospital employees, the ones who care more about my feelings than the scandal playing out in front of them, greet me awkwardly.

When we finally reach the front exit, Derek stops in front of the sliding glass doors and turns to me. Constance and Bob stop, too. "This is as far as I go," Derek says, meeting my gaze. "I'm sorry we have to part ways under these circumstances." He offers his hand for me to shake.

I shrug. "My arms are full. I've enjoyed my work at Asclepius, Mr. Piedmont. Goodbye."

I walk past him toward the glass doors, and as they slide apart, I remember again that night at the farmhouse and my unfulfilled desire to march over to Bobby Allan's house. Then I remember the night after Eliot's birth when Kelly's glare told me to back off, and I did. Like a slideshow, all the times in my life when I wanted to defend myself, to have the last word, but didn't, flash before me.

Pausing, I turn around before I can think twice. "I just want to say that you'll be sorry one day that you didn't stand behind me in this. You won't find a better person for my job than me. I worked my ass off for this hospital, and I would've continued to do so. Yes, I broke the rules, but there were extenuating circumstances. Too bad you couldn't have seen that. As far as I'm concerned, the hospital is the real loser here."

Before Derek can respond, I swivel toward the open doors again and walk out with Constance and Bob following behind me.

"Bravo, Maggie," Constance says when the doors shut behind us.

"Way to go, Miss Mahoney," Bob adds.

I glance back at them. "I'm sorry if—"

"Don't apologize." Constance smiles at me. "I loved it."

"So did I," Bob says with a gruff chuckle.

Standing up for myself feels good. Unfortunately, it won't pay my mortgage.

CHAPTER THIRTEEN

*T*he lunch crowd has thinned by the time I reach the diner. Only a few stragglers lag behind. Stay-at-home mothers, retirees, unemployed people, like me. A couple of young men, college students most likely, bus tables on either side of the room.

Serenaded by conversations and the clatter of dishes, I order iced tea and scan the menu, trying to keep my mind occupied. But I'm more nervous than I thought I would be, and watching the door is too tempting. I prop the menu behind the napkin container again.

More than once, I catch myself thinking I'm about to meet Paul, not his brother. I imagine him entering the diner, his earnest brown eyes searching each table, each face. Paul, but more than two decades older than the last time I saw him, his golden hair shorter, sprinkled with silver. His body thicker, a few signs of age on his face. Different, yet the same. The tiny white scar on his chin will still be there, the one I used to trace with the tip of my finger. The dimple in his left cheek. The cowlick at his crown. He'll have the same brisk walk, the same habit of drumming his fingers on the tabletop and bouncing his knee, like Eliot does, because he can't sit still or he's nervous. And that thing he did that always got to me most will not have changed – how he'd smile with his eyes while his mouth formed only the slightest curve on one side.

The man who pushes through the door wearing jeans, a camel brown button-down shirt, and cowboy boots isn't Paul. His gaze narrows in on me almost instantly – an unfamiliar gaze – and I'm reminded that Paul is dead. I'll never see him again. Maybe I wouldn't have anyway, but the possibility always lurked at the back of my mind. And in my heart.

As Mark Reeves approaches my table with long, unhurried strides, I notice he's taller than Paul, his hair a bit wavy and chocolate brown rather than straight and golden. He's rougher around the edges than Paul.

I stand, nod at him, lift a hand.

When he pauses at the table, I notice that his eyes are sky blue, not brown. His smile is wide and crooked, a nice smile, dazzling even, but there's no dimple in his cheek. "Mark?"

"Yes, and you're Maggie, I'm betting."

We shake hands. His palm feels slightly callused, his fingers a little rough. Maybe he still works alongside his construction crew instead of just shuffling papers.

"Thanks for meeting me."

"I'm glad I could." He pulls out the chair across from me and we both sit. "It's green, by the way."

"Pardon me?"

"Your shirt," he says. "It's green. You told me blue."

"Oh." I glance down, then up again. The corner of his mouth twitches. I tilt my head. "Has your optometrist ever mentioned that you might be color blind?"

"Never." He holds my gaze. "How about yours?"

Nervousness makes my heart beat too fast. "I'm willing to compromise and call the shirt turquoise."

"That works for me." He laughs.

Well, well. This isn't how I pictured our meeting would proceed. I expected him to be curt with me. Angry about the secret I kept from his brother, his entire family. He doesn't seem the least bit perturbed. Maybe he's bluffing to throw me off guard. Playing nice so I'll be relaxed when he lowers the boom. No chance that I'll relax, though.

I cross one leg over the other, fold my hands in my lap, trying not to gawk at him. But I can't help studying him a little too closely. I doubt I would ever have pointed him out in a line-up and said, "That's him. Paul's brother." Yet something about him seems familiar. Maybe it's the tilt of his head as he contemplates me. Or the shape of his nose, although it looks as if it's been broken at least once. Strangely enough, the imperfection makes him more attractive.

"I'm sorry," I say. "I don't mean to stare. It's just that you and Paul—"

"I know. I don't look like him."

"No. But there's something . . ."

"Yeah, we heard that a lot." That smile again – quick, easygoing, open. So unlike Paul's cautious, assessing one. "I've always been the proverbial black sheep of the family. Paul was the white knight."

I can't help wondering if I've tarnished that image of his brother.

My thoughts must show on my face, because after a few moments of silence, Mark says, "White knights are human, too. Everyone makes mistakes. Even the good guys."

Defensiveness jolts through me, stiffens my spine. Is that how Paul referred to Eliot and me? As *mistakes*? Pushing aside that insulting possibility, I say, "That's why I'm here. To try and stop a mistake."

"Okay."

I fold my hands on the table. "I want to discuss the job offer you made Eliot."

I pause when the waitress arrives. Mark and I each take a menu from behind the metal napkin canister, scan it then place our orders. The woman refills my tea glass then leaves.

"Did Eliot tell you he's been accepted to medical school?" I ask. "He was going to start in August on a partial scholarship."

He gathers the menus, replaces them behind the napkin holder, leans back. "He told me. That's a smart kid you raised."

"Yes, he is. And ambitious. At least, he was."

"Was?" He scowls.

"You're right. I shouldn't have said that. Eliot's still ambitious. Keeping Will is proof of that. What I meant is, now he's talking about throwing his plans for school away to go to work for you."

The waitress appears again with Mark's iced tea. He thanks her, then pours a good amount of sugar into it.

"I wouldn't necessarily say his coming to work for me is throwing anything away. It's more like a change of direction. And you're right that Eliot's still plenty ambitious." He chuckles, and I notice deep laugh lines around his eyes. "Hell, he's already pointing out ways we could streamline my construction operation."

I stare at him, speechless. Unamused.

Mark stops stirring his tea and places the spoon on the table. "I don't mean to make light of your concerns."

"I hope not. This is Eliot's future we're talking about. Will's future. Not some game. Eliot has a job at a clinic. The doctors told him the position is his for as long as he wants it, and he can go part-time while in school. He's making valuable contacts there and gaining experience that will help him later in his career. He won't get any of that working construction."

"Believe me, he'll get *plenty* of hands-on experience." Mark Reeves chuckles again. "So much, he'll wish he had another set of hands."

I take a moment to tap down my temper. "I think you know what I mean."

Mark stops laughing, pinches the bridge of his nose. "I'm not handling this right. Of course, I know what you meant. Eliot won't gain the type of experience working for me that he could draw on later as a doctor. I understand."

"He's wanted to be a surgeon for as long as I can remember."

He takes a long drink, sets down his glass. "Are you sure?"

"About what?"

"Is becoming a doctor Eliot's dream, or your dream *for* him?" His question stuns me. Before I can catch my breath to respond, Marks leans in closer toward the center of the table and adds, "Why don't you sit down and talk to him about it? Better yet, let him do the talking and you listen."

Though he says this calmly, I'm anything but calm. "We *have* talked. What do you know about any of this? You don't have the right to insinuate—"

"You're right. I don't." He shrugs. "All I can tell you is that I'm hearing a different story from Eliot about what he wants than what you're telling me."

I hesitate, then ask, "What did he say?"

"He said he isn't sure what he wants to do. But I have to tell you, he seems pretty damned excited about learning the ropes at Reeves Construction and getting his hands dirty for a change. A young man *needs* to get his hands dirty now and then. Eliot's don't look like they've ever touched much more than a computer keyboard."

I glare at him. "It sounds as if I'm not the only one steering him in a direction."

"All I did was make Eliot an offer. He took it on his own. Look at the situation from his point of view. He'll be able to support himself and his son without having to rely on anybody, even you. That has to look pretty appealing to him. Seems like it would to you, too."

"I'm a lot more worried about Eliot's future than I am about money. I don't want him to have regrets some day over what he gave up." I reach for my purse. "I didn't come here for you to advise me on how to handle my son."

Mark frowns. "Are you leaving?"

"I'm going home."

As I push back my chair, I hear my name called. Sheila Barnhill, the brown-noser Alice believes is trying to snag my job, walks across the diner toward us.

"Oh, shit." Dropping my purse and ignoring Mark's surprised stare, I pick up the menu and open it to cover my face, hoping Shelia will take the hint. No such luck.

She stops beside me. "Hi, Maggie."

I lower the menu. "Shelia. What a surprise."

Her eyes shift to Mark and linger a moment before coming back to me. "What are you doing here?"

"Eating. How about you?"

"The same." She laughs. "I guess that was a stupid question." She lowers her voice, adds a pinch of compassion to it. "I just never guessed I'd see you out and about today after what happened this morning." Her gaze flicks toward Mark again as she says, "I'm so sorry, Maggie."

"Thanks." I will myself not throw my iced tea in her face. It's been that kind of a day.

"No one at the hospital can believe that they fired you, especially the way they did it. Oh, my god. I was mortified for you. Truly." I give her a blank, unblinking stare, and when I don't respond, Shelia says, "Pardon my manners." She reaches an arm across the table toward Mark. "Sheila Barnhill."

He takes her hand. "Mark Reeves."

"Maggie and I—"

"We're former co-workers at Asclepius Hospital. Or more accurately, I was Sheila's boss," I say.

She shifts her gaze back and forth between Mark and me, as if waiting for one of us to explain *our* relationship.

"The hospital's loss is my gain," Mark says. "Maggie's an old friend of my brother's. He always said great things about her, and I've been trying to get her to come to work for me for years."

I gape at him.

"What kind of business are you in?" Shelia asks him with genuine interest.

Mark smiles his crooked smile. "Which one?"

Laughter bubbles up in me as Sheila's eyes widen then narrow in on Mark with even greater interest. I almost forgive him for everything he insinuated a few minutes ago.

"How many businesses do you have?" Sheila asks, but the waitress arrives with our food and interrupts the conversation.

"I wish we could talk longer," Mark says amiably, "But Maggie and I have a lot of business to discuss and only a short time to do it in." He checks his watch. "I have to see a man about a dog in an hour." Smiling at Sheila, he adds, "It's been nice meeting you."

"You, too." She grins and turns her attention to me. "Maggie, I don't know what to say."

"Then don't say anything." I lift my napkin, shake it open, place it across my lap. "Have a nice life, Sheila."

"Pardon me?" Her chin snaps up. She tosses her hair back. "Excuse me for worrying about your welfare." Swinging around, she stalks off in the direction she came.

"Enjoy my job," I call after her, my appetite gone.

"Hey, good for you," Mark says quietly and chuckles.

He redeemed himself somewhat with the way he handled Sheila. In fact, I actually like the man when he isn't telling me how to behave with my son. But I'm too embarrassed to resume our conversation. "I'm sorry about that," I say. "Thanks for saving face for me."

"No thanks necessary. I've had plenty of experience dealing with her type." He bites into his burger but stops chewing when I push back my chair again and stand. "You're still leaving?" he mumbles around a full mouth of food.

"There's no reason to waste more of your time. Or mine. Where Eliot and Will are concerned, we obviously disagree. I don't see that changing. Goodbye, Mark. And thanks again." I duck my head and start toward the door.

"What about your sandwich?"

"You can have it," I call over my shoulder.

On the drive home, all that's happened today comes crashing down around me, and the thing that hurts the most is Mark Reeves' implication that I'm a domineering mother. I know Eliot. If he thought I was pushing him toward something he didn't want for himself, I would've figured that out a long time ago. And if I didn't, he would have told me.

After two decades of never crying, I can't seem to stop. Tears gush from my eyes so fast I have to pull off the highway into a furniture store parking lot because I can't see the road. Ignoring the wary stares of a young couple passing by, I shriek and hit the steering wheel repeatedly until the heels of my hands throb.

I leave the boxes I brought from the office in the trunk of my car. I'd like to forget about them, at least for awhile. With my purse slung over one shoulder, I take the mail from my curbside box before starting up the walkway to the house.

When I've almost shuffled through to the bottom of the stack, I feel a soft brush of fluff skim between my ankles and look down. The stray orange cat has her face tilted up, peering at me. She's thinner than the last time I saw her. "I was right. Eliot was feeding you, wasn't he? The sneak."

I start up the walkway again, intent on ignoring the cat. But the sound of a tiny *meow* stops me short. I look over my shoulder. "I know you're probably hungry." *Not to mention lost and lonely.* "But I can't help you. I'm allergic. Even if I wasn't, I don't like cats." My father's face flashes before me, the anxious look in his eyes the last time I saw him, the kitten he left me before he disappeared from my life.

A horn honks down the block, and it occurs to me that I've been conversing with an animal in my front yard. I start up the walk again.

Meow.

"Stop it," I yell without looking back. I step onto the porch.

"God, what is wrong with me?" Dropping the stack of mail and my purse to the bricks at my feet, I turn and sit down on the porch, my feet on the sidewalk.

The cat steps cautiously toward me.

"I'm allergic!" I sob, glaring at her.

She takes another wary step.

"I couldn't even keep my dad's cat, what makes you think I'll keep you?"

Two pale amber eyes stare into mine.

I taste salt on my lips, wipe my face on the sleeve of my jacket. "I couldn't keep Shep's cat. I couldn't keep it." I cry harder. "I couldn't."

The orange tabby is filthy, but I pick her up anyway, hold her in my lap, pull her close to me. Sniffing and shaking, I stroke her head. Her warmth and purring soothe me, and gradually my breathing steadies. When I hear a vehicle pull up across the street, I ignore it, telling myself they won't see me sitting here if I don't look up. A door slams. Then I hear footsteps moving up the walkway toward me. So maybe the vehicle wasn't across the street.

Two cowboy boots enter my field of vision. Size elevens, at least, the leather tips aimed directly at my red painted toenails, eight inches away, maybe less. I tilt my head back.

Mark Reeves frowns down at me. He holds two Styrofoam containers. "Your lunch."

I look at the cat again, mortified.

Mark clears his throat. "Can we start over? I think I might've been a little too direct with you about Eliot."

"A little?" Shifting my hold on the cat, I put my purse on my shoulder and scoop up the mail. Then I stand and walk to the door, realizing I don't have a hand free to unlock it.

"I'll take the mail," Mark says from behind.

I turn around, wait while he stacks one container atop the other. Then I hand him the cat.

Seconds later, as I'm twisting the key in the lock, he says, "Eliot said you don't like cats."

"I don't. I'm allergic." The door swings in. Shifting,

I take the stray from his arms and walk into the house, leaving the door open and Mark on the porch.

When I reach the living room he calls, "Can I come in?"

"Suit yourself." After dropping my purse on the floor, I toss the mail onto the coffee table and sit at one end of the sofa.

Mark enters the room and sets the containers on the coffee table alongside the mail. He sits in the chair across from me. "I didn't have the right to say those things to you at the diner. You're Eliot's mother. You know him better than I do."

"I know Eliot's upset with me about what I led him to believe about his dad. I guess I don't blame you if you are, too." I shrug. "I wish I could, but I can't change anything now."

"If you think I'm mad at you, you're dead wrong. What happened between you and Paul is none of my business."

"You really expect me to believe you're not the least bit upset with me? Eliot has the same rare blood type Paul had, did you know that? He might've—" I stop abruptly, unable to admit aloud that, because of me, Eliot was unable to save Paul's life.

"Listen." Mark sits back, covers his chin and mouth with one hand, taps his upper lip with his forefinger. After a few seconds, he lowers his hand, and sounding profoundly sad, says, "I would've liked watching my nephew grow up, but the fact that I didn't is as much Paul's doing as it is yours. He wanted Eliot to be placed for adoption, and if that had happened, I wouldn't have known him, either. As for Paul's blood type – he knew he had a son. We brought up to him the option of trying to find Eliot to see if he might be a donor match, but Paul wouldn't do it. The fact that you raised Eliot instead of adoptive parents wouldn't have changed that. Paul didn't want to ask his kid to do something so serious."

The doorbell rings. *What now?* "Excuse me."

Carrying the tabby with me, I head for the door, mulling over all that Mark Reeves just said.

The man on my porch asks if I'm Maggie Mahoney. When I tell him I am, he hands me an envelope then turns and leaves without another word. I read the letterhead. *Rigby & Teal Attorneys At Law*. Repositioning the cat, I tear into the envelope, pull out the letter, read *Dear Ms. Mahoney . . .* The message beneath my name scrapes through me like a dull razor. I stare at it for at least thirty seconds before laughter seizes me. By the time I make it back to the living room again, I'm hysterical.

Mark grins at me. "Hey, I like a good joke. What's so funny?"

"I'm being sued." I toss the letter at him, toss the cat on the sofa and sink down beside her.

Mark scans the letter. "You find this amusing?"

"It's either laugh or shoot myself."

"Who is Elizabeth Enlow? If you don't mind my asking."

"She's Will's mother. Liza."

"That's right. I remember her name now." Mark stares at me, and as if my laughter is contagious, he chuckles. "Eliot told me she filed the grievance."

"Week before last." Gasping for a breath, I add, "And today — today I got escorted out of my workplace. That's what Sheila was talking about at the diner."

Mark frowns, then blurts a short laugh. "They escorted you out? No kidding?"

"No kidding. Took my badge first. Then I was formally escorted from the hospital by the head of security and a couple of company hotshots."

Mark laughs along with me now. "This isn't your day."

"This isn't my *month*. Finding out about Will and bringing him home in the same week. Losing my job. Now Eliot wanting to move."

"That's a lot of stress."

Our eyes meet, hold a moment before I look away. I excuse myself and go to the bathroom for a tissue, bring back the box, offer him one.

Sobering, Mark studies me. "You okay?"

"Better than I would be had I shot myself." I giggle.

He holds up a hand. "Don't start that again."

Reaching for one of the containers he brought, I ask, "Is this one mine?"

"Take a look and see."

I open the lid, find his burger inside, hand the container to him and reach for the second one. "That's going to be cold. You can nuke it in the microwave if you want."

He bites into the burger then grimaces. "I'll take you up on that."

"In there." I point toward the kitchen.

While he's gone, I take a bite of my club sandwich, then set it aside. It occurs to me I'm in the house alone with a man I don't even know, that I'm letting him prowl around my kitchen as if we're old friends. I try to recall some snippet of information Paul might've mentioned about his brother, but it's been too long; nothing comes to mind.

The microwave dings. "You mind if I get myself some water?" Mark calls.

"Go ahead. Bring me some, too, would you? The glasses are to the right of the sink."

When he joins me again, Mark eyes my untouched sandwich. "It's no good?"

"I'm just not hungry anymore."

He sits, lifts his burger then puts it down. "Me, either." Glancing at the cat, he says, "She doesn't look picky. You want me to feed it to her?"

"I think a saucer of milk might be better. I'll get her some in a minute."

Mark leans back. "I'm sorry you lost your job."

"I've been on leave the past week while they made up their minds about my fate, so I've had time to get used to the idea." Which isn't exactly true, but I'd rather pretend I'm not upset than start bawling again.

"You plan on looking for another hospital job?"

"Eventually." My rainy day savings won't hold me over for long, but I don't tell him that. "It might be nice to do something different for a few months, though. I could use a change of pace."

"Any ideas?"

"I haven't given it much thought yet."

The way he looks at me, as if he's trying to figure me out, makes me uncomfortable. "Thank you for saying what you did about Paul not wanting Eliot to be a donor."

"No need to thank me. It's the truth."

"So, you thought Paul's son had been adopted?"

"Yes. That's what he told me."

"I guess that means Paul talked about the two of us?"

Mark nods. "When he and Kelly divorced, she and Andrea

moved back to Oklahoma City to be close to her parents. Paul ended up in Red Lake pretty soon after that. He told me about you then. He talked about finding Eliot, but he wasn't sure he should."

"Why not?"

"He thought Eliot might not want to be found. And he felt guilty. Like he didn't deserve to be a part of Eliot's life since he encouraged you not to be."

"Encouraged? More like pressured." I blink at Mark as all the old confusion and pain rises up in me again.

"Paul regretted that, Maggie. He said, deep down, he knew you wanted to keep the baby, but he pushed you toward adoption because he was afraid."

I study Mark's eyes a moment, then look away, not wanting him to see the turbulence in mine.

"He wished he'd handled things differently. He knew he should've told you he'd help you if you decided to keep the baby. He would've if you'd stood your ground."

"So, what? It's *my* fault?"

Mark winces. "I didn't mean it's your fault. Neither did Paul. Had he known you kept the baby he would've helped you. He would've been involved and been a dad to Eliot."

"No offense, but that's easy to say now that he's gone."

"That's what he told me."

"And that was easy for him to say after the fact."

His brows draw together. "Paul's not here to explain himself. But I believe him."

The cat enters the room and hops up in my lap again. I let her stay. "Was he sick for a long time?"

"A couple of years. Mom took care of him."

"Is she okay?"

Mark hesitates before answering, "I'm not sure she'll ever be okay when it comes to losing Paul."

"I'm so sorry."

We sit in silence for at least a full minute. I want to ask about Paul's marriage. Why he and Kelly split up. But those questions seem too personal to ask someone I've just met. Oddly, though, he doesn't feel like a stranger; maybe he has more of Paul in him than what shows on the surface, and I'm picking up on the similarities without even realizing it.

"Paul's daughter," I say to him. "Does she look like him?"

"She looks like her mother."

"She's beautiful then."

"Yes. And a sweet girl, too. She and Eliot hit it off right away. I bet they would've been close if—" He catches himself.

"If they'd grown up knowing one another," I finish for him. "Because of the choice I made, they both grew up without siblings."

Until recently, I never considered how my decision might've affected Paul. I didn't question how it could've affected his daughter, either.

He scoots to the edge of the chair, his elbows on his knees, his hands steepled.

"I did what I had to," I say.

"I understand. I assume you did what you thought was best for Eliot. And I want what's best for him, too. I love my job. Eliot should love what he does for a living, too. If that's being a doctor, then I sure don't want him to give up his chance to go to medical school. And I know he's giving up a lot more than that by moving to Red Lake. He'll miss having you close. He'll miss his friends. I'll encourage him to think it over some more before he decides." Mark pauses, then adds, "I wouldn't complain about having a doc in the family."

Something tells me Eliot will listen to Mark Reeves when he won't listen to me. Relieved, I say, "I appreciate that."

"I'll talk to him tonight."

"Good." I begin gathering our trash, and Mark stands and helps me. We carry it into the kitchen and throw it away, then take turns washing our hands at the sink.

"I guess I should head out. You better now?" Mark asks.

"I am."

"Sorry again about the lawsuit."

"I have a good lawyer."

I lead him out of the kitchen to the front door. When I extend my hand, Mark takes it and holds on longer than required for a handshake.

"Thanks for lunch," I say.

"Any time. I'll make sure Eliot and Will get an early start tomorrow."

Stepping back, I turn to open the door then face him again. "He's doing okay? With Will, I mean?"

"Seems like he has two left hands sometimes, but Will doesn't act like he minds. And like I said, Andrea and Mom are helping, too. Mom's happy to have a baby to fuss over again. She's eating it up."

"Thank her for me, would you?"

"Sure." He gestures to the cat at my feet, and one corner of his mouth curves up. "Just for the record, you haven't sneezed once since I've been here. I won't tell Eliot."

He turns away before I can respond. I wouldn't know what to say anyway. Because, he's right, to my surprise. Reaching down, I lift the cat into my arms.

A black pickup truck sits at the curb. The sign on the side of it reads Reeves Construction. "Mark," I call to him as he reaches for the door.

He pauses, looks back.

"I want you to know I loved Paul." I draw one corner of my lower lip between my teeth.

He doesn't say anything, just looks at me and nods.

CHAPTER FOURTEEN

*T*he next day passes in a flurry of preparation. I go all out, as if Eliot and Will have been away a year rather than only a week. I want their homecoming to feel like a new beginning. I want our home to be a place they'll be happy to stay. I want Eliot to look at me and know that I welcome them with open arms, the way Nanny and Chick welcomed me on that day I showed up at the farm, pregnant and afraid. I never expected to be raising a baby at this stage of my life. It's not a path I would have chosen. But since it chose me, I'll make it work. We both will — Eliot and me.

By five p.m., I've set the table. Shrimp creole simmers on the stove, filling the house with the spicy scent of cayenne pepper and tomato. As I stand at the front window and watch for Eliot's Jeep, clouds move across the sky.

The stray orange cat weaves in and out between my ankles. I pick her up. Bathing her was an experience I'll never forget thanks to the battle scars I'll probably have when the scratches on my arms heal. But, despite our power struggle in the tub, we've become fast friends. I try not to analyze that fact.

Holding the cat in the crook of my arm as I watch the road, I imagine Eliot's face when he steps from his Jeep, imagine a sheepish avoidance of my eyes, a muttered, *I'm not sure what to do anymore. Maybe Will and I should stay here, and I should go to medical school.* I see us eating supper, discussing the advantages and disadvantages of him moving to Red Lake and accepting Mark's job offer, Eliot deciding against it. I see us both relaxing then, our laughter floating across the table and up to the bright lights on the fixture above. Will sleeps in his carrier on the floor at Eliot's feet while gray rain patters outside. The storm doesn't touch my family. We're in the cocoon I've built around us, warm and dry. Safe. Protected from the world. With his decision made and the tension behind us, Eliot and I go on to talk about . . .

That's where my fantasy stalls. After he decided to stay here and go to school, what would we say to each other to fill the space of an entire meal? Our conversations dwindled when he crossed the line from little boy to young man. Too often, we floated together, brushed the surface of one another then drifted apart. *You need any salt? How was your day? The mail's on the kitchen counter; you got something from the school.*

Memories spark in my mind – a slideshow of our past.

Eliot at six at the dinner table. "Mom?"

I looked up from a work memo I was reading.

"Everybody's dads came to school today."

"What for?"

"To talk about their work."

My heart skipped. "No moms came?"

"That's next month. Will you do it?"

"Ask your teacher what day, and I'll see if I can get off."

Eliot put his fork down and looked across at me. "Where's my dad?"

"I've told you that I don't know where he is."

"Did he have a heart-tack and die like Megan's dad?"

"No, he just . . . He couldn't live with us. He had to go away."

"Can I go see him?"

"No." I concentrated on cutting my pork chop into little pieces.

"Why not?"

"We'll talk about this later, Eliot. Eat your dinner, and I'll take you for ice cream later, okay?"

Another spark...

Eliot at ten, the two of us on Christmas vacation in Mexico, an afternoon on the beach. I was working toward my Masters in Nursing and brought along homework. I glanced up from a page, saw him standing at the edge of the water.

Further down the beach, a boy yelled, "Dad!" and a man threw a Frisbee toward him. Eliot watched, dragging a toe in the sand.

I put down my notebook, stood, jogged over to him. "Hey, kiddo. Let's get in."

"That's okay." He darted a glance at the father and son.

"What's wrong? I thought you'd love the ocean."

"I sort of wanted to have Christmas at home this year. With a tree and stuff. Like Russ's family always does."

"Why didn't you say so?"

"You didn't ask."

I blink, and Eliot is fifteen.

He sat at the kitchen table, books and papers spread out around him. I walked by and spotted within the clutter a copy of the career aptitude test the school gave sophomores. I picked it up. "So what's the verdict?"

"I tested strong in abstract reasoning. That means I'd be good in jobs like design or drafting."

"See this?" I pointed at the test results. "Your score in spatial

relations and mechanical reasoning is just as high." I flipped a page to the definitions. "You might also do well in medical school." I slipped the test under his nose.

"Oh, yeah?" He glanced at it briefly, then back at his textbook.

"You should think about that, Eliot. When you were younger, you talked about becoming a surgeon. You're smart enough." I smiled. "Nanny told me once that Uncle Ned had wanted to be a doctor, and my mom wanted to be a nurse."

"Those tests don't mean anything. Maybe I'll just be a farmer like Chick was so I won't have to worry about chemistry anymore."

"Chick worked his butt off."

"And surgeons don't?" He yawned. "Varsity's playing in Tulsa on Saturday. Will you drive Russ and me to the game?"

"I can't. I have to work."

"You worked last Saturday."

"We're short of staff. I'm filling in."

A lightning bolt cracks the sky. Thunder booms. The cat squirms in my arm as I step away from the window. I catch sight of my reflection in the entry hall mirror but can't look myself in the eye; I'm too afraid that everything Mark Reeves said to me at the diner has merit.

I move up to the window again and cradle the cat against me, stroke her head, worried about Eliot and Will traveling in a rainstorm. With any luck, Will is asleep and Eliot isn't too tense driving alone. I'm not sure what kind of highway driver he is; I can't remember a time when we've traveled together that I let him drive, and he never asked.

Rain falls in plump, lazy drops that thump like a million tiny fingers against the roof and windows as Eliot's Jeep passes in front of the house and turns into the driveway, the headlights slicing the gloom. I open the door, step outside onto the porch beneath the overhang, smile and wave at Eliot's blurred image behind the rain-streaked Jeep window.

The headlights dim. His door opens. He darts across the yard to join me, head ducked against the wet onslaught from above. When he jumps onto the porch beside me, he shakes his hair, splattering water onto me and the cat.

"Hey!" Setting the cat down, I laugh and hug him. "How was the drive?"

He eyes the orange tabby with a baffled frown. "Okay. The storm didn't start until I hit the city limits." Reaching down, he picks the cat up. "What's going on here?"

"I can't figure it out. She doesn't affect me like other cats do."

"Right." Eliot smirks. "I'm starving."

"I made the creole. And hush puppies from a mix. They're good, too. I saved you one," I tease, wishing he'd tease back, that our exchange wasn't so awkward. But he only says, "Let's eat," and starts around me.

I reach for his wrist to stop him from opening the door. "Aren't you forgetting something?"

Eliot turns to me. "I'll get my bag when the rain lets up."

"I mean Will."

"Will didn't come."

"What? Where is he?"

"He stayed in Red Lake with Patricia, Mark's mother. He was acting all cranky, like he didn't feel good. Since I'm headed back tomorrow, I didn't see any reason to bring him."

It doesn't appear to occur to him that I might be a reason. "You're going back so soon?" I ask.

"I need a couple of days to move into Mark's garage apartment before I start work."

"So, you haven't changed your mind." Disappointment threads through me.

"I told you that was the plan."

Lightning strikes, the quick white splash of it illuminating the resentment on Eliot's face. The clap of thunder that follows makes us both flinch.

Eliot slips his arm from beneath my hand and opens the door. "Let's go in. That one could've split us in two."

I've already done that, I think, following him into the house. I started building a wall between us a long time ago. A wall made of secrets, questions I refused to answer, questions I avoided asking my son.

What would you like to do when you grow up, Eliot? What interests you? Does seeing that father and son down the beach make you sad? What questions do you need answered about your own dad that would wipe the bitterness from your eyes?

I guess Mark didn't tell Eliot that I lost my job or that Liza filed suit against me; during dinner, he doesn't mention either incident. I decide not to bring it up. I don't want him to think I'm trying to guilt him into changing his mind about moving. And those two latest catastrophes are still too raw to share. I need time to let it all sink in before I decide my next step.

"So tell me about Will." I sip my tea.

"Let's see . . . He smiled for the first time our second day in Red Lake. A real smile. Not gas."

I laugh.

"I tickled his chin, and his bottom lip curved up." He pops a hush puppy into his mouth.

I pick at my creole and watch him, enjoying the lift in his voice whenever he mentions Will.

"I think he recognizes the sound of my voice. When I say his name, he gets all quiet and still."

"Of course, he does. You're his dad. He knows you. How is he sleeping?"

"He slept six straight for the first time last night. We stayed at Patricia's. Will had been cranky all day, and she thought he might have an earache or something."

I set down my glass. "What's Patricia like?"

"She's nice."

"How old is she?"

"I don't know. Seventy, maybe? Seventy-five?"

"She's good with Will, I gather."

He shrugs. "Yeah."

"And you like her?"

Annoyance flickers in his gaze. "I said she's nice."

I sit back, search for a non-controversial topic. I'm proud of Eliot, but I also feel a little left out, upset, worried about his future. And dreading mine. What am I without my nursing career? What will I do without Eliot around for the first time in twenty-one years? Did Mark even talk to him about staying home and going to school? Eliot seems more confident than when he left. I'm glad, but I wish he could've found that same self-assurance here. I can't help thinking he might have if I'd handled everything differently.

After dinner, he falls asleep on the couch while I'm loading the dishwasher. I wake him at ten and we both go to bed. The rain falls off and on until dawn.

By mid-afternoon the next day, the sun has burned away the morning clouds and the sky is a deep brilliant blue. Eliot packed the Jeep earlier, as well as a small trailer he rented for the baby furniture, and he's ready to start back to Red Lake. We stand beside the vehicle while he fidgets, tapping his fingers against the side of his leg, nibbling his lip, obviously impatient to get on the road.

"Will you come visit?" I ask.

"It might be a while. I have a lot to take care of."

"I'll miss you both. I already do."

As if he just thought about my leave of absence, he asks, "Have you heard anything about your job?"

"Not yet." It's just a small lie. It will be easier to tell him I was fired over the phone.

"You sure you don't want me to talk to Liza?"

"My lawyer said it wouldn't be a good idea."

"Okay. I'm sorry about what she's doing."

"It isn't your fault."

His gaze shifts downward, away from mine. "I'm sorry I'm such a disappointment to you."

"Eliot," I say in just above a whisper, taking him by the shoulders. "Don't ever think that; it isn't true. I'm so proud of you. You're the best thing that ever happened to me. I just don't want you to make a mistake that you'll regret. I'm referring to school, not Will."

He meets my gaze. "What I'm doing . . . I think it'll be okay."

"I hope so. I want you to be happy." Struggling for the right words, I say, "It seems like there's so much we haven't talked about that we should have."

"Like what, Mom?"

"I love you, for one thing."

"I know. I love you, too. It's not like I'm moving across

country. I'm four hours away. We'll see each other. We'll talk on the phone."

"Will we? You don't want my advice. You don't seem to want to hear anything I have to say." When he flinches and steps back, I look down at my shoes. "I'm sorry. Old habits die hard, I guess." Choking out a laugh, I say, "Come here."

His Adam's apple bobs. He steps toward me.

As we hug, I memorize the feel of his arms around me, his familiar scent. "Drive carefully. Call me when you get there, okay?"

"I will." Eliot ends our embrace, ducks his head, swipes at his eyes with the back of one hand.

After he leaves, I go inside and sit in his empty room, weighed down by silence.

CHAPTER FIFTEEN

*L*ong before sunup the next morning, I set out for Juniper, and almost three hours after backing out of my garage, I'm across the Texas state line and approaching the city limits of my hometown.

More than twenty years have gone by since I sold the farm and left. Nothing remained in Juniper for me anymore. At least, that's what I thought.

Two decades ago, as I passed the city limit sign while going the opposite direction, I imagined returning one day. I would pay off all of my dad's old debts. I would tell everyone who'd listen that I'd become a nurse; I'd fulfilled the dream that death stole from my mother.

If any of the people I used to know still live here, there's nothing to stop me from doing those things now. I could also show off Uncle Ned's Bronze Star; I brought it with me, locked it safely away in the car's glove compartment.

But this trip isn't about redemption, it's about my family. Maybe my grandparents' essence still lingers here. My mother's, too. Even Uncle Ned's. Maybe it will seep into my parched soul and restore me so that I'll remember who I am and all I'm capable of surviving.

I hardly recognize Juniper's town square. The once stately courthouse could use a fresh coat of paint, and the stretch of lawn in front of it is patchy and overgrown, not the trimmed green blanket of grass I remember. Turning the corner, I see that Ray Allan's businesses no longer exist. One is a fabric store now. Another, a liquor store. Farther down the way where his hardware store used to sit, only a vacant lot remains. The wind tugs a dust devil up from the dirt, and the mini-tornado spins across the empty expanse, gathering speed with each rotation. Next door to the lot, Riley's Diner, where I once worked as a waitress, is now a Dairy Queen.

I push harder on the accelerator, anxious to glimpse something familiar, my stomach tossing like the leaves on the trees. At the far edge of town, I turn left off the highway onto a dirt road, travel two more miles then follow the curve, imagining what I'll see around that bend.

There will be a field plowed into rows as narrow and thin as brown corduroy. In the field, a thin old man with hunched shoulders will be sitting on a tractor, a ribbon of smoke curling up from the cigarette that dangles from one corner of his mouth. I'll see a two-story, whitewashed house tucked into the edge of the field, as cozy and neat as a Rockwell painting. There will be a vegetable garden beside the house, sporting haphazard shoots of green in various sizes. Long-stemmed purple and yellow iris will sway gently in the flowerbed lining the front porch.

At the clothesline out back, a woman in a loose blue housedress and dingy sneakers will turn at the sound of my car, both hands gripping the corners of the white sheet that flaps around her knees.

The image dims, and my breath rushes out as the road rises,

and I complete the turn. Hitting the brake, I sit for a moment then ease to the road's shoulder and park. Signs of discarded life litter the field. Rusted refrigerators lie on their sides. A primer gray truck fender. More than one rotted couch. Upended tables and chairs. Toys and televisions and stained mattresses. A rumbling backhoe scoops a mound of dirt and lifts it.

A small metal building sits where the house once did. The sign beside it reads, "Juniper Landfill."

At Juniper's one and only grocery store, a checker informs me that a refrigerator at the back of the produce section contains a small selection of flowers for sale. I locate it and choose two limp red roses, each surrounded by a couple of sprigs of baby's breath and tied together with a curly white ribbon.

"You find everything you need?" the teenaged boy at the register asks when I return to the front.

"I did. Thanks." The nametag on his shirt reads *Cody Allan*. I take a closer look at him. When I was sixteen, I spent too much time gazing into a pair of green eyes exactly like his. "Are you related to Bobby Allan?" I ask.

"Bobby?" Cody laughs, studies me with curiosity. "He's my dad. Nobody except my mom ever calls him Bobby, though, and only when she's mad."

I smile at him. "What do people call him?"

"Bob."

"Well, he's Bobby to me. We went to school together. I grew up here. Tell him hello from Maggie Mahoney." *And tell him I forgive him for dumping me way back when.* Or maybe I should ask the kid to *thank* his father, instead. Nanny was right; it was for the best.

"Okay, I'll tell him." Cody rings up the sale.

I pull cash from my wallet. "Is this your family's store?"

"No, I just work here."

"I thought your grandfather might own it. He owned a lot of businesses in town back when I lived here."

"Dad had to sell them after Granddad died."

I try to remember Ray Allan's face, the sound of his voice, but can't. Strange. He taunted me in my dreams for years; now, he's barely a memory. "I'm sorry to hear he passed away," I tell Cody, for the sake of good manners.

"It was a long time ago. Ten or more years, I guess. I was in elementary school."

I hand him the money and return my wallet to my purse. "What's your dad doing now?"

"He works at the bank for my other grandfather."

"Mr. Courtland?" I recall the town banker, a tidy man who always wore a bow tie.

"Yeah, that's him."

"So, Bobby Allan married Shelly Courtland," I say quietly to myself.

"Yeah, she's my mom."

They seem like people from a previous life. I can't imagine myself still living in Juniper, married to someone I've known since kindergarten. "Tell your mom hello from me, too."

"Okay."

After I pay for the flowers, I say goodbye to Cody and start from the store. In the parking lot, I pause to look at the building across the street. It used to be a bar my dad frequented. Now it's a coffee shop. An idea strikes me – one that makes me uneasy.

Taking a chance, I go back into the store and ask Cody what happened to the man who once owned the Lucky J.

"Mr. White?"

"Yes, that was his name." I'd see him around town with Shep sometimes. He was the only person I knew of in Juniper who spent time with my father.

"He works at Jiffy Lube now," Cody tells me. "I see him all the time. If you're looking for him, he has lunch every day at the Dairy Queen. You can't miss him; he always reads a book while he eats."

Uncertain what I intend to do with that information, I thank the boy and leave, pointing my car in the direction of the cemetery. I wasted so much energy for so many years trying to prove my worth to the people here. I'm surprised by how little their opinion means to me now.

At the cemetery, I place one rose on Nanny's grave, the other on Chick's. Facing their headstones, I sit on the ground between them, my legs crossed, my hands on my knees. "Okay, you two. Give it to me straight. What do you make of this mess I'm in? I'm floundering. What should I do?"

I study the names engraved in the marble and wait. *June Malloy Hester. Beloved wife, mother, and grandmother. William "Chick" Hester. Beloved husband, father, and grandfather.*

"I pushed Eliot away," I whisper. "I don't want to lose him."

The sun beats down, beading my forehead and neck with perspiration. A fly buzzes around my head. A strong gust of wind catches a nearby tree, and the rustle of branches sounds like distant applause. The roses blow off the graves and tumble toward a neighboring tomb. The baby's breath scatters.

Pushing to my feet, I dust off my jeans and weave my way around marble and rock, headed for my parked car. Even if the farm still stood, my grandparents would not have been there, just as they aren't in this graveyard. They never were. They've been with me all along.

———

At twelve-thirty, I order a burger at the Dairy Queen and carry my tray to a table in the restaurant's far corner. A grizzled, old cowboy sits in the booth across from mine. If not for the paperback novel in his hand, I would never have recognized Mr. White.

He glances up from the book and tips his battered hat. "How ya doin'?"

"Fine, thanks. And you?"

"Fair to partly cloudy."

I laugh. "Sorry to hear that."

Black eyes twinkle against his leathery face. "Ma'am, at my age, that's something to celebrate."

"I see."

He squints at me. "You look familiar." Closing the book, he reaches across the aisle and offers his hand. "Hank White."

"I'm Maggie Mahoney." We shake. "I used to live here."

"Well, I'll be." His eyes narrow-in on my face. "You're Shep Mahoney's girl."

I prepare for the twinkle in his eyes to extinguish, for him to politely excuse himself and return to his book. "The Hesters were my grandparents. They raised me," I tell him.

He smiles, and the twinkle remains. "June and Chick were good folks. The best. So were your mama and Ned." He pauses before adding, "Your dad was a good man, too."

"You don't have to say that."

"I mean it. We grew up together. I was a little older, but everybody knew ol' Shep. He was a charmer back in school. Had a big heart, too. Your old man woulda given a stranger the shirt off his back if they needed it." Hank makes a huffing sound. "Lots of folks 'round here seemed to forget that when he came home from the war needin' a little help himself."

"That didn't give him the right to steal from them," I blurt out. Embarrassed, I lower my gaze to the tray on the table in front of me and begin to unwrap my burger. "Thanks for trying to save my pride, but I've known for a long time what my father was."

"And what is that, Maggie?"

"The consensus around town seemed to be that he was a coward."

Hank curses under his breath. "Folks who said that weren't over there."

"Where?"

"'Nam. Or any war, most of 'em."

I feel his gaze on me as I force down food I don't taste. After a moment, I look up and meet his gaze. "I don't mean to be rude. It's just that Shep and I weren't close."

"Did you ever go to your dad and ask what happened to him?"

"I was a kid. He should've come to me."

"You're right about that, and I'm not defending him for stayin' away. But I think you ought to know that he was ashamed to face you."

The knot of ice in my chest shifts a bit. "Did he say that?"

He pauses then says, "You remember I owned the Lucky J?"

"I remember."

Mr. White studies me closely as he says, "You probably know

that your dad came into my place from time-to-time. When nobody else was around, sometimes Shep would talk to me."

"Were you with him in Vietnam?"

"We went over together. Me, Shep, and Ned, your uncle. But we didn't serve in the same outfit."

I sigh and shove the remains of my meal aside. "Okay, tell me about him."

With the book in one hand – a mystery novel — he stands and steps over, slides his lanky frame into the booth seat across from me. Removing his hat, Hank says, "Shep did Long Range Recon Patrol."

"I don't know what that means."

"He was part of a six-man team sent ahead of the others to scout out where the enemy was hidin'. Sometimes they'd do ambushes and raids, too. It was high risk. A lot of them that did it didn't survive long enough to tell the tale."

I cross my arms, realize I'm shaking, that my heart thumps too hard. A carload of kids pulls into the parking lot outside, the bass on their stereo throbbing. Hank and I both shift to watch them.

"Shep was in and out of the hospitals over there," Hank continues, looking at me again. "Each time for something worse than the time before. First was a broken nose, I believe, then a flesh wound, then he got hit in the shoulder. The docs and nurses would patch him up, get him on his feet again, and back out he'd go."

He pauses, as if to give me time to respond or ask a question. But the ice in my chest has moved up to my throat, and I can't speak. I'm afraid. Afraid he'll confirm the whispered rumors from my childhood that haunt me. Afraid the ice will melt, and

I'll feel the old shame again, the hot, harsh sting of it that I've managed to numb for a very long time.

Hank pulls a napkin from the canister, folds it into a tiny triangle. "After the third time in the hospital, when they sent him back out to rejoin his unit, Shep started losin' his mind a little." He pauses, nods and greets a young couple who pass by and say hello to him. Then he lowers his voice and says, "Your dad felt sure the next grenade or bullet or land mine had his name on it. He was twenty, Maggie. Just a kid." Exhaling a loud breath, he adds, "The things we saw over there, the fear we lived with, there was no dodging it. It stays with you night and day. There were times it almost did me in, too. And I didn't have the kind of dangerous duty Shep did."

"Wasn't it *all* dangerous?"

"Sure, it was. But some of it was worse than others."

Hank holds my gaze. I can't look away, even though I dread the rest. I sense hearing it won't be easy, that it will change me. But a part of me has always wanted to know; that's why I came to the Dairy Queen today. I hoped I would find this old friend of my father's, and he would either confirm or disprove all those whispers from my childhood, that terrible story I had always struggled to acknowledge. "What happened?" I ask.

"Shep blinded himself." He tosses the paper triangle aside. "Your daddy put his own eye out, hoping they'd send him home."

We're silent for several seconds. My heart thumps so hard I hear it. "How did he do it?"

"You don't want to know the details. They don't matter. What does matter is that afterward, he knew he'd screwed up, that he couldn't live with himself if he got to go home while others were trying to survive in that hellhole. He begged them to send him back out."

"But they didn't."

"No." Hank pauses, watching me. "He got drunk one night after comin' home and told a so-called buddy what happened. The news spread fast after that."

I turn to look outside. The wind has kicked up. It blows even harder now than it did at the cemetery. A tumbleweed skips across the Dairy Queen parking lot then onto the road. Running away.

Like my father did.

Like I did.

"So, he *was* a coward. Everyone was right."

Hank's startled expression tells me that he thinks I'm being harsh, and maybe I am. But despite my newfound pity for my father and the anger coursing through me over all the terrible things he went through, I can't let go of my bitterness toward him. I've held onto it tightly for so long.

"No, Maggie. Shep wasn't a coward."

"How can you say that after what you just told me?"

"I can't judge him, and no one else has a right to, either. Your dad fought bravely over there. But he was just a boy. And human. He had his limits, and when he reached 'em he made a bad choice." Hank sits forward, clasps his hands together on the table, unclasps them. "Shep bawled like a baby when he told me that story. Said he didn't deserve you. That you were ashamed of him, and you had a right to be. He told me he didn't deserve your mama, either."

"If he loved her so much, why didn't he keep his promise? Why didn't he marry her before he went over there?" I swipe at the tears on my cheeks.

"I can't answer that. Shep never said." The booth squeaks as Hank shifts his weight.

"What became of him?"

"I don't know. I haven't seen or heard from Shep since he left Juniper."

We sit for a while, neither of us speaking. Not looking at each other. Finally, I ask, "Could you tell me something about him from before the war? Before he changed. Something good." I blow my nose into a napkin.

Our eyes meet. He grins. "I could tell you a lot of stories. But the one that comes to mind is when he fell for your mama. After he graduated, we both worked a construction job south of town, and we carpooled out there together every day. One afternoon, we were headed home after a long day. Shep was drivin'. He spotted Leanne window shoppin' on Main. She'd grown up over the summer, and Shep couldn't take his eyes off her."

Hank chuckles and slaps his thigh. "He was so busy watching her that he missed the street curve and drove right through the plate glass window of Ray Allan's hardware store. I can still hear the song that was blaring on the radio when the car came to a stop. "Pretty One," I think it was called."

"Roy Orbison?"

"Yeah, that's who sang it. Shep was crazy about that guy's music."

"So am I."

"Once, in high school, his cat scratched up his Orbison album and—"

"He had a cat?"

"Yeah, he did for a while. Somebody dumped a litter out at his place, and all but one of 'em died." Hank shakes his head. "Shep loved that cat. I always thought it was because he was

195

lonely. You knew about his folks and how he was raised, didn't you?"

"No. I don't know anything about his family."

"He didn't have any brothers or sisters. His old man wasn't around much, and his mother died when Shep was little. Shep spent a lot of time alone. I always figured that cat was the only company he had at home."

I think of the kitten my dad gave me before he disappeared. I understand now; finally, the cat makes sense.

For the next half hour, Hank tells me stories that make my father seem human to me in a way he never did before. Shep and I have more in common than Roy Orbison, I discover. We share a sweet tooth, among other things. As Hank talks, I begin to picture a funny, mischievous young man. Imperfect, but with a big heart. A young man who had loved to laugh and make others laugh, too. I'm torn between resentment that I never knew that side of him, and happiness over learning it existed.

After some time, Hank reaches for his hat, slides across the booth seat, and stands. "Well, I got to get back to work now. I'm late."

"I'm sorry I kept you so long."

"No, I enjoyed it. Will you be around town a while?"

"No, I'm heading back to Oklahoma City in a few minutes."

"You live there?"

"Yes, I'm a nurse at a hospital there," I say, before I remember that's no longer true. "My son is grown now. He has a son of his own."

"You're a grandma." Hank shakes his head and chuckles. "Hard to believe."

"You can say that again."

He squints at me as he puts on the cowboy hat. "You gonna be okay?"

"Yes, I think I am." I smile.

"I'm glad. It's been good seein' you, Maggie."

His palm feels rough against mine as we shake. "You too, Hank." He starts away from the table, but before he reaches the door, I call out to him, and he turns. "Thank-you for telling me the truth. And for being a friend to my dad." *My dad.* I can't remember the last time I called Shep that. Maybe I never did.

"You're welcome, but no thanks necessary. You want to hear any more stories about Shep, you give me a call, you hear?"

"I will, Hank."

Fifteen minutes later, I glance at Juniper in my rearview mirror. I have a lot of information about Shep to process, but even so, I feel a sense of relief. I doubt I'll ever come back this way, but as I did the last time I left, I'm taking my memories of Nanny, Chick and Uncle Ned with me. And, this time, I'm taking something else. A new image of my father. He made a mistake for a heartbreaking reason and suffered for it for the rest of his life. Maybe someday I'll be able to completely forgive him for causing so many others to suffer along with him.

I guess this trip wasn't for nothing, after all.

I think I understand now why Eliot is staying in Red Lake. He doesn't have memories of Paul, good or bad, to carry with him. Mark, Andrea, and Patricia Reeves are all he has of his father. He needs to walk the same streets Paul walked. To breathe the same air and search for his father's essence. To find a part of his heart that's been missing.

CHAPTER SIXTEEN

*T*wo days following my trip to Juniper, Mark Reeves calls in the middle of the afternoon.

"Hi, Maggie, how are you?"

"Fine." I turn down the television volume. "Is something wrong?"

"No, everything's fine. Eliot and Will are doing great."

"Oh." *Then why are you calling me?* "What's up?"

"I've been going back and forth with myself about whether or not I should call." He clears his throat. "I don't want you to think I reneged on talking to Eliot about moving here and giving up school. I asked him to think it over some more before he decided, but his mind was made up."

I stare at the image on the television screen. "Thanks for trying, Mark. I appreciate it."

"I'm sorry things didn't work out how you wanted." He pauses. "Any news about the lawsuit?"

"Not yet. My lawyer keeps telling me it'll take time."

"Whenever lawyers get involved that's usually the case. They're paid by the hour." He laughs. "I used to rile up Paul by saying that." I hear a horn blare and decide he must be in his car. "How are your allergies? Have you tossed that cat out on her ear?"

I detect the hint of a smile in his voice. "No, I haven't." As if on cue, the tabby slinks by the couch and bats a paw at the skein of yarn that rolled from my lap to the floor earlier. I reach down and stroke her soft fur. "She's not making me sneeze. If that should change, though, she's history."

"Yeah, I bet." He waits a beat, then adds, "You're flipping me off, aren't you? For bringing up the cat."

"Wouldn't you like to know?" Alarmed by the teasing, almost intimate tone of our conversation, I change the subject. "How is Eliot liking his job?"

"Hasn't he told you?"

"We haven't talked since he left here the other day. He hasn't called."

"You have his number, don't you?"

"Yes, but I think he should call me first." I nibble my lip, then add, "I don't want to seem like I'm prying."

"You're his mother. It's your job to pry. Or did *my* mother just brainwash me by telling me that years ago?"

I don't answer him. I feel too defensive. And wary. My last discussion with Mark Reeves about Eliot didn't go so well. I'm not interested in a repeat of that scenario.

"Is this a bad time?" Mark asks. "I could call back later."

"No, that's okay. Sorry to be so quiet, I'm just busy."

"Doing what?"

I don't think I've ever met a more forthright, inquisitive man. He acts as if we're old friends. I glance at the How-To book lying open in my lap and pick up my needles again, feeling a tug at the opposite end of the yarn. On the floor at my feet, the cat is tangled up in a piece of yarn she managed to pull from the skein. I reach down to try to unravel her mess. "I'm knitting a blanket," I tell Mark.

"You don't seem like the knitting type."

"I'm not." I remember Tim calling me a granny and me telling him there'd be no knitting going on at my house. Judging from the knotted mass I tug from around the cat, there may *not* be any knitting going on until I visit a yarn store.

"Interesting. You're allergic to cats, but you've taken in a stray. And you don't knit, but you're making a blanket?"

"That's right. A baby blanket. My grandmother started it for Eliot. She died before she finished it, so I'm going to finish it for Will."

"That's nice. What else are you doing to keep busy these days? Are you looking for a job?"

"Not yet. I've been gardening a little. Oh, and watching television." I set the blanket and tangled yarn on the end table. "Did you know Thomas Magnum was married once?"

"You mean Tom Selleck?"

"No, the character he played. Magnum P.I. I've been watching the reruns. He married this woman who —"

"When's the last time you left the house?"

"A couple of days ago. I took a little drive to my hometown. Why?"

"When do you plan on leaving the house again?"

"When I reach the bottom of the peanut butter jar or put on makeup. Whichever comes first." I turn off the television. "I've never had the chance to just stay home and be lazy. It's kind of nice not to wake up to an alarm and rush off to work. And—" My throat tightens, and before I can stop myself, I blurt out, "And I don't know what to do with myself. I'm not used to living alone. I feel as if I've lost my son." *Oh, God. Not again. I will not cry.*

"You haven't lost Eliot." Mark sounds panicked that I might fall apart on him. "Call him, Maggie. He's just being a guy – he's clueless. He doesn't mean to hurt you. Better yet, come visit."

"Not until he invites me. And don't *tell* him to. I want the idea to be Eliot's."

"Until he wakes up and asks, maybe you should do something away from the house."

And maybe Mark Reeves should mind his own business.

"I'm going to look for a job," I say, aware of the defensive tone of my voice. "I'm just not ready yet."

"I don't mean to butt in."

"Yes, you do." I laugh.

"Okay, maybe I do. I'm worried about you."

"Why? You barely know me."

"You're Eliot's mother and Will's grandmother. And I know how it feels to be alone."

The warmth in his voice weaves through me, soothes me as much as the cat's soft vibrating purr. "Why are you being so nice to me all of a sudden?"

"Haven't I always been?"

"No."

"Fair enough. I was an idiot. Like I said, I'm being nice to you now because you're Eliot's mom and Will's grandmother. Besides, I like you."

"Like *I* said, you barely know me."

"True, but you pretend to hate cats while it's obvious you have a soft spot for a particular orange one. And your eyes shoot daggers when you put people in their place, like that Sheila woman you used to work with. And me. Aren't those good enough reasons for me to like you even though we haven't known each other long?"

I smile, and before I can think twice about the wisdom of becoming even more personal with Mark Reeves, I ask, "You think if we'd stayed in our marriages it would've been better? The loneliness of being alone, I mean?" When he doesn't answer right away, I wince. "Sorry. I didn't mean to sound as if I'm assuming anything about your marriage."

"It's fine. He pauses, then adds, "I didn't know you were ever married."

"Only for a year."

"How did you know I'm divorced?"

"Eliot mentioned it." And Doug Dowlen, but I don't tell him that.

"So, your ex—"

"Left me. It was mutual, really. He was an insurance broker and a good guy. A *really* good guy. I just married him for the wrong reasons. I was lonely. I liked him, but he really *loved* me. Most importantly, though, he cared for Eliot." A sigh rushes out of me. "I know it wasn't easy for Stephen living in this house. He said he felt like an intruder, that there wasn't enough of me to go around; I gave all I had to Eliot and my job. When he left, I was sad, but I didn't shed a tear. Not one. That's when I knew that I'd married him so Eliot would have a good father, not because I loved him."

"Even when it's mutual, divorce is tough."

The understanding and sympathy in his voice feels like a hug; until now, I didn't realize how much I needed one. Still, I'm embarrassed that I've gone on too long, revealed too much of myself.

"In answer to your question," Mark continues, "I don't think staying in our less-than-stellar marriages would've been better than living alone. One reason being, if we had, I couldn't ask you out to dinner. What are you doing tomorrow night?"

I freeze. "Um, I'm sorry, Mark. I'm busy tomorrow night."

"Doing what? Knitting and watching Magnum P.I. reruns? I'll be in town on business, and I thought I could just stay afterward, and we could go someplace nice. You choose where."

"I'm out of the loop when it comes to nice places for dinner. Besides, that would put you home so late. It's a four-hour drive."

"I'll get a hotel room."

"I can't, Mark."

"Why?"

"Because . . . I don't know. I feel . . . it doesn't seem right."

"Because I'm Paul's brother? Is that it?"

"No. I don't know. Maybe."

"You and Paul were together a long time ago. He's gone. But you're not, and neither am I. This isn't about him."

"What *is* it about?"

"I like your company."

"You might want to seek counseling," I scoff. "At our one short meeting, I argued with you, walked out on you, and left you with the lunch tab. Not to mention the fact that I bawled like a baby and laughed like a maniac."

"That's what I mean. I've never met a more interesting woman."

"Ha! You're the one who needs to get out more."

"Sleep on it. I've got to go." The sound of a door slamming follows his words. "I'll call you tomorrow."

"Mark – I don't need to—" He breaks the connection.

I drag myself from bed before sunup the next morning. With coffee in hand, I check a local job search site online, avoiding anything medical. Even if I could land a nursing job, I don't want to go that route yet.

I print several pages, then circle an ad for a clerk at an independent bookstore, another for a baker's helper, one for a salesclerk at a quiet antique shop where I've browsed many times. Satisfied, I fold the sheets in half and put them in my purse.

An hour later, I head out the door. Although the standard procedure is to apply online, I decide it can't hurt to show up and talk to the person who's doing the hiring face-to-face. At each place, I fill out an application and am told they'll "be in touch."

At ten o'clock, I'm sitting at a red light, scanning the job site on my phone again. A horn honks behind me. I glance up and see that the light has turned green. I start across the intersection and notice a sign ahead on my left that reads *Milsap's Greenhouse,* and beneath it, *HELP WANTED.* I pull into the parking lot and go inside.

Humid air, and the earthy scents of plants and damp soil surround me. Visions of Nanny's gardens flash through my mind, and a feeling of calm flows through me as I make my way to a front counter where a middle-aged woman with frizzy brown hair talks on the phone. She smiles at me as I approach, lifting a finger as if to say she'll be with me in a second.

When she ends the call, she asks, "Can I help you?"

"I noticed your sign out front. I'd like to apply, if you're still hiring."

The smile on her unadorned, freckled face spreads wider. "I'm Kay Milsap."

"Hi, Kay. I'm Maggie Mahoney."

She comes around the counter, and we shake hands. "Let me get you an application." Returning to the other side of the counter, she opens a drawer, retrieves a clipboard with the application attached, and hands it to me along with a pen. "I'll be in back if you need me," she says.

Ten minutes later, Kay glances over the information I've provided and asks me a few questions. The pay she quotes isn't much – less, in fact, than I had considered accepting – but the moment I stepped inside the greenhouse, I knew I not only want the job – I need it. I need to spend time in this peaceful place with a down-to-earth person like Kay, a woman I instinctively like. "That sounds fine," I tell her.

"Can you start the first of the month?" She tucks a strand of hair behind one ear, tightens the sash on the gardening apron over her jeans. "A week from today?"

"How about Monday, instead?"

"Great! Monday, it is. See you at nine."

I exit the nursery, pausing to smell a rosebush just outside the door, thinking of how quickly life shifts, the changes sneaking in behind your back so that when you turn around, you're caught off guard.

During the drive home, my cell phone rings. The display tells me it's Mark. I don't answer. The rings soon stop, but in less than a minute, start up again, and I see that it's Tim now; he and Alice often call to check on me. They stopped by the house yesterday, and I told them about Eliot moving and why.

Answering the call, I say, "Hey, Tim."

"What are you doing?"

"Driving home. I just landed a job. I'm going to work in a nursery."

"Sweetie! I'm so happy for you. Take *that* Derek." He laughs. "I knew you could do it, Maggie. What hospital?"

"Not a *hospital* nursery, a *plant* nursery."

A pause, then, "Maggie . . . you're a nurse, not a gardener."

"I want to take care of flowers for a while instead of people. Plants don't file lawsuits."

"Good point. We should celebrate. I'll call Alice."

"Okay. I could use some fun for a change. I'll cook dinner."

"We'll bring the wine. What time do you want us?"

"We'll start early. Come over when you get off work."

I make chicken piccata, prosciutto-wrapped melon, a big green salad, and garlic bread.

As promised, Tim brings wine and two wrapped gifts. He also brings a huge photo of Derek that he had enlarged at an office supply on his lunch break. Alice supplies the darts. After we eat, we carry the wine out onto the backyard patio where we take turns throwing the darts at the poster-sized image of the hospital's Director of Corporate Compliance.

Tim, who owns three dogs, two cats, and a hamster, expresses his approval that I've kept the stray cat.

I take aim at Derek's throat and send a dart flying. "I just hope I don't end up one of those sad, lonely women whose only reason for getting up in the morning is to feed twenty animals."

"Oh, you won't." Alice sets her wine glass on the patio table and lifts a dart to take her turn. "Tim and I are making a list of available men who are likely prospects to end your celibacy." I start to protest when she quickly adds, "When you're ready, of course. No pressure."

"Maybe a little pressure," Tim interjects. "I saw that blanket you're knitting on the sofa." He crosses his arms and scowls at me. "You promised, Maggie."

I refill my glass. "It's for Will. And I have to admit, I'm enjoying learning to knit."

Tim glances at Alice, lifts his brows, and says, "We'd better hurry up with that list of prospects."

We soon grow tired of punishing Derek and his face is shredded, Alice excuses herself, goes into the house, and returns a minute later carrying the two gifts Tim brought and another bottle of wine. She sets everything in front of me.

"What have you done?" I ask, touched by their gesture.

"I took off early to do a little shopping," Tim says.

"I couldn't get away." Alice cringes when she adds, "I had to trust him to pick out my gift. I apologize in advance."

I laugh, and start to open the top package, but Tim stops me.

"First, a few toasts." He reaches for the wine bottle.

I cover the top of my glass with my palm. "I'm already plastered."

"On a glass and a half?" Tim scowls at me. "This is a *celebration*. Don't be a spoil sport."

I frown at him for a second, then remove my hand and he pours the wine.

He sits back and lifts his glass in a toast. Alice and I follow suit. "To your new career," he says. "May your thumb turn green and your life be serene."

"Here, here," Alice adds, and we all tap glasses.

Tim sips, then raises his glass again. "As you plant and water and toil, may no worms invade your soil."

Alice smirks. "Lord, that was bad, Tim. Really, incredibly bad."

"But offered in the right spirit," I say, laughing, relieved to be silly after the seriousness of the past few weeks. "Thank you, Tim. However, the right worms aren't a bad thing."

"On second thought, *you* might be the one who needs to lay off the wine, Tim," Alice interjects.

"I'm not the least bit drunk. Besides, I'm just getting started." Tim winks at me and lifts his glass again. "Another toast." He clears his throat. "Here's to it and from it and to it again. And if you ever get to it and don't do it, may you never get to it to do it again."

The toasts continue, each one more absurd than the last. We're laughing hysterically when I hear a noise at the gate, it opens, and Mark Reeves walks into the backyard. The table falls silent.

Mark stops in the center of the yard. "I rang the bell. Nobody answered." He shrugs, glances at the table. "I heard a commotion back here. Sounded like a party. Looks like I was right."

A jolt of alarm has me sitting up straighter, and I realize that I'm a little drunk. One second, I'm worried about looking like a mess and embarrassing myself, the next, I'm irritated that Mark Reeves showed up at my house without calling first. Then I remember not answering his call earlier today when I saw his name on my cell phone screen.

I glance at Alice, then Tim. Tim stares at Mark with pursed lips, his head tilted to one side. When he realizes I'm watching him, he turns to me and raises a brow. "Guess we can tear up that list of names, Alice," he says. "Where are your manners, Maggie? The man looks positively thirsty."

"Come join us, Mark," I say, feeling awkward and off guard.

He starts over, and I make introductions, then say, "I'll get another wine glass."

"I'll get it." Alice stands, turns her back to Mark and winks at me. She starts toward the back door.

"You got here just in the nick of time," Tim says. "Maggie's about to open her gifts." He pulls out the chair beside him and pats the seat. "For you," he tells Mark.

Mark shifts his gaze between Tim and me as he rounds the table and sits. "Is it your birthday, Maggie?"

"No."

Alice returns with a wine glass for Mark and plops down again.

"What are we celebrating, then?" he asks, glancing at the destroyed poster of Derek. "Or are you all just practicing up on your torture techniques?"

"I got a job today." I tell him about it, and he congratulates me.

Alice points at the packages on the table. "Open mine first." She pours Mark's wine. "It's the one with the yellow bow."

I pick it up, remove the bow, turn the box over, peal back the seam.

"Oh, *for the love*, would you just rip into it?" Tim groans with an exaggerated roll of his eyes.

I tear off the paper, open the box. "A photo album." I grin at Alice. "I love it."

Her silver hair ruffles in the breeze. "For all your pictures of Will. I know the two of you will make lots of memories together."

Drawing my lower lip between my teeth, I look down at the album, my good mood swept away by a sudden deep sadness.

"You will, Maggie. Trust me," Alice says quietly. "I have four grandkids. I'm an old pro at this." She hiccups.

I feel Mark's gaze on me as I lean over to kiss her cheek. "Thanks, Alice."

Tim claps his hands together. "Enough already. Open mine."

He slides his package across the table, and I pick it up. "I'm a little scared, Tim," I tease while ripping off the paper.

"Trust me. You're gonna love it," he says.

Staring at the picture on the box of clay animal with something like hair sprouting out of it, I say, "I hate to ask, but what is it?"

"A Chia Pet." Tim takes the box from me, turns it sideways, points, and adds, "The grass growing out of it is the animal's hair. I didn't believe you'd keep the cat, so I thought this would be the next best thing."

"Hmmm." I stare at it, speechless.

"Such unimaginative friends, I have." Pouting, Tim sits back and crosses his arms.

"Maybe he has the right idea, Maggie." Mark chuckles. "A pet that doesn't bark or poop sounds good to me."

"Hey!" Alice gestures toward the battered poster of Derek. "After the grass grows, we could give it to Derek to use as a toupee!"

Mark watches the three of us with an amused expression as we dissolve into laughter again.

"Thanks you, two," I say, composing myself. "I love the gifts. And I love you." I stand to gather the discarded paper and bows.

Mark glances at the poster again. Derek has a dart in each nostril and one in his Adam's apple. "Who *is* that poor guy, anyway?"

Tim gestures at the image of Derek with his glass. "Someone

who doesn't deserve your pity. In fact, I should've found a full body shot so we could've thrown darts at his—"

"Tim! You're terrible." Trash in hand, I start for the house. "Not a bad idea, though."

"Wait, Maggie." Mark leans forward to reach into the back pocket of his jeans. "I have something for you, too."

Surprised, I return to the table, set the wrapping paper on it, and take the envelope from Mark. Opening it, I slide out a stack of photographs.

"They're of Will and Eliot," he says.

"Oh, good!" Alice leans over to look. "You can put them in the album."

A knot of emotion lodges in my throat. In the first picture, Eliot, his smile relaxed and wide, holds Will up to face the camera, their heads side-by-side. Will barely resembles the same baby we brought home from the hospital; his cheeks are rounder and rosier, his eyes alert and bright. He looks so much like Eliot, even more than he did as a newborn. I swallow and keep my gaze down as I shuffle through the rest of the stack. "Thank you, Mark."

"I'd like to take credit. But when I told Mom I was coming, she had the idea for me to bring them to you."

I'm struck by how happy Eliot looks in every shot. I *want* him to be happy. But the contentment – no, *joy* – on his face also makes me sad that he couldn't find that same happiness here with me. That I can't be with him to share it. And that's my fault.

As I return the photo stack to the envelope, I'm aware of the silence around me. Alice touches my arm.

I look up at Mark. "I love these. Your mother's very kind."

Pushing away from the table, I take the envelope and escape

into the house and my bedroom. Closing the door, I sit at the edge of the bed, my head pounding.

A few minutes later, a knock sounds on my door. Alice says, "Maggie? May I come in?"

"Sure. It's open."

She crosses the room and sits beside me. "You okay?"

I nod. "Other than being drunk and—" A sob slips out of me. "I'm an idiot. I don't know why I ran away. It's just—"

"I understand." She pats my knee. "We all do."

"I'm selfish, aren't I? I should be glad Eliot's happy. I *am* glad. I guess I just feel excluded. How juvenile is that?"

"Not juvenile, at all. Human. I'm sure Eliot doesn't mean to exclude you."

"I'm not." I turn away, embarrassed by my emotional state.

"Have you called him?"

"No, I don't want to interfere."

"Interfere? He wouldn't think that. Eliot loves you."

"I know he does. But if he wants to talk to me, he'll call. He thinks he's a disappointment to me. That's what he said before he left."

"I bet he's doing the same thing you are. Waiting for you to reach out to him. Sometimes it's hard to make the first move after a fallout. I know he misses you."

I nod, but I can't face her.

Alice stands. "Tim and I will clean up the kitchen."

"No, that's okay. It'll give me something to do besides feel sorry for myself. I'm afraid I'm not very good company anymore. You two go on. I'll call you tomorrow. Take a cab. I don't want either of you driving."

"Good idea." She hiccups. "Lord, I haven't been in this condition since Tiny Tim tiptoed through the tulips."

I laugh. "It's been a while since I drank so much, too. It was fun, but I'll probably pay for it in the morning."

"If you need me, shout. I'll be at home."

"Thanks, Alice." I look up at her. "I don't know what I'd do without you. Tim, too. Thank him for me, okay?"

"Of course."

"Is Mark still here?" I ask as she starts for the door.

"Yes, he says he's going to stick around for a bit. He wants to apologize."

"For what? Tell him he doesn't need to do that."

"I'm not sure he'll go, Maggie. I think he has a stubborn streak." She opens the door, looks back at me. "If I were you, I'd jump that man's bones before he gets away."

"*Alice . . .*" My face heats.

"I mean it. You're too serious. You could use a little fun; it would cheer you up. And it's obvious he's willing. Did you see how he looked at you?"

"No." I make a face.

She scoffs. "If you didn't, you're blind. He was wishing you were one of those packages on the table so he could unwrap you."

"Yeah, right. Even if I were interested—"

"Why wouldn't you be? He's—"

"Eliot's uncle."

"So what?"

"Getting involved with him could cause a lot of problems for everyone concerned. Eliot most of all."

"Would you quit being the perfect virgin mother, for once? It's really exhausting." She says this with a teasing tone, but something tells me she means it.

"Yeah, right. I've been anything but a perfect mom." I exhale a noisy breath. "Was I out of line, Alice? Keeping Eliot and Paul apart?"

"It's easy to second guess yourself now, but it won't get you anywhere."

"I can't help wondering if I misjudged what kind of father Paul would've been."

"What do you mean?"

"Did I really spare Eliot the pain of having a somewhat neglectful dad, or did I rob him of the attention of a loving one?"

"You did what you thought was the right thing for him at the time. Now you have to do what's right for *you*. Quit being so damned independent. It's okay to need someone, Maggie. To lean on someone. Mark seems like a nice man. Give him a chance."

She lets herself out, leaving me alone and woozy. And as exhausted with myself as Alice claimed to be.

CHAPTER SEVENTEEN

I find Mark climbing down the treehouse ladder in the yard. When he hears the back door close, he turns, sees me, and jumps the rest of the way to the ground.

"Eliot and a friend built that." Crossing my arms, I approach him, my attention on the branches above his head. "They were eleven."

"Not a bad job. Not pretty, but sturdy as hell. Next time there's a tornado, if I were you, I'd hole up in there."

"They spent a fortune on nails."

After a long pause, Mark says, "About those photographs—"

"Thanks for bringing them. I'm glad to know that Eliot and Will are happy and doing well." I shrug. "I am a little jealous, though."

"Don't be. Eliot misses you."

"Does he?" I focus my attention on the treehouse. "He still hasn't called."

"That doesn't mean anything. Guys his age forget to call their mothers. I know, I used to be one. Hell, sometimes I still forget."

"I had the impression you and your mother are close."

"We are."

I shake my head and look at him. "I don't get it."

His eyes crinkle at the corners when he smiles. "Guys are dense when it comes to relationships. Most of us, anyhow." Mark leans against the tree trunk. "So, you're going to work in a greenhouse?"

"Starting on Monday."

"You won't miss being a nurse?"

"I pretty much gave up the aspect of nursing I loved most a long time ago."

"What was that?"

"Patient care. When I went into the administrative side of things, I lost that one-on-one contact with people. I knew I'd miss it, and I did."

"Then why did you give it up?"

"Because it was part of *the plan*." I huff a humorless laugh. "What you said that day at the diner was pretty much on target. I had everything mapped out. For myself *and* for Eliot. Don't ask me why. I'm not completely sure. It's all tied up with a lot of baggage from my past and a pathetic need to prove myself." A warm breeze blows hair into my face. I tuck a strand behind my ear.

Mark studies me during the long stretch of silence that follows. A dog barks somewhere in the distance. Children's voices and laughter drift to me. He looks up at the treehouse. "You game?" Turning, he grabs hold of the ladder and wiggles it.

I scowl at him. "We're a little old for treehouses, don't you think? Besides, I had too much to drink; I'd probably fall on my ass."

His expression conveys what Alice said aloud: I'm too

serious.

Lifting my gaze to the branches overhead, I say, "Okay, fine. Why not? I'm game if you are."

He climbs, and I follow. When we reach the top, I sit on the railing, and Mark stands beside me.

I scan the empty space. "I haven't been up here in years. It was right after Eliot and his friend Russ finished it. There used to be some lawn furniture. Who knows what else."

"I bet Eliot spent a lot of time up here."

"For a while. Especially during the year I was married. It was a good place for him to avoid Stephen and me." I slide off the railing, stoop to pick up a small, dead tree limb from the floor, toss it down to the ground. "Did you have a happy childhood?" I ask, wondering more how Eliot would answer that question than Mark.

"Yeah, it was pretty good, I'd say."

"Mine was good, too. I mean, there were bad things. Hard things."

I tell Mark that my grandparents raised me and why, uncertain what drives me to so readily share my personal life with him. As I talk, the tree sways and we sway with it, the unsteadiness beneath my feet matching what I feel inside.

"Nanny and Chick were what made things good," I continue, trying to fill the silence so I won't dwell on what I see in his eyes — the same surprising connection that I'm feeling, that I've felt since that day he came to the house after our disastrous first meeting at the diner. "I wasn't an easy kid, but they never made me feel I was a burden to them. Or a disappointment. Apparently, I didn't make Eliot feel as secure." I cross my arms and avoid Mark's gaze. "Did I tell you he apologized to me the other day for being a disappointment?"

"Eliot is dealing with some tough things right now. He'll find his way back to you, Maggie."

A sparrow lands on the railing's far end. "Like birds," I say.

"Birds?"

"My grandmother had a thing for them. They go away but they always come back – that's what she told me. She thought they were just about the only thing a person could rely on." Heat creeps up the back of my neck. "She said they could lift you up, that they could save you."

"Maggie . . ." Mark's hand comes to rest on my shoulder.

I turn to him, my heart full of so many unspoken things it might burst.

He draws me into his arms, and when I abruptly pull away, he lets go of me and steps back. "I apologize if—"

I silence him by lifting onto my toes and kissing him.

Without breaking contact, Mark pulls me to him again, and I lean against the railing, wrap my arms around his neck. Our kiss is tender and comforting, and I don't want it to end.

When it does, I say, "Please tell me you really had business here today. You didn't drive four hours just to bring me those photographs, did you?"

"I had business here. I could've done it by phone, though." He brushes my lower lip with the pad of his thumb. "I've been thinking about you all week, Maggie. Come back to Red Lake with me. I'll bring you home before you have to start your job on Monday. Or you can follow me in your car if that's more comfortable."

I lower my arms from around his neck. "I can't. Eliot didn't invite me."

"*I'm* inviting you. You can stay at Mom's."

"Your *mom* didn't invite me."

Mark steps aside to give me some space. "Is it Tim?" His eye twitches.

"Tim? He was my assistant at the hospital."

"I liked him, but I don't have a clue how to compete with a metrosexual."

I laugh. Mark doesn't seem like the sort of man who'd know that word, much less what it means.

He feigns a look of offense. "That's what I hear they're called."

"They?"

"Guys who wear jewelry and get pedicures."

I tilt my head and study him, amused. "Tim's just a good friend." I smirk at him. "And I'm one hundred percent sure he's not a metrosexual."

"No kidding." Mark smirks back at me.

I swat at his arm. "You were teasing me about Tim."

"Was I?" He takes my hand. "If you won't come to Red Lake, then I'll just have to come back here. When's your first day off?"

"This is crazy." I look away, my nerves on edge. "We barely know each other."

He shakes his head and sighs. "That again."

"Well, it's true. We don't."

"We can change that. All I'm asking for is dinner. Maybe a movie. A walk. What could that hurt?"

"It could hurt Eliot. I'm already on shaky ground with him."

"I'm only asking for a date, not marriage." His cheek twitches. "Not yet, anyway."

I tilt my head and narrow my eyes at him, my heart beating unsteadily. "Even a date might be awkward for him."

"I think you're borrowing trouble."

"Maybe so, but it just doesn't seem right. I mean, Paul

and I—"

Mark takes my hand. "You aren't saying we can't be friends, are you?"

"No, I'm not saying that. I'd like to be friends."

"We'll see where it goes from there," he adds.

I purse my lips and try not to laugh.

"Well, I guess I should hit the road."

He lets go of my hand, and we climb down the ladder. "Thanks again for the pictures," I say, turning to face him when we reach the ground. "And for listening."

"Anytime." He tucks a strand of my hair behind my ear, his fingers brushing my cheek. "Call Eliot."

"I will."

The feel of his fingers on my skin lingers in my mind long after he leaves through the gate.

After I wash dishes and clean the kitchen, I dial Eliot's cell phone number, and he picks up.

"Hi." I grip the receiver.

"Hey, Mom."

"How are you? I haven't heard from you in a while." Wishing that hadn't sounded so much like a reprimand or an accusation, I wince.

"I'm good. I've been busy with work and everything."

"How's Will?"

"He's good, too."

I hold my breath, wait for him to go on, and when he doesn't, I ask, "Do you like your job?"

"So far."

"That's good." I pause again. "Is the apartment working out okay?"

"Yeah. It's small, but it'll do."

Frustrated by how little he has to say, I grapple for a way to jumpstart the conversation. "How's Will's colic?"

"He's been kind of fussy, and he's sort of off his bottle, but he's asleep right now. I usually don't put him down this early, but he was really tired. Patricia said he didn't nap much today."

"I won't keep you long, then. You probably want to sleep while you can. I hope he's not getting a cold. Does he still wake up a lot at night?"

"Sometimes he sleeps longer. And he's getting fatter." Eliot's laughter sounds awkward and forced. "His knees have dimples."

I laugh, too. "He *is* getting fatter. Your uncle stopped by today and brought pictures. He's adorable, Eliot." Tension buzzes in the stretch of silence that follows, and the sudden realization of what I said — and how he might interpret it — punches into me. "*Will's* adorable, I mean. He looks like such a happy baby."

"Why was Mark there?"

"He had business here, so he dropped by. He's a nice man. I like him." Remembering the kiss Mark and I shared, I wince.

"Yeah, he is." Suspicion cloaks Eliot's voice. I'm sure he must wonder what possible reason Mark and I would have to meet up other than to talk about him. I'm relieved that he doesn't ask any questions.

"I think it's great that you're getting to know your dad's side of the family," I say.

Muffled noises drift across the line. Eliot clears his throat. "Yeah, it's been nice."

I stare at the clock, count the seconds as they tick by. "Tell me about your job."

"Right now, I'm doing concrete work."

"I bet that's a big change from working at the clinic." I keep my voice light.

"Yeah, I have calluses on my hands now instead of paper cuts."

"Do you and Will need anything? Something you left behind? I could mail it to you."

"No, we're fine."

"If you think of something, just let me know." I start to tell him goodnight when it occurs to me that he doesn't know about what happened at the hospital. "I should probably tell you that Liza filed a lawsuit against the hospital, and I lost my job," I say.

Silence, then, "Mom, I—"

"It's okay."

"No, it isn't. It sucks. You love your job."

"Maybe I loved it too much. I know I always worked more than I should have." I take a breath. "Something good might come out of this. Maybe I'll learn to slow down."

He groans. "I feel awful."

"It's not your fault, and I'm doing okay. I've already found another job. On Monday I start work at Milsap's Greenhouse."

"A greenhouse? What do you know about plants? No offense, but our flowerbeds look like shit."

I laugh. "Not anymore. I've been working on them. They look pretty good now. Anyway, I'm a fast learner. It'll be fun." I pause, then add, "You and I are both taking off in new directions."

"Why would the hospital fire *you* over Liza suing *them*?"

"It's corporate politics." Before I can talk myself out of it, I say, "And you might as well know that Liza is suing me, too."

Eliot curses. Twice. "What is *wrong* with her?"

"Maybe she thinks it's a matter of principle. Who knows?" What I don't say is that I think Liza is angry at him and taking it out on me.

"I'm calling her," he says.

"Don't, Eliot. I know you want to help, but it might do more harm than good." I rush to change the subject. "I know you're really busy, but I'd love to see you and Will as soon as you have time."

"I'll try, but I don't know when I can get away."

"Just come when you can."

I dream I'm standing on the dirt road bordering Nanny and Chick's farm. A lightning bolt shoots out of a cloud and strikes the house with a thunderous CRACK, leaving a yawning, smoking mouth in the center of the roof. The walls wobble, and the house falls in on itself, spewing dust into the sky.

An engine rumbles beyond the dust. When the air clears, I see a bulldozer move slowly toward the rubble. The dozer's blade lifts, aims at the pile of wood.

Running toward it, I scream and wave my arms. All that I am, good and bad, lies beneath those splintered planks.

I reach the remains of the house in time to scoop up all that's important: a wounded sparrow, Chick's walnut cradle, Nanny's half-finished butter-yellow baby blanket, a broken guitar string, a crumpled paper bag filled to the brim by Mary Nell with things I once desperately needed for Eliot.

As the blade descends, I strap all I've taken on my back and leave everything else on the pile. I start running again, this time away, with no destination in mind. I move so fast that soon I'm weightless, and my feet leave the ground. As I pass over Juniper, I look down and see only a fading sweep of color and light.

Wind rushes past me as I soar away from all that's below, the sound of it soothing me so much that I'm not startled by the sudden shriek that pierces the silence. Turning toward the sound, I see a blackbird flying beside me, wings flapping gracefully, gliding . . . gliding.

I rise with the blackbird above the clouds, and as we fly, the bird faces me, and his glossy black eyes stare into mine. His beak opens, and a second caw emerges, the sound transforming into a baby's cry.

I jolt up in bed, my heart banging in my chest, my gown soaked with perspiration. The phone rings on the nightstand. I grab the receiver and glance at the clock. *1:10 a.m.* "Hello?"

"Mom?"

"Eliot? What's wrong?" Reaching for the lamp, I turn it on.

"Will has a fever," he says, talking fast. "A hundred and two."

"Do you have that baby Tylenol I sent with you?"

"I gave him some about thirty minutes ago, but it hasn't helped. Mark isn't home yet. I reached him on his cell, and he said he got a late start leaving the city. I just hung up from Patricia. She's coming over."

I push aside the covers. "Listen, Eliot—"

"She says I should rub Will with alcohol until she gets here."

"Don't do that," I say quickly. "He could have an adverse reaction."

"Should I put him in a cold bath? She said—"

"No, that could make him shiver so hard his temp could rise

even more." I keep my voice calm, not wanting to increase Eliot's anxiety. "Is Will awake?"

"Barely. He woke me up crying, but after I changed his diaper he quieted down. He seems really sleepy. Like he can't keep his eyes open. And he's breathing sort of fast and making a wheezing sound."

"Take off his clothes and look at his chest," I tell him.

Muffled sounds echo across the line. "Okay. I'm looking."

"When he takes a breath, do the muscles draw inward?"

"Maybe a little."

"What about his lips and fingers? Are they blue or gray?"

I hear Will whimper. "They're pink," Eliot says.

"That's good." The fact that his breathing is rapid still concerns me. "How far does Patricia live from you?"

"Not far." He pauses, then adds, "I think she just pulled up."

"More than likely Will only has a cold. I'd rather not take any chances, though. Especially since he had that little respiratory problem when he was born." I hear a knocking sound across the line. "Is that Patricia?"

"Yeah, I'm letting her in."

"I want the two of you to take Will to the ER."

A woman's concerned voice drifts to me, and Eliot says to her, "It's my mom. She says we should go to the hospital."

"I'm just being cautious," I say to him. "Lots of things can cause a baby to run a fever. Will might just have a cold or an ear infection. I'd rather play it safe, though. When you get to the ER, tell the nurse about the problem he had with his breathing."

"I will."

"I wish I was there with you."

Eliot pauses, then in a choked voice says, "Can you come?"

Standing, I hurry over to the closet. "I'm on my way."

CHAPTER EIGHTEEN

I break every speed limit and arrive in Red Lake with the sunrise. Eliot and I spoke on our cell phones a few times during the drive. The hospital hasn't sent Will home, which concerns me. I call Eliot now to let him know I'm in town, and he gives me directions.

Mark is waiting outside the entrance as I cross the parking lot, his face lined with fatigue. "How's Will?" I ask as he ushers me inside.

"They're moving him from the ER to a room."

I take stock of the hospital. "I wasn't expecting such a large facility."

"Red Lake's small, but the hospital serves a bigger area. All the little towns for miles around."

I'm relieved that it isn't the typical small community clinic so that Will can, I hope, get whatever treatment he needs.

My tennis shoes squeak against the tiles as we hurry down a hallway. "Is the room he's being moved to in ICU?"

"No, a regular room on the pediatric floor."

"Good. What does the doctor say?"

At the bank of elevators, Mark pushes the *up* button. "It's pneumonia, but it isn't severe." The doors slide apart, and we step together onto the empty elevator. "I'm sorry I wasn't home when Eliot needed me," Mark says. "When I left your house yesterday evening, I swung by to see friends and stayed a while."

"You don't have to explain."

When the elevator doors open onto the third floor, we step off into a waiting area occupied by six people. A tiny, slender woman with short, choppy red hair sits on one of the vinyl couches. She sees us and rises, and I know at once that she's Patricia, Mark's mother. She has Paul's intense expression, his mouth. She crosses to meet us.

"Mom, this is Maggie," Mark says.

Cautious, curious eyes meet mine. "Hello, Maggie." She offers her hand, and after an awkward hesitation on my part, I clasp it. "Eliot will be so relieved to see you," she says.

"I'm glad you were with him, Mrs. Reeves."

"Where is he?" Mark asks his mother, drawing her attention away from me.

"Room 303. They were getting Will settled. I was in the way, so I stepped out." Patricia glances at me again. "You should go on in. Eliot is waiting for you."

Matching double doors grace both ends of the waiting area. "Which way?" I ask, and she gestures toward the right.

After pushing through the doors, I pass the nursing station, looking for room 303. I find it and step inside. With his back to me, Eliot watches a nurse who stands beside a crib. She leans over the tall stainless steel rails.

I touch his shoulder, and he turns, emotions playing across his face that I identify as relief and scared gratitude.

"Hey, Mom."

We hug, each of us grasping tight to the other, as if we've finally found our anchor. "How're you doing?" I ask, stepping back to look at him.

Eliot swallows hard. "Okay."

His eyes are bloodshot, his face clenched tight as a fist. "You don't look okay."

"I've been better." He glances toward Will's crib. "What's she putting on him?"

Hearing his question, the nurse looks up at us and smiles. "It's called a pulse oximeter," she says.

"It checks his oxygen saturation level," I add, and the woman's smile transforms to curious regard. I introduce myself, tell her I'm a nurse. Something flickers in her eyes, something I recognize from my own experiences of dealing with patients or family members with medical backgrounds. An *oh, great, you'll be questioning everything* look.

Eliot eyes the small board that mobilizes Will's arm and the plastic line inserted at the inside crook of his elbow. "Why does he need an I.V.?"

"The fluids will help keep him from getting dehydrated," the nurse explains. "And all his meds are administered through it." She finishes with Will then starts from the room. "The doctor should be up in a few minutes. Call me if you need anything."

When the squeak of her shoes against the floor tiles fades, Eliot crosses to the bed and stares down at Will with a helpless expression. "What kind of meds are they giving him?"

I move up alongside him. "Until we talk to the doctor, I can't answer that. Mark said they told you Will has pneumonia, so it's probably an antibiotic."

"How long do you think he'll have to be in the hospital?"

"Nobody answered these questions for you?"

Eliot scowls. "They didn't tell me *shit*. And the little bit they did, I didn't understand." He makes a scoffing sound. "Some doctor I would've been. I didn't even know what to ask."

I wrap my arm around his shoulder. "You're stressed out. Nobody expects you to think straight right now. When the doctor shows up, we'll ask him all our questions."

Eliot tilts his head to the side, rests it against mine, and we stand that way for a while, watching Will sleep. Side-by-side, my arm around him, our heads together. Minutes go by before he says, "If I hadn't called you, I would've done what Patricia said. I could've hurt him."

"She meant well. My grandmother used to swab me with alcohol and put me in a cold bath when I had a fever, too. I survived. Sometimes I even got better. Will probably would've been fine, too."

"Why did they do that if it's dangerous?"

"They didn't know the risks back then."

After a moment, he murmurs, "Thanks for driving here. I knew you'd know what to do.

I tighten my arm around him, relieved and pleased that I'm the one he turned to, the one he trusted. "I'm here, Eliot. For as long as you and Will need me."

A half hour later, the doctor leaves Will's room, and I convince Eliot to go to the small cafeteria to eat something.

"Maybe Patricia and Mark will go with you. Or tell them they can come in here with Will and me if they want."

I walk him to the door, stand just outside in the hallway and stretch my arms overhead as he disappears around the corner. A young woman steps from the room next door and bursts into tears. I hesitate a moment, then go over to comfort her.

Minutes later, Mark rounds the corner, and I squeeze the worried young mother's hand then excuse myself. "Thanks," she calls after me. "You've been a huge help."

I glance back at her. "Anytime. I'm right next door if you need anything."

Mark watches the woman as she wipes her eyes and enters the hospital room again. When I pause in front of him, he shifts his focus to me. "Someone you know?"

"No, just a scared mom. I've comforted my share of them over the years."

"Before you went into administration?"

"Yes."

"You're obviously good at it."

"Maybe." I shrug.

"Too bad you gave it up."

"I helped people working in administration, too," I say, feeling a sudden need to defend myself.

He studies me for a few seconds, then says, "Mom went to the cafeteria with Eliot."

"Good. He could use the company."

"He said Will probably only has to stay the night?"

"That's what the doctor said. Getting him here quickly for treatment made all the difference."

"Thanks to you."

"No, thanks to Eliot. He had the foresight to call me. I think he sensed it was more than a cold. I'm sure your mom would've figured that out soon enough, too. Anyway, the doctor said Will can easily be treated at home, but because of his respiratory scare at birth, he wants to watch him overnight as a precaution."

"That's great news. That little guy scared me to death." He motions toward the door. "Can I see him?"

"Sure." He follows me into the room, and we stand at the side of Will's bed.

"Eliot's lucky to have you," Mark says quietly. "You plan to stay in Red Lake a while?"

"Until he's well. Which reminds me . . ." I glance at my watch, see that it's almost eight. "I need to make a few calls. My new boss at the greenhouse, for one. I won't be able to start on Monday."

"You think that'll cause any problems?"

"It shouldn't. It was my idea to start work so soon. She was planning to give me at least a week." Looking down at my rumpled clothes, I add, "I'm going to have to buy a few things. I was in a hurry and left without packing. I didn't even bring my toothbrush or a hairdryer."

"Mom wants the three of you to stay with her. Eliot's apartment only has one bedroom, and you'll all be more comfortable at her place while Will's recovering."

As far as I'm concerned, a cramped efficiency apartment is preferable to several days and nights under Patricia Reeves' roof. During our brief meeting earlier, she was nice enough, but when she looked at me, I felt as if she was trying to imagine me as Paul's girlfriend all those years ago. I'd be crazy to think she doesn't resent me, that she doesn't blame me for the fact that Paul never knew his son. Considering that Eliot would've most likely been a donor match for a kidney, she might also blame me for Paul's death.

But this isn't about me, it's about Will, and I know Mark is right; if Eliot's apartment is as small as he says, taking care of the baby will be easier at Patricia's house.

"Thanks," I say to him, despite my reluctance. "Your mom's nice to offer her home to us."

"You're family."

"No, Eliot and Will are." A knock at the door interrupts us. "It's open," I call, and a girl about Eliot's age looks in. It's as if I've stepped back in time, and I'm staring at Kelly again. She has her mother's shiny blond hair, the same big eyes and slender build.

"Hi, Andrea," Mark says.

"How is he?" she whispers, pausing just inside the doorway.

"He's doing okay," Mark says. "He should go home in the morning. Did Grandmom tell you?"

"Yes." Her eyes flick to me, then back to her uncle. "I wish someone would've called me last night. I should've been here with Eliot."

"Sorry. There was a lot going on." He motions her further into the room. "Come meet Eliot's mother."

After Mark makes introductions and we greet one another, Andrea returns her attention to the baby, dismissing me.

"Eliot told me you've been a big help with Will," I say to her.

"I haven't done much. Will's sweet. Eliot, too." Her words are like pin pricks, quick and sharp.

I'm sure Andrea told her mother about Eliot and Will. What did Kelly say about me, I wonder? Nothing good, obviously.

Mark's cell phone rings. He pulls it from his back pocket, and after a short conversation, he ends the call. "Sorry about that."

"You really aren't supposed to have those turned on in here," I tell him automatically, then wish I hadn't when I catch sight of Andrea's look of disdain. I start to tell her I issued the reprimand out of habit, thanks to my job, but I balk at the thought of explaining myself.

"It's off now." Mark returns the phone to his pocket. "I need to make a few more calls. I'll go outside." He excuses himself and leaves me alone with Andrea.

Every muscle in my body tenses, and I admit to myself that she isn't the only one in the room harboring unresolved feelings of contempt. My knotted emotions regarding Eliot's half-sister catch me off guard. After so many years, I'm surprised they still exist. Andrea is the child Paul chose to raise instead of ours. Maybe that's a distorted way to describe what he did, but that's how it felt for too many years. Looking at her now, a pretty girl with worry clouding her eyes, the knot inside me unravels a bit.

"Andrea?" Her gaze slides my way. "You and your grandmother and Mark have been wonderful to Eliot. The way you've embraced him and Will means a lot to him. I appreciate it, too."

Her brows tug together. "They're family. Of course, we'd embrace them."

Family. Mark said the same thing. Is it as simple as that for the Reeves clan? Paul's long-lost son shows up and they accept him as one of their own without a single conflicted emotion? Why couldn't it have been that simple for me when I found out about Will?

"I've wanted to find my brother for a really long time," Andrea murmurs, shifting her gaze to Will again.

"I'm glad Eliot has your support. This has been hard on him. Not only Will's illness, but finding out he's a father and learning about his own father all in the space of a couple of weeks."

"Dad would've loved knowing them. He would've been so happy." Her voice falters. She lowers her head.

"Your father was a good man, Andrea." She glances up at me with narrowed eyes, and I add, "I know I don't have to tell you that. I wish he and Eliot had met, too. I'm sorry I waited too long to try and make that happen. I'm sorry about a lot of things."

I glimpse a change in her expression, a crack in the ice. "Dad said the exact same thing when he told me I had a brother," she says.

Eliot sleeps in the recliner at the foot of Will's bed. I'm nodding off in the chair across from him when his cell phone trills softly from the ledge beneath the window. I wait for Eliot to stir, and when he doesn't, I pick up the phone, stand, and walk toward the door.

"Hello."

After a short hesitation, a girl says, "I was calling for Eliot?"

I step into the hallway, close the door behind me. "He can't talk right now. I'd be happy to give him a message."

"This is Liza."

Dread settles like a stone in the pit of my stomach. I turn my back on the nursing station and stare toward the window at the end of the hallway. "Hi, Liza, this is Maggie."

"Oh." Her voice is quiet, almost timid. "Russ called me. He said the baby's sick?"

"Yes." I explain Will's condition.

"I'd come, but–" Her voice quivers. "I don't know what to do, what's right."

I don't like the thought of her showing up here. "Will's going to be fine. He'll go home in the morning, and I'm staying to help take care of him until he's completely well."

"How is Eliot?"

"Tired, but he's doing okay. He has a lot of support here."

"Russ told me Eliot met his father's family."

"Yes, and they've been great." Her sudden chattiness surprises and annoys me. Has she forgotten that I'm the woman she's suing?

"Would you tell Eliot I called?" Liza asks. "That I'm thinking about him and Will?"

"I'll tell him."

She clears her throat. "Ms. Mahoney . . . about, well, everything else."

"I'm not sure this is the time to discuss any of that, Liza." My words are pinched. Leaning against the wall, I close my eyes. Since arriving in Red Lake at sunup, I've been running on adrenaline. Now, exhaustion drops down on me like a gavel. "Your lawyer would probably tell you not to discuss it at all."

Talking fast, she says, "I've been really confused about a lot of things. I know you don't have to, but would you keep me posted about Will?"

"I'll have to ask Eliot if he's okay with that."

"I understand." Seconds slip by before she says, "Goodbye, Maggie."

"'Bye, Liza." I break the connection.

I keep my back to the wall, my eyes closed. Emotions collide inside me. The hospital fired me because of her. Losing my career because I didn't allow her to keep a secret from my son about something he deserved to know feels like a kick in the gut. I don't care what the law says, in this case, I was right in breaking her confidence; nobody will ever convince me otherwise.

Opening my eyes, I see Mark standing a few feet away.

"Has something happened with Will?" he asks.

"No, he's fine." My lower lip quivers.

Mark rushes over and takes my arm. "What's wrong?"

I pull back, whisper, "Eliot's in there. I don't want him to see me so upset." He leads me down the hallway. "That was Liza on the phone. Will's mother."

"She called *you*?"

"She called Eliot. This is his phone. He's asleep so I picked up. She seemed different. Concerned for Will and remorseful, in a way."

"About time," Mark huffs.

I put the phone in my pocket and dig a tissue from my other one. "I must look terrible. I should go wash my face." I blow my nose, and when I turn toward Will's room, Mark catches my shoulder. I face him, and he pulls me into his embrace. I don't resist. It feels good to be held, to draw from his strength. He smells like laundry soap and shaving cream. "I'm sorry for being such a mess," I say. "Liza's call was the last straw."

"You're allowed to cry, Maggie. And to lean on somebody else for a change."

"You sound like Alice. That's what she told me again when I called earlier and asked her to feed the cat and water my lawn. She and Tim are taking turns doing my chores and lecturing me." I manage to laugh as I step back, keeping my hands on his arms. "I have to hold it together for Eliot."

"You're doing fine. I doubt he expects you to be Wonder Woman."

"That's good. I'd never fit into the outfit." I laugh again and wipe my eyes.

"Take Eliot to Mom's, and both of you get some rest. She made a big chicken salad earlier and a lot of other food. I'll stay here with Will."

"Eliot won't leave."

"You go, then. I'll keep him company."

"I don't know." I smile. "I'm sort of afraid of your mother."

"Mom? She's five foot two."

"Something tells me that didn't stop her from keeping two rowdy sons in line. I bet she's as tough as my grandmother was. I mean that in a good way."

"You're right. But you don't have anything to worry about. Mom's on your side."

"Is she?" I cross my arms.

"There was a time when she might've confronted you about keeping Eliot from Paul. But she's softened a lot since he died."

"Okay, I'll go," I tell Mark.

I can't imagine what Paul's mother went through when he died, what she still endures. I've felt lost and alone since Eliot moved to Red Lake, but the void his absence left in my life doesn't compare to the one Patricia faces every day.

CHAPTER NINETEEN

The modest, ranch-style brick home Mark and Paul grew up in sits at the end of a street lined with identical houses bordered by perfectly square yards. Inside, everything is spic-and-span clean and comfortably cluttered, with his-and- hers matching recliners in the living room, a crocheted afghan folded over the back of the couch, and magazines in neat stacks on the coffee table.

Patricia refuses to let me help clean up the kitchen after I finish my meal. Holding a cup of coffee, I wander into the living room and study the framed family photographs that fill every space. The walls, the bookcase, the end tables. Everywhere I look, I see Mark and Paul at various stages of life, from infancy to college. Many of the shots include another man resembling Mark. Their father, I'm sure.

When Patricia joins me, I return a photo of a boyish Paul with a missing front tooth to the fireplace mantel and meet her gaze. "Thank you."

"It was nothing." She waves me off. "That salad's a cinch to make."

"It was wonderful. But I'm not just thanking you for the meal."

She gazes at me over her reading glasses. "For what, then?"

"For accepting Eliot."

"He's my grandson. Besides, I like him." Patricia walks over to the coffee table, pulls open the center drawer, and takes out a pack of cigarettes, a lighter, and an ashtray. With a sheepish wince, she says, "My hiding place. Mark lectures me like a Sunday school teacher about smoking. I'm down to two a day. One after lunch, and another after supper. And never in the house." She nods toward the sliding doors that open onto the back yard. "Want to join me?"

"Sure."

We sit facing each other across a picnic table on the patio. Patricia taps a cigarette out of the package and lights up.

"Thanks for being so nice to me. I wouldn't blame you if you weren't," I tell her.

She stiffens. "Why wouldn't I be?" Avoiding my eyes, she takes a drag off the cigarette.

I shrug. "A lot of reasons."

Patricia turns her head and blows out a menthol-scented stream of smoke.

"You must be wondering what kind of mother I am that Eliot's so eager to move away from me when he should need me most."

"That's no mystery. I raised two sons. Eliot needs to prove he's a grownup. To you and to himself. He wants to handle things on his own."

The woman is wise. I felt those same things at Eliot's age. I told myself I didn't need anyone, that I could handle things, make a life for myself and Eliot on my own.

Patricia's eyes flick to me, then away again. "Eliot wore out the floor tiles pacing 'til you got to the hospital."

I hate imagining his distress. But I'm pleased to hear her confirm that I'm the one he needed most, the one he wanted by his side in a crisis.

A warm breeze rustles the leaves on the elm tree in the center of the yard, and a chattering squirrel darts up the trunk. Gathering my courage, I ask, "Did you know about me?"

She tenses again, and I realize she doesn't want to talk about Paul. "My boys didn't share much with me about their personal lives," she says.

"It must run in the family. I thought I knew Eliot, but in the last month, I've realized he had a lot going on that I knew nothing about."

"It doesn't just run in the family, it runs in the entire male species. That's the way with most mothers and sons, the best I can tell."

"You probably know by now that I kept secrets from him about his dad. He's mad at me about that."

Patricia's brows lift slightly. After a final drag, she stubs out the cigarette in the ashtray.

My heartbeat kicks up as I add, "Maybe you're mad at me, too."

"I'm not." She pushes the ashtray aside and shrugs. "I do think Eliot and his dad deserved to know each other, though."

"Don't even get me started on what *I* deserved from *him*," I snap. "And I'm not referring to Eliot." I'm immediately ashamed of implying anything bad about Paul to his mother, but the words were out of my mouth before I could stop them.

Without so much as a flinch, she says, "I know that. Forget

what I said. I guess every life has a different path to take. You've done a good job with Eliot, Maggie. Quit beating yourself up."

I turn away, my face on fire.

"So, Eliot's mad at you," she says. "Just like a man to think he knows best. Did you do what you thought was right for him?"

The times over the years that I almost told Eliot who his father was, the times I almost picked up the phone to call Paul, rush back to me. I had so many fears. Fears for myself, yes, but they weren't what stopped me most. My fears for Eliot did that.

"Yes," I tell Patricia. "I've always had Eliot's well-being at heart. But I'm not sure that helped me make the right decisions. The truth is, I worried about myself, too. About what would happen to me if I told either of them the truth."

"That's only human."

"Sometimes being human gets in the way of honesty. That, and pride."

"If Eliot thinks he's going to be the world's first perfect parent, I'm afraid he's in for a rude awakening. He'll change his tune once he's walked a mile in your shoes." Patricia stands and picks up the ashtray. "I'll be right back. I have to dispose of the evidence in the dumpster." She sends me a sly look and excuses herself.

She's different than what I had imagined. In spite of the fact that she's keeping me at arms-length, despite her earlier implication about Paul's rights, I like her better than the prim, perfect woman I always used to picture when I thought of her, the one who stirred jealousy in me because she had Eliot and Will nearby.

She returns moments later and sits across the table again. We talk about the weather for a while. A safe and comfortable topic.

I spend the night at the hospital, and just before dawn, awake to find Eliot standing beside Will's bed. Leaving the recliner, I join him. "Everything okay?"

"The nurse just checked on him," he whispers. "She said he looked good." I take his hand and he adds, "He seems so frail. It's crazy. A couple of months ago, I couldn't have imagined having him. Now I can't imagine *not* having him."

"I know that feeling." After a moment, I say, "I forgot to tell you that Liza called yesterday while you were asleep. I answered your phone."

"I wish you wouldn't do that." He frowns at me, then asks, "What did she say?"

"Russ told her Will's sick."

"I asked him to."

"Why?"

"I don't know. It seemed like I should."

"Liza gave Will up, Eliot. If some couple she didn't know had adopted him, they wouldn't even consider calling her about this."

"But some strange couple didn't. *I'm* raising him."

I sigh, uncertain about his motivation for including Liza in this. Does it have to do with the fact that I didn't include Paul in *his* life? "Do you think she should be here?" I ask.

"It doesn't matter to me one way or the other, except that I'm pissed at her for what she's doing to you." He shrugs. "I guess I just thought it was her right to decide whether or not she comes."

I don't agree, but it's his decision to make, not mine. "I got the feeling she doesn't think it's her place to be here."

"Good. I wanted her to know, but I don't want her to think I need her here, or that I can't take care of Will without her."

I blink at him. "It's okay to miss her."

"I don't." He lifts a shoulder. "But sometimes I wonder if things would be better for Will if we were together. Kids raised by single parents are more likely to have all kinds of problems. In school and with drugs and—"

"You turned out fantastic, in my completely unprejudiced opinion," I say with a smile, interrupting him. I reach into the crib and brush a palm across Will's head. "Will wouldn't be better off with the two of you together unless you and Liza would want to be a couple even if he didn't exist."

He looks relieved to hear those words.

"What about Ann?" I ask.

"She broke up with me. We need different things right now."

"I'm sorry."

"It's okay." He turns away, trains his attention on Will.

Hurting for him, I listen to the quiet voices drifting to us from the nurse's station. "Liza wanted someone to keep her posted about Will's pneumonia. I told her that was up to you."

"I'll call her."

Nodding, I say, "Will's stronger than he looks, Eliot. And he has genetics on his side. He has a determined dad." I smile. "His grandmother Mahoney is a survivor, too, if I do say so."

Eliot's Adam's apple bobs as he turns to me. "Yeah, you are."

I take a deep breath. "His grandfather Reeves was a fighter, too." When Eliot doesn't respond, I add, "School wasn't a breeze for your dad. It took Paul two tries to get into law school. He wasn't a quitter. He didn't give up on anything easily."

Eliot's face twists. "He gave up on us."

"No, Eliot. Not really."

"Mark told me my dad pushed you to place me for adoption, even though he knew you didn't want to."

"Yes, but he wasn't taking the easy way out or being cold-hearted. He was scared. And Paul really believed it was the best solution for all of us. Especially you." I wait for him to look at me, and when he does, I say, "Your dad was a good man, Eliot. We both made mistakes. I'm only sorry you paid the price for them."

He clears his throat. "Mark also told me that my dad decided not to try to find me to see if I was a donor match. I couldn't have saved him even if he'd known you kept me. I was upset when I said those things to you."

"We both said things."

"You're right. And just so you know, I did want to go to medical school. You didn't push me to do anything I didn't want to do."

"You can still go."

"Maybe I will someday. But everything's changed now. I want a different sort of life, at least for a while. I don't want to be so busy. You know, so tied up with school."

"Just so you're sure. Don't give it up because you think it's not a possibility anymore."

"I'm sure. School will still be there if I'm ready again someday." He tucks Will's blanket more tightly around him.

"Eliot . . ." He looks at me. "I hope you didn't decide to keep Will because you thought your dad deserted you."

"Maybe I did at first. Before I saw him." He returns his attention to Will. "I'm glad I kept him. I know it's going to be hard. It already is. But I wouldn't go back and change anything." After a stretch of silence, he asks, "Was my dad like Mark?"

How many times over the years have I heard the same need

in his voice and ignored it? How many times did I evade his questions to spare him more disappointment? That was my biggest mistake. Not knowing is so much worse than the truth. After learning the facts about my own father, I understand that now.

"No," I tell Eliot. "Your dad didn't look like Mark, if that's what you mean. He looked like Patricia." With a rush of sudden realization, I scan Eliot's face. "So, do you. That shouldn't surprise me, I guess. I always did think you looked like your dad." Laughing, I add, "With a little of Chick sprinkled in."

I squeeze his fingers, thinking of my mother – how Nanny and Chick brought her alive for me. How much that meant. "Something about Mark's smile reminds me of Paul, though," I say. "And the way he tilts his head when he talks. They have the same kindness in their eyes."

"Mark says my father was an athlete."

"He was. When I knew him, he only played sports for fun, not competition. Basketball, mostly. You're like him in that way. He met his friends a couple of times a week for a game or to shoot baskets, just as you do."

Eliot smiles, then sobers. "Were you ever this scared with me when I was a kid?"

"You were healthy. I was lucky about that. But, yes, I got scared sometimes. Or maybe 'worried' is a better word. I still do."

He reaches into the crib again and touches Will's tiny forearm. "I don't want him to hurt," he says, his voice little more than a whisper. "I want to make everything right for him. For him to be happy."

"I know you do."

"What if I can't?"

"You're already a good dad. You love him. You're doing your best. That's all you can do and all that matters."

"What if I make mistakes?"

"You will. All parents do."

"At least I have help. You didn't have anyone."

"I had you." I wrap my arm around his shoulder. "I did the best I could, and when I made a mistake, I kept trying. That's what you'll do, too. Keep trying. And don't beat yourself up. I wasn't so good at that part. It's great advice, though. From your grandmother."

"Nanny?"

"Patricia," I tell him. "She gave it to me today."

Mark shows up before the doctor does. He hands me a sack with a new toothbrush and toothpaste inside. "Mom thought you might want these."

I take the sack. "Thanks."

"I'll bring you two some breakfast from the cafeteria. What would you like?"

"I'm not hungry," Eliot says.

"He never eats breakfast," I add.

"How about you?" Mark asks me.

"I can wait."

"Go on, Mom," Eliot says. "Get out of this room and eat something. I'll call your cell when the doc shows up."

"No, I'll stay." My stomach growls.

Mark nods toward the door. "I won't take no for an answer."

"I won't either," Eliot says.

"Well, okay, if you're going to gang up on me. At least let me brush my teeth first." I go into the adjoining bathroom.

A few minutes later, I'm sitting across a table from Mark eating scrambled eggs and toast. "You're a very persistent man."

"You have no idea."

"Just because you bought me eggs don't think I'm going to go out with you." I squint at him.

"I don't recall asking."

Looking down at my plate, I take another bite, embarrassed.

"Will you?" he asks.

"Will I what?"

"Go out with me when Will is better?"

"You know the answer to that." I take another bite, then change the subject. "I like your mother."

"You sound surprised."

"I am, a little." I look up at him.

"If you go out with me, we could take her along to chaperone." His cheek twitches.

"Maybe she and I will go out and leave *you* at home."

Mark feigns offense. "I'm a lot more fun after a couple of beers than she is."

"That's one of the things that worries me."

One corner of Mark's mouth curves up. He sips his coffee. "Mom likes you, too."

"That also surprises me."

"You shouldn't shortchange yourself."

"Maybe it's her I was shortchanging," I tell him.

"She's honest about her feelings; I respect that. And she might be one of the least judgmental people I've ever met."

Mark huffs. "You wouldn't say that if you'd known her when I was sixteen."

I laugh. "I liked her house. But I can't imagine Paul growing up there, for some reason. I can see you there, though. It looks like you."

"Rough around the edges, you mean?"

"I was thinking laid back. Comfortable." Finished, I push my plate aside.

Mark eyes the triangle of toast I left. "You're not going to eat that?"

"I'm stuffed. If you want it, it's yours."

He slides the plate toward him, reaches for two packets of grape jelly and spreads it on thick. Keeping his focus on the toast, he says, "I look comfortable, huh?" He takes a bite, chews, swallows. "I was hoping you might think I look sexy. Or hot, maybe."

I do, on both counts, but I'm not about to admit it.

He looks up at me. "I'd settle for mildly attractive. Cute, even."

Smirking at him, I say, "You look comfortable in your skin. That's a compliment, by the way."

"Why wouldn't I? I've been living in this skin for forty-five years."

"I don't know." I pick up my fork, lay it down again. "Most people don't ever reach that comfort zone."

"What about you? Are you comfortable in your skin?"

"Sometimes I am. Other times, I feel like it's smothering me."

"Hmm." He finishes off the toast, pushes the plate toward me again.

Squinting at him, I ask, "What does that mean? That *hmm?*"

"I'm just trying to decide if you're always so serious, or if it's just that I've only been around you under serious circumstances."

Alice's and Tim's similar accusations come to mind, and I feel a need to defend myself. "I'm not always serious." I lower my gaze to the plate, glance up again, find him watching me with narrowed eyes. "I'm *not*."

"I didn't say anything." He lifts his coffee cup, takes a drink.

"But you don't believe me."

"Nope."

"Why?"

Setting down his cup, he reaches across the table and touches the space between my brows. "This little wrinkle right here. It's cute, but it looks like it took a lot of contemplation to make it."

I scoot back, jostling the table and sloshing coffee over the rim of my cup. "You're teasing me."

"Who? Me?"

I scoot up to the table again, take another drink of coffee, pout. "What about the other night when you showed up at my house – uninvited, I might add – when Tim and Alice were there? I wouldn't call that serious."

"You were drunk."

"Tipsy." I glare at him.

He chuckles. "You were having a good time, but . . . I don't know . . . it seemed rare. Like you weren't used to laughing and having so much fun."

I tap my foot beneath the table. "It wasn't rare."

"When was the last time you danced?"

"I don't dance."

"Went swimming?"

"I can't remember, but—"

"Went to an amusement park, or took a hike, or rode a horse?"

"I'm afraid of horses."

"Made love?"

My breath catches. "None of your business. You're a snoop."

"And you're blushing." Undaunted, he continues, "If you want, I'll skip work, and we can do all of those things."

"In that order and all in one day?" I tilt my head to one side, determined not to let him see that his teasing rattles me. "Maybe we should pace ourselves. You're forty-five, remember? I wouldn't want to wear you out."

Before he can say anything, my cell phone rings. Relieved to have the interruption, I fumble beneath the table for my purse but can't find it. Mark has a way of loosening me up, but I'm afraid I'm about to unravel completely.

Wearing an aggravating smirk, he lifts my purse from the side of our table. "Here."

I pull out the phone and answer it. "Hello?"

"Mom?"

"Oh, uh, Eliot. Is everything okay?"

"The doc just left. Will can go home."

"Oh, that's fantastic! I wanted to be there to ask him a few things, though."

"Patricia's here. She asked a lot of questions. We both did."

"Good. I'll be up in a minute."

"Take your time. I have to sign some paperwork before we can leave."

I break the connection, lay down the phone.

"Everything okay?" Mark asks, his voice sober now.

"Will's been released."

"That's great. We'll take him home and get him settled in. With you and Mom pampering him, he'll be good as new in no time. Then I'll show you around Red Lake. I hope you can stand the excitement."

I fold my napkin into a square, ready to put an end to our flirtation before it gets out of hand. "I don't think that's a good idea."

"Why? And don't tell me it has anything to do with Paul, because I don't believe that."

"He's the only reason we're together. He and Eliot."

"They may have brought us together, but they don't have anything to do with the rest."

I lift my purse and stand. "There is no *rest*."

"There could be. I'd like to see if there might be." He stands, too. "I like you, Maggie. A lot. I don't tell women that every day, believe me. I can count on one hand the number of women I've spent time with since my divorce."

I find that hard to believe. He's a good-looking man. A nice, fun man. A smart, charming, accomplished, and irritating man. If only he wasn't Eliot's uncle. "Why don't you spend time with women?"

"I haven't met anybody who can take what I dish out and sling it back at me. My ex sure couldn't."

"And I can? I thought you said I'm too serious."

"Not when you forget to be." He chuckles. "What you just said about wearing me out was funny."

Embarrassed all over again, I start away from the table, and he follows. "This isn't the time or place to talk about this."

"I agree."

"Good." We exit the cafeteria, make our way toward the bank of elevators.

When we reach them, Mark pushes the button and says,

"When and where would you like to get together to discuss it further?"

"Could you stop joking for even one second?"

"I'm not joking."

The doors slide apart, and we walk onto the elevator, followed by a group of four other people. The old elevator takes forever to kick into gear and start its ascent from the hospital basement, where the cafeteria is located. We take a rattling, jostling ride up to the first floor in silence. When the doors open again, everyone else gets off, leaving Mark and me alone. I stare at the numbers overhead as the doors slide together.

"Maggie?" Mark grasps my arm gently. "I know you've had a tough few weeks. I'm not trying to pressure you into anything you don't want." He hesitates. "Do you feel like I'm pressuring you?"

"Yes." I don't look at him. The elevator jerks, starts to rise.

"I owe you an apology then," he says, releasing my arm. "It's just that, after forty-five years, I've learned that life's too short to waste time pretending. When something seems right-"

Before he can finish his sentence, I turn, lift up on my toes, and kiss him on the mouth. And then his arms are around me, and he's kissing me back, and I taste everything that's been missing in my life. Everything I've needed but have avoided for so many years. Everything I've convinced myself I shouldn't pursue because I might make another mistake. And maybe that's exactly what this is — a mistake. But I can't stop myself.

I lean into him, shove my fingers into his hair at the nape of his neck, make tiny desperate noises born of relief and desire and a need so strong it aches all the way to my soul.

Another jostle, a ding. We pull apart at the same moment the doors do.

Andrea stands outside, looking in at us.

"Hey there," Mark says a little too brightly, and my heart vaults up to my throat.

Her eyes widen, then narrow in on me. "Will's going home," I stammer.

"I heard," Andrea snaps, moving past us onto the elevator. When she turns around, she looks at Mark as if I'm not there. "I'm going to get coffee."

Facing forward, side-by-side, Mark and I step off the elevator onto solid ground again. But as the doors close behind us, it feels as if the floor wobbles a little beneath my feet.

CHAPTER TWENTY

*M*ark heads to work from the hospital. Patricia goes home. Eliot, Will, and I make a stop by the garage apartment behind Mark's house to pack some things to take to Patricia's. While Eliot is inside, I wait in the car with Will. I'm so relieved that he's better that I find it difficult to take my eyes off of him.

The moment I do, I see that the neighborhood is old and lined by stately trees. The houses have a forties and fifties feel. Some appear to be newly renovated, while others show their age. Mark's place has been scrubbed, polished, and spruced up like a dignified old gentleman. The two-story white house is trimmed in a pale, muted green. The wrap-around porch makes me think of lazy summer evenings with chirping crickets, iced sweet tea, and the spinning of tall tales. Evenings like the ones I spent on the farmhouse porch with my grandparents so long ago. It's easy to imagine Mark here. I envision him telling stories like my grandmother once did, with a teasing twinkle in his eye that reminds me of Chick.

The image unsettles me. I turn my attention to Will again,

see that he's still sleeping peacefully in his carseat, then shift to look at Eliot's apartment. It sits over the garage at the end of the driveway, set back from the house. When he emerges carrying a suitcase, a diaper bag slung over one shoulder, I'm hit by the fact that this is his home now, his first place to live without me.

I'll have to get used to that – the two of us parted in so many ways now. Both adults. Still joined by blood and love and memories, but also living our own, separate lives. Which makes me melancholy, a little scared, proud. Proud of Eliot and of myself. We've come a long way together. Though life hasn't always been easy, we've not only survived, we've thrived.

When we arrive at Patricia's house minutes later, she leads us to a bedroom at the back of the house. A small pressed-wood crib, painted pale blue, sits at the foot of a double bed. A faded sticker of a lamb adorns the headboard, pressed there years ago, I suppose, at a haphazard angle. Inside of it, a folded quilt lies on top of the smooth, fitted sheet.

"This was Mark's bedroom," she tells us. "He pulled the crib down from the attic last night." She touches the railing gently, as if it's made of fine china rather than battered wood. "Both my boys slept in it. It's old but sturdy." She gestures to the corner at a rocking chair. "That, too."

"Everything's great, Patricia. Thanks," Eliot says.

"Yes," I agree, thinking of the beautiful walnut cradle Chick made with skilled, loving hands, sitting empty now back at my equally empty house. There had not been room in the trailer for Eliot to bring it. I try not to dwell on the sorrow that brings me, tell myself memories are more precious than possessions. The ones this run-of-the-mill crib embodies for Patricia are equally as special to her as the ones the walnut crib hold for me.

We settle Will down for a nap, and while Eliot showers,

Patricia leads me across the hall to a slightly smaller room. "You can sleep in here," she tells me, her gaze flicking to mine, then away, and I realize it must be Paul's boyhood bedroom.

"Thank you, Patricia." I place my purse on the bed beside a pink flannel robe and a pair of matching slippers.

"I thought you might want me to freshen up your clothes. I'll toss them in the wash while you shower, and you can wear those." She gestures at the robe and slippers, then sizes me up. "It might be a little short; you're taller than me."

"It's fine. Thank you so much."

She starts for the door. "I'll fix us some sandwiches."

After my shower, I wander into the kitchen wearing the robe and slippers. Eliot sits at the table across from Patricia, eating as if he's starved.

"I hope you like roast beef," Patricia says to me.

"I love it," I tell her, though I'm still full from breakfast with Mark at the hospital cafeteria. I sit in front of the plate she made for me and force the food down while we make polite small talk. Polite. That's what we've been to one another since we met. Two strangers linked together by her son, and now, by Eliot and Will. It occurs to me that Patricia and I have yet to mention Paul's name to each other, even though we've talked vaguely about him.

Exhausted from the hospital stint, Eliot goes to bed after lunch and sleeps the rest of the day, while Patricia and I take turns tending to Will and continue our mannerly dance with each other. Late in the afternoon, I leave for a visit to Red Lake's shopping mall, where I buy toiletries and a couple of casual outfits to tide me over until I return home.

Just after dark, Eliot wakes up when Mark and Andrea arrive with Chinese takeout. I rise from the recliner with Will in my arms. "That smells wonderful. I'll go put him down so I can eat."

"I'll hold him," Andrea says.

"Okay." I take Will to her as Mark heads for the kitchen carrying the food, with Patricia and Eliot at his heals. Andrea doesn't look at me when she takes Will from my arms. She sits on the couch. "Do you need anything?" I ask.

"No." She glances at me briefly, and her eyes seem to say, *yes, I need you to drop off the face of the earth.*

"I like your sandals," I say, motioning toward her feet. "Where did you buy them?"

Andrea shrugs. "I don't remember. I've had them forever." She keeps her eyes on Will.

"There's a great new shoe store close to my neighborhood in the city." I tell her the name. "You should check it out."

"I've been there."

I realize my friendliness seems forced, that I'm trying too hard. But I can't seem to stop myself. Because she's Eliot's half-sister, I'd like to win Andrea over. But if she's determined our relationship is only going to be civil, I guess I'll have to accept that. For Eliot's sake, I wish it could be more.

After dinner, Mark asks if I would like to join him for a walk. I only hesitate a moment before saying yes. As we make our way down the block, neither of us mentions what happened on the elevator earlier today.

Mark points to a house identical to his mother's, except for the color of the trim. "The summer after seventh grade, when I was twelve and Paul was almost eleven, that place was empty. We snuck in one night and smoked our first cigarettes. A week or so later, we went back with more cigarettes, a couple of six-packs, and a kid named Ricky Biltmore. The next morning, we nursed our first hangovers." He shakes his head. "God, we were stupid."

"Ten and twelve?" I study him. "So you were wild kids, huh?"

"We tried to be. Or Paul tried. I didn't have to try; it came a whole lot easier for me. I was a bad influence on him."

"Why doesn't that surprise me?"

He hooks his arm through mine. "We used to have some great block parties here. All the dads on the street would barbecue while the moms made potato salad, baked beans, and banana nut ice cream."

"Sounds like Red Lake was stereotypical small-town America back then."

"It still is, in a lot of ways. The good ones and the bad ones." Glancing at me, he adds, "Mostly good. It's still a decent place to grow up, and as far as neighbors go, you can't beat the folks here. Take Mr. Gramercy over there." He waves and calls out to a stooped old man walking a dog down the sidewalk across the street. "He jumped my old El Camino more than one winter morning during senior year when I was late getting to school and Dad had already left for work." Mark laughs. "Holy cow, can that man cuss. From time-to-time, I still stop by and beat him in a game of dominoes. He doesn't like to lose."

I suspect Mark's Red Lake stories are meant to ease my mind about leaving my son and grandson here. They do ease my mind, if not my heartache. They also endear me to Mark even more.

We turn a corner, and a park comes into view. Mark points to a gazebo. "Got my first French kiss in there."

"You don't say?" I look up at him, amused.

"Yep. Seventh grade. I was twelve."

"How was it?"

He purses his lips, frowns, contemplating. "Wet." I laugh, and he adds, "Not nearly as good as the one with you this afternoon. Not by a long shot."

My pulse jumps, and I abruptly stop laughing. "That was an eventful year for you, seventh grade," I say quickly, wanting to steer the conversation in a different direction. "First smoke, first hangover, first French kiss. The girl was someone special, I hope."

"You might say that. I married her ten years later after a whole lot of drama. Breaking up, getting back together, breaking up again." He huffs a humorless laugh. "I shouldn't have ignored those red flags."

We spend some time on the park's old merry-go-round, then sit in two swings and watch the sun go down. When we finally turn the corner onto Patricia's block again, I'm laughing, relaxed, and completely at ease.

Mark stops me at the edge of a yard, pulls me beneath the shadow of a neighbor's tree, and kisses me softly. "Finally," he murmurs, his voice a low rumble, his breath warm against my lips. "It's about time I get to make the first move instead of you." He pulls back slightly, and one side of his mouth curves up.

"So, you think I'm a loose woman?"

"Why do you think I like you so much?"

"Hey! You're the one who—"

Mark shuts me up with another kiss, then steps back and looks into my eyes. "Goodnight, Maggie."

"Aren't you coming in?"

He nods. "I have to get Andrea. We came together. But I knew you wouldn't want me to tell you goodnight in front of everyone. Not like this." He brushes his mouth against mine again.

I lean back, stroke a finger across his chin. "I appreciate that."

We make our way to his mother's house. Above in the blue-black sky, the moon sits on a cushion of wispy clouds and shines down on us. A sign, I wonder? Nanny would say so, I'm sure. Too many years have gone by since a man made me shiver with only a look, and never like this. This feels like more than a shiver.

On his mother's front porch, I lift onto my tiptoes, lean forward, and say my own goodnight to Mark. I take my time.

Over the next two nights, I find it difficult to sleep, though Will is stronger, and Eliot has returned to work. Both nights, in the wee hours, I make my way to the bedroom window and stare into the shadowed backyard. Sometimes I glimpse movement below, and a tiny glow of orange shimmering in the darkness surrounding the patio.

While looking down, I wonder if Paul ever stood at the window, what he thought about, dreamed about as he watched the sleeping town? I've searched my soul for any remnant of the resentment I once felt toward him, but it's shriveled like a dead weed now, dried up and ground to dust. I've also searched my heart for any of the love I once felt for him and found that I'm free of it, too. My love for Paul has transformed into a memory as cherished as the cradle Chick built. As precious as the stories Nanny told to guide me. As special as Chick's quiet love and gentle, unpretentious wit.

During my weeklong stay at Patricia's house, when I do sleep, my dreams are full of birds, of Chick on the farmhouse porch, laughing as he plays his guitar and sings funny songs to me. Sparrows dip and circle in the sky above us.

Then there's the dream of Chick on his tractor, plowing the fields. He forms the tip of a 'V', guiding the geese that fly behind him.

And, sometimes, I dream of Chick walking down the road toward the farmhouse for the very first time. He stops beside Nanny in her vegetable garden; a plump little baby sits on the ground beside her. She stands and shields her eyes from the sun. *"I'm William Mahoney,"* he says, moving toward her on legs thin as twigs, dark eyes twinkling above a nose as long and pointed as a beak.

He spreads one arm wide and his baggy sleeve flaps in the breeze like a wing as he wraps it around Nanny. Together, they stoop, and he lifts the baby from the ground – my uncle Ned.

A feather flutters up from beneath my grandfather's collar and floats skyward. Nanny follows it with her gaze. *"I'll call you Chick,"* she says.

Tonight, though, the dream is a new one. Nanny tends the flowerbeds around the farmhouse, pulling weeds, faster and faster, as the sun sets behind her and a wrecking ball slowly swings back, aimed at the porch. She looks up at me, motions me over. Her lips move, but I can't hear her words, can't understand what she's trying to tell me.

I wake with a start in the stuffy room, feeling smothered, my heart thumping like a drumbeat.

Wearing the robe Patricia loaned me, I walk quietly through the dark house to the back door, sensing she's outside, that she can't breathe, either. Despite our cautious friendliness with one another, tonight I feel drawn to this woman I barely know. I'm not sure what's been disturbing me since I've been here, why my sleep is so restless, my dreams so strange. I wish I could easily leave every single hurtful thing from my past behind, as I did in the dream of flying beside the blackbird, so light of heart, so free.

The door creaks when I open it. Patricia sits at the picnic table on the patio. She turns to me, her face pale and gaunt in the moonlight, and for an instant, I wonder why she can't sleep, why her eyes hold so much pain. But, out of nowhere, I hear Nanny's voice in my mind on the day we buried Chick.

"When your Mama died, I never thought I'd hurt as bad again. Lord, I was wrong."

And my own words from when I was a little girl come back to me. *"If I'd been big enough, I woulda' saved Mama."*

I suddenly recognize the pain in Patricia's eyes; I've seen in before in my grandmother, and I'm struck with the realization that they both lost a child — children they would've given anything to save. Maybe that's what connects all mothers most — the need to protect our children from heartache and pain, no matter how old they are. It's a heavy burden to bear because it's impossible to succeed.

I close the door, go to Eliot's grandmother, sit beside her, take her hand. "Are you okay?"

"I was just thinking about Paul," she says.

I don't respond, just squeeze her fingers.

Together, we watch the sun rise.

CHAPTER TWENTY-ONE

*O*n my last day in Red Lake, we move Will and Eliot back into the apartment; I'll stay with them on tonight and sleep on the sofa. Mark has everyone over to his place for dinner and cooks burgers out on the grill. After we eat, Patricia, Andrea and Mark clean up while I help Eliot give Will his bath in the apartment.

Squeezed into the tiny bathroom, Eliot and I stand side-by-side in front of the sink. Will lies on his back on the bathing sponge I bought for him. Eliot places a washcloth over Will's lower body, then squeezes warm water from a second washcloth onto him. The baby coos and kicks his feet.

I laugh. "I see you're keeping that thing covered up now."

"I only had to be sprayed in the face once to learn my lesson."

I pour baby shampoo into my palm then gently lather it onto Will's scalp. "You're great with him, Eliot."

Keeping his attention focused on Will, he says, "I still have so much to learn. Before he got sick, Patricia showed me a lot." Eliot looks up. "But not as much as you."

I meet his gaze briefly.

"You haven't started your new job yet," he says. "There's nothing to keep you in the city. You could move here. Mark knows everybody in town. He could help you find a job. You could drive back to meet with your lawyer about the lawsuit when you need to."

Taken off guard by his suggestion, I rinse off Will's head, silent for a while. "Doug Dowling called earlier today," I finally say to him. "Liza dropped the lawsuit."

His eyes widen. "Mom, that's great!"

"When I called to tell Constance, she said she was sure I could get my job back at the hospital."

Eliot reaches for a towel on the rack behind him and holds it out. I lift Will into his arms. "I know how much your job means to you," he says.

"I'm not sure I want to go back. So much has happened. Oddly enough, I'm looking forward to working at the greenhouse and getting my hands dirty."

I think of the last dream I had about Nanny, the one with her pulling weeds, motioning me toward the garden before the wrecking ball dropped, her lips moving silently, trying to tell me something. She was a simple woman. Surely her lessons were simple, too. I've only made them complex. Complicated them, as I have everything else in my life.

Eliot wraps the towel around Will and holds him close. "I'll miss you, Mom. We both will."

Tears blur my vision. I smile. "I'll miss you, too. But, as you said, we'll only be four hours apart."

He hesitates, then says, "Living in Red Lake, my new job, it all feels right for Will and me. At least for now. I'll be able to support us. I'll have time to spend with him, and we'll have a lot of family around." He winces. "I didn't mean—"

"No, don't apologize. Don't ever be sorry for doing what you think is right. If you're happy, I'm happy. That's all I've ever really wanted for you, Eliot."

"I *am* happy."

I turn my head away from him, say in a quiet voice, "Were you before? Growing up?" Taking a breath, I face him again. "Were you happy, Eliot?"

"*Yes.*" I hear his distress that I would ask such a question, see that same distress in his eyes. "I wondered about my dad. I wished you would talk about him, tell me about him, but I didn't think about him all the time. I was too busy being a kid." He lays a hand on my arm. "You were always there for me, Mom."

"I was always working." My voice wavers. "Always trying to prove I didn't need Paul. I'm so sorry about that."

"If I needed you for something, if something was really important, you were always there for me. I came first before your job. I knew that."

The tears fall now. "School plays *were* really important. And driving you and your friends to games on weekends. I wish I hadn't put work before those things that meant so much to you. I missed them. I'll never get them back. Neither of us will." I press my lips together. "I hurt you."

"You didn't, Mom. I was safe. You took care of me. I knew you loved me."

I swipe at my eyes. "I hope so."

He shifts Will to one arm and hugs me with the other. After a moment, when Will cries a little, Eliot steps back and bumps into the wall. He laughs. "What do you say we get out of this bathroom?"

"Okay." I nod at him, smile a watery smile. We walk into the apartment, and Eliot lays Will on the bed. "Let me dress him in his pjs," I say. "You go back down with the others. I'd like a little time alone with my grandson."

"Sure."

When he leaves, I place a soft gown over Will's head, fuzzy socks on his pudgy, little feet. Then I sit at the edge of the bed, pick him up, and hold him close to me. I lay my cheek against his down-soft head and close my eyes. A song plays through my mind, one Chick used to sing to me and strum on his guitar when I was a girl. I rock back and forth, sing it to Will now.

"You, you, you. I'm in love with you, you, you. Tell me that you love me, too. I'm in love with you, you, you. We were meant for each other, sure as heaven's above . . ."

Sensing a presence in the room, I break off and open my eyes.

Mark stands in the doorway, watching me, a tender expression on his face. "That's one very lucky little boy. I'd change places with him right now if I could."

I lay Will in my lap. "Mark Reeves. Always the jokester, aren't you?"

He crosses the room and sits beside me. "Who says I'm joking?" Placing his index finger in Will's palm, he asks, "Are you okay?"

"Yes. I will be." I tell him about Liza dropping the lawsuit.

"Good thing Miss Enlow wised up," Mark says. "I've been thinking I might have to go have a little talk with her." He takes a breath. "I've been thinking, too, about all you've been through. Sometimes I'm not the smartest, Maggie, and maybe I've come across as insensitive. I hope I haven't made things harder on you by—"

"No. You didn't. You've helped me. Really. You make me

laugh. I don't know if I would've made it through all this in one piece without you."

"Sure, you would've." He looks up from his and Will's hands at the same time I do. "I meant what I said about wanting a chance to see where this thing between us might lead."

I touch one of the little chicks on Will's pajamas. "I was thinking of my grandparents when I bought this gown," I say. "I've been thinking about them a lot since Will's birth. I keep dreaming about them. It's as if Nanny's trying to tell me something but I don't know what."

"Is this about the birds?" I'm surprised that he remembers what I told him that day in the treehouse. "You said she told you they left but they always come back. That they can save you." Mark pauses, but before I can answer, he says, "Eliot doesn't have to return to the city to come back to you, Maggie."

"I know that. He came back to me this week, I think."

"He never left." His brows tug together. "I know you have to go home, but I'll see you again, won't I? Sometime soon, I hope."

"I don't know. I'm mixed up about things right now. Us included. I've never been very good at relationships. And I've been alone for a long time."

"Maybe too long."

"I've made a lot of mistakes with men."

"Me, too." He smiles. "Made mistakes, that is, with the opposite sex." He pauses, then asks, "Can I call you? Maybe come for a visit?"

I keep my eyes on his. "Let's hold off on the visit. But you can call. I'll be upset if you don't."

He nods. "I'll take that."

Will brings Mark's finger to his mouth, and I laugh. "I think it's time for a bottle. No beans or carrots in there, big guy."

I lift Will from Mark's arms and stand. "My grandmother grew vegetables. I used to gripe about all the weeds she'd have me pull when she made me help her in the garden. She once told me gardens are like life. A person has to dig through a lot of weeds and rocks and toss them aside to get to the good stuff."

Mark stands and places a hand behind my neck, then kisses me softly. "There's lots of good stuff ahead for you, Maggie. Just let it happen."

Eliot and Will see me off the next morning. The Reeves family, Mark included, said their goodbyes the night before. I'm thankful. I want this time with my son and grandson, although Eliot and I both hate long goodbyes.

I stand in the driveway beside my car with Eliot beside me and Will in my arms. The sun shines bright above us. The breeze is warm and as gentle as a whisper against my skin.

I kiss Eliot's cheek quickly. "Take care of yourselves."

"We will. You, too, Mom."

Brushing my lips across Will's head, I say, "Don't grow up too much before I see you again." With an aching throat, I hand him to Eliot. Then I hug them both at once. "I love you."

"I love you, too, Mom."

"I better leave before I start bawling." I step away from them.

Eliot blinks back tears of his own. "Good idea. Be careful."

"I will," I say, opening the car door.

"Mom?" I glance up at him. Eliot raises a hand. "Goodbye, Tonto."

I laugh, touched that he remembers. "Goodbye, Kemosabe."

CHAPTER TWENTY-TWO

*wo Months Later*

On my first Saturday off from Milsap's Greenhouse, I work in the flowerbeds surrounding my house. I've become obsessed with weeds over the past weeks, with searching them out, uprooting them, tossing them aside. I'm vigilant in my attack.

Crisp autumn air, thick with buttery sunshine, crinkles and curls against my skin. I smell the sharp promise of winter in the breeze, hear it in the leaves that rustle like stiff orange and yellow petticoats as they dance along the street. At the end of the block, neighborhood children play makeshift hockey in a circular driveway. Their shouts and laughter drift to me, along with the occasional crack of the puck against their wooden sticks.

I've enjoyed every second spent at Milsap's these past three months, and every second I've worked in my own gardens at home. Nanny's stories have finally started to make sense to me, the reasons she spent her life outside with her eyes on the birds, her face in the breeze, her hands in the earth. These are the pulse of life, and there's no escaping the beat, good or bad. Maybe happiness can only be found by moving with the rhythm instead of trying to change it.

Still, I've become as restless as the weather over the past couple of days. Something's missing. Eliot and Will, of course, but something else.

When I hear an engine slowing behind me, I turn to see Eliot's Jeep pulling into the driveway. Releasing a squeal of surprise, I push to my feet and run to meet him. It's his first time home since I left Red Lake.

He emerges from the vehicle grinning, and I throw my arms around him. "Why didn't you tell me you were coming?"

"I wanted to surprise you."

Stepping back, I peek through the Jeep's rear window. "Ohmygosh!" I tug at the back door handle. "Look at how much Will's grown."

My grandson breaks into a smile when I lean in, offering me a toothless, drooling, chubby-cheeked hello. Brilliant and beautiful to behold. Impossible to look at without smiling back. He gurgles and shrieks, pumps his dimpled legs, and opens and closes his fists as I unbuckle him from the carseat.

"Look at you!" I take him out. "Eliot! He's fantastic."

"More like a handful."

"Of course, he is." And an unexpected blessing, I think, as I start for the house, realizing how much I've learned, how much has changed for the better, since he came along. "Let's go in and have something to drink. Are you hungry?"

A half hour later, I give Eliot Nanny's baby blanket that I finished knitting for Will. He thanks me, then heads out to the Jeep for his bags. When he returns, he lays an envelope on the sofa beside me and takes Will from my arms.

I glance at the envelope, frown up at him. "What's this?"

Mark sent it for you. Holding Will up in front of him, he says, "Come on, big guy. Let's find you a bottle." They head for the kitchen, but after only a few steps, Eliot stops and looks back at me. "You know how I had to decide for myself what I wanted?" He pauses, but I only blink at him. "You have to do the same thing for yourself, Mom. And whatever it is, I'm okay with it."

"What's this all about, Eliot?"

His brows lift slightly. "I know, Mom."

My heartbeat kicks up. "What do you mean?"

He gives me an *as-if* look. "I *know*. And I'm good with it."

As he turns toward the kitchen again, the cat appears out of nowhere and hops up onto the sofa beside me. Unsure what to think of Eliot's revelation, I lift the envelope and start to open it, then hesitate.

On my first night at home after leaving Red Lake, Mark called, and I made all the same old excuses. It would be too complicated for us to start seeing each other. Too many other people could get hurt. He disagreed, said everyone in the family except Will was an adult, and if they had a problem with us spending time together, they would just have to get over it. I insisted that I had been alone too long, that I was used to being on my own. I had failed twice before in my only two serious relationships with men. Maybe I wasn't cut out for it.

What I didn't admit is that I'm a coward. Which made no

difference, because Mark already knew that it was fear driving my resistance,

"Everything worthwhile in life is a risk, Maggie," he said.

He called twice the following week, and he's called every night since. We talk about everything except what's really foremost on my mind, and his too, I suspect. Our growing feelings for one another, the fact that they've taken root and not even my sharpest gardening tool could pry them from my heart.

Outside, I hear geese honking far off in the distance. Taking the envelope with me, I go out into the backyard and stare up into the twilight sky, but I can't see the birds. A cool breeze wafts over me as I break the envelope's seal, and I shiver as I lift out a folded piece of paper.

My hands shake a bit as I open the sheet. They continue to shake as I read the printed email message to Mark from Helen Ward, one of the nurses who took care of Will at the hospital in Red Lake.

Hey Mark,

I was wondering how to get in touch with your nephew's mother, Maggie. Do you think she might be interested in a position at the hospital here? There's an opening in labor and delivery. I remember her prior position was as a nursing director, and this would be sort of a step down the ladder from that, but she seemed smart and good with people. Plus, I liked her.

At the bottom of the email, in cursive, Mark has written,

Maggie,

This might be some of that "good stuff" you said your grandmother

mentioned. I hope you'll consider the job. You'd be able to do the kind of work you love most again. Eliot and Will would have you closer. Selfishly on my part, so would I. This over-the-phone stuff isn't enough for me anymore.

Speaking of your grandmother, I've been thinking over what you've told me about her bird stories, and it seems to me she was a very wise woman.

The longer we're apart, the harder it is for me to fly without you. Be my wings. Let me be yours. We could lift each other up. Come back to me.

I love you,

Mark

"Mom?"

I turn. Eliot stands on the patio holding Will in his arms, studying me with a concerned expression. "You're crying. What's wrong?"

"Nothing." I laugh, press the letter to my chest, feel the quick flutter of my heartbeat, the cat rubbing against my ankles.

Eliot lifts something from the concrete. "I wonder where this came from?" He holds up a dark gray feather.

A calm certainty settles over me. My heartbeat slows. "It's a message from Nanny," I tell him, then shift my gaze skyward as the geese call out again.

The End

If you enjoyed this story, please leave a review on Amazon.

And be sure to read *What I Left Behind* - A Novel About Love and Family.

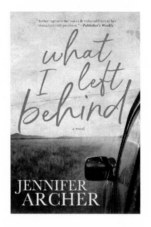

Don't miss the Sneak Peek of *What I Left Behind* on the next page.

SNEAK PEEK OF "WHAT I LEFT BEHIND"
- A NOVEL ABOUT LOVE AND FAMILY

Prologue

pril 6, 2005

Dear Nick,

If you're reading this, my cancer won and my worst fear of leaving you too soon has come true. I want you to know you were my world, the best thing that ever happened to me, my heartbeat. Raising you has been my greatest joy. I wouldn't trade one second of the past sixteen years!

I hope you will meet life's challenges with courage, grasp opportunities with self-confidence and deal with temptations wisely. Always be true to yourself, Nick. You know what's right for you and what isn't. Learn your boundaries and stay within them.

When you were four, you asked about the "little voice" in your head that warned you were about to do something "bad." I said it was God, guiding you. I still believe that. Trust that voice. When you make a mistake, don't beat yourself up like you're so prone to do. You're human, and humans screw up. Learn from your mistakes, then make changes. That's the key to success. We've dealt with some of that already. (You know what I'm talking about). You've come a long way, and I'm proud of you.

Nancy and Randy have a place for you until you're old enough to be on your own. Give them a chance. But, if being with them doesn't turn out to be right for you, I want you to look up a woman named Allyson Cole in Portland. She owes me, and I'm trusting what my heart tells me; that she'll want to know and help you. Read my journals and you'll know me better too. Goodbye, my sweet boy. Be happy. I will always be with you.

I love you,

Mom

CHAPTER 1

Six Weeks Later

I slide a bubbling vegetable pizza from the brick oven, scenting the kitchen's warm air with garlic.

"Allyson?" Joleen, my newest employee, though she's worked here four years, steps up beside me. "There's a lady at the register who wants to say hello."

As Joleen hurries back to work, I set the pizza on the work counter and turn. My heart slides to my toes at the sight of a young woman up front with long auburn hair. But then I realize it isn't this woman Joleen speaks of, but my neighbor Mary Keller, the blonde beside her.

Mary waves and calls, "Hi!"

I smile, wave back, then breathe again.

I've been seeing them everywhere today. On my early morning run before breakfast. In the car next to mine at a light on the way into work. On the sidewalk outside the café when I opened up. Girls and young women with red hair, skin as pale as milk. They're all ages. Gurgling toddlers, gangly, gap-toothed preteens, laughing college students, stressed-out mothers approaching middle age.

Why am I startled each time I catch that flash of color so like autumn leaves? These girls, these women, have stalked me before. Many times. But always, always, each year on this very date. Today of all days, I should expect them.

I've learned only one thing helps drive their image from my mind. Work.

Concentrate, Allyson.

On the aromas of yeast, onion and sweet red pepper, the clatter of pots and pans, the rise and fall of voices and laughter in the adjoining dining room.

Empty your mind.

Get caught up in the rhythm of chopping and spreading, of pouring and slicing.

Behind me, the café hums and buzzes. Today, like all Fridays at the Slender Pea, my gourmet health-food café, the lunch crowd seems noisier than any other day of the week. People are pumped up for the weekend ahead, ready to relax and have fun.

I'm pulling double duty today since Guy Ward, the young man who shares the cooking with me, is off on day five of his weeklong leave of absence. Guy and his wife, Kylie, just had their first child, and he's home getting to know the baby. A girl, by the way. Pink-cheeked, mostly bald and squirmy. A gorgeous, living, breathing doll. And difficult to look at.

At least for me.

Her sparse hair is feathery brown, not red. And though I didn't hold her when I stopped by their house to visit last night, I know exactly how she'd feel tucked in the crook of my arm, a warm, satin weight against my breast. I stared at those tiny fingers, wrapped so tight around Kylie's thumb, and I knew that years from now, when the baby is grown and off living a life of her own, her mother will still feel that gentle grip, that connection.

Work. Concentrate.

When the kitchen wall phone rings for the sixth time, Teena, who is twenty-seven years old and has been with me since I opened the café's doors ten years ago, picks it up as she passes by. "Ally-thon, i'th for you," she says, lisping due to her recent tongue piercing. She presses her palm over the mouthpiece to muffle all the noise. "I'th your thith-ter. Beverly."

As if I don't know my only sister's name. "Tell her I'll call her back when things slow down."

"I can cover for you." Teena jabs the receiver at me. "Here. Joleen hath everything under control out front."

Giving in, though I'd rather not talk to Bev or anyone else right now, I place a second pizza on the work counter behind me. "Thanks. I'll take it in my office. Shout if you need me. And refill the raspberry-tea dispenser, would you?"

I grab a stalk of celery from Teena's hand as I pass by. Seconds later, I collapse in the chair behind my desk and scan the frames lining the opposite wall. There's a magazine photo of me standing in front of the café on the day of the grand opening, certificates proclaiming the Slender Pea Portland's best casual-dining choice for lunch five years running, a newspaper article recounting my "journey to success."

I bite off another chunk of celery, slip on my reading glasses then pick up the phone. "Hey, Bev, what's up?"

"I'm on my break, thank God." As usual, she sounds hurried, dramatic and cynical. All signs that my sister is happy. "After a decade of teaching, my last-period class has me seriously considering a new career."

"Like what?" I ask, knowing she loves her work and would never give it up.

"I'm not sure. Something less stressful. Police work, maybe? Brain surgery?" She sighs. "I was thinking I'd drive over for the weekend and see if you can come up with any better ideas."

My sister lives in Washington. Walla Walla. A long drive

away just to cheer me up. I know that's her true reason for wanting to come.

My appetite gone, I throw the rest of the celery stick into the trash. "If you're worried about me being alone tonight, don't be. Warren and I have a date."

"*Good.*" At my mention of Warren, her voice bounces up. Sometimes I think she likes him even more than she likes me. "I hope he has something special planned. You know, to take your mind off things."

Closing my eyes, I picture the silver streaks in Warren's dark, wavy hair, his teasing blue eyes and runner's body. Not bad for fifty-six. Not bad at all. "He doesn't, but I do."

"Please say you're going to tell him you'll marry him."

"*Marry* him?" Shuffling through a stack of mail, I huff a laugh. "He hasn't asked. Not lately, anyway. He finally knows better. I'm happily single and staying that way. Forever."

"Then what's your big plan?"

"I'm going to ask Warren to move in with me."

Beverly sighs again. "Oh, Ally."

"*What?* I think I'm at least ready to take things that far. That is, if he'll agree to live at my place. I worked hard for that house. I finally have it just how I want it. And, no way am I tackling the junk in my attic again."

"I don't understand why two people who want to live together don't get married."

"No marriage, no divorce. What better reason do you need?"

"Great attitude."

"Marriage is just so…I don't know…*permanent.* What if one of these days I decide I want to move to Timbuktu and he doesn't?"

"Ally…"

I don't have to see my sister to know she's rolling her eyes and twirling a lock of silver-gray hair around her forefinger. She's always been jealous of my slow-to-gray brunette hair, while I've always envied her for doing everything right and in the right order. She met the right guy at the right time—after graduating college with honors—married him and raised two great kids—both girls—then went to work teaching school after they both fled the nest.

"Isn't it Warren taking off to Timbuktu that you're really worried about?" she asks. "History's not going to repeat itself, Ally. You won't wake up some morning and find out he's gone."

"How do you *know* that?"

"Because I know Warren. He's not some immature kid. He's a responsible grown-up who loves you."

"It doesn't matter. Him leaving isn't what worries me. That happened a long time ago. And I'm long over it."

"Then, what's the problem?"

Shoving the mail aside, I chew the inside of my cheek. "I don't know. You just make it sound so simple."

"It's not simple, but it's not as difficult as you make it, either." Bev slips into counselor mode, a role she knows well with me for a sister. "Go into a marriage with the mindset you'll work out any differences you face along the way and, chances are, you will."

I want to believe she's right. I want to marry Warren and live happily ever after, to have what Bev has with her husband. Trust. Stability. A love that endures through the bumpy times as well as the smooth ones. But I'm afraid, for me, that fairy-tale existence is not meant to be. "I've never had a good relationship that lasted. Not even with Mom and Dad. Why should this one be an exception?"

"That's not true. I've known you since I was two years old. Our relationship is good, isn't it?"

I laugh. "You got me there. So, you're different."

"And things could be different with Mom and Dad if you'd forgive them. They aren't getting any younger, Ally. They know they handled things badly. They've been beating themselves up over it ever since." Her voice softens. "I'm sorry. I know it's hard. But it's been a long time."

My heart closes off at the mention of my parents and forgiveness in the same breath. *Tough luck,* I think. *Too little, too late.* "Don't start with me about that, Bev. Not today."

For several seconds she doesn't say anything, then asks, "What prompted this decision about Warren?"

I swivel my chair to look out the window. Not a redhaired female in sight on the street beyond. No green eyes boring into me. Accusing, questioning, dismissing. Maybe it's a sign. "It's time I moved on, don't you think?"

"What do you mean?"

My throat knots. "She's thirty-five years old today, Bev. *Thirty-five.* If my daughter wanted to meet me, I would've heard from her by now. I made it easy enough for her to find me. All she has to do is contact the adoption agency. I have to quit waiting for a phone call that'll never come."

A family that will never exist.

"She could still contact you." My sister sounds concerned and as sad and doubtful as I feel. "But you're right that it's time to move on. You've got to quit punishing yourself. Allow some happiness into your life that doesn't involve work." She pauses.

"Warren's going to want to get married. You know that, don't you? You can't put him off forever."

"Who knows…maybe some day." I smile. "When I'm older."

Beverly snorts. "Older?"

"Okay, so we can twine rosebuds around my walker for the trip down the aisle."

"*Trip* being the word of concern here. It'd be nice if you married while your vision's still strong enough to see your groom smiling at the end of that aisle."

I cock my head to one side and drum my fingertips on the desktop. "Think about it. Something old, something new, something borrowed, something blue. Warren could be the something old and my hair could be the something blue. Blue-gray, that is."

"Tacky."

As if on cue, Teena pokes her dyed-pink head into the office. "Ally, we have a problem out front."

"Hey! Here's the something I can borrow now. Teena's nose ring. It'll look great with my blue hair."

Scowling, Teena mumbles something about my sanity. "Ally, I'm ther-iouth. You know that little roach problem we're having?"

"Roaches?" Beverly says with disgust. "Did I hear Teena say you've got roaches?"

"Water bugs, not roaches." I scowl at Teena. "And only one. A *tiny* one. When you run a restaurant they go with the territory. They come in with the boxes of food. You just have to stay on top of it."

Teena sniffs. "A cuth-tomer just found our one *water bug* thwimming in hith thoup."

Groaning, I remind myself to call the exterminator again when I hang up. "Tell him no extra charge for the added protein. And lunch is on me."

"No way." Shaking her head, Teena turns to leave. "You tell him."

I groan again. "Gotta go, Bev. I have to see a man about a bug."

After I pop the question to Warren, we decide to skip dinner and go straight to dessert.

He dips a strawberry into the whipped cream, slips it into my mouth then unbuttons the top of my blouse. "Why do you want us to live together, Ally?" His eyes hold mine.

Leaning back against the bed pillows, I swallow the strawberry and reach for his waistband. "Because of your great —" grinning, I grab his belt buckle "—big—" I begin to unfasten it "—*throbbing*—" I slide the belt through the first loop "—heart." Warren chuckles, and I add, "Because we're good together."

He frees the second button of my blouse, his knuckles skimming across the sensitive space between my breasts. "Try again."

I close my eyes, feel the third button release. "Because I'm ready. Because we have fun." *And you made me feel beautiful... young...alive.* My breath catches as he opens the clasp between my bra cups. "Because I can't stand waking up in the morning without you beside me."

"Not good enough," he mutters just before his lips brush across the top of one breast. "Try again."

Seconds pass in a silence broken only by the sound of his breathing and mine. "Because I love you," I finally whisper.

His head lifts. I open my eyes, and he looks into them, grinning the dimpled grin I adore. "Finally. It took you long enough."

It's true. I love Warren Noble. Funny, fabulous, fifty-six-year-old divorced father of two grown kids. Wonderful conversationalist who challenges me. Skilled surgeon with a great bedside manner both in and out of the hospital. Marathon runner. Owner of magic hands. And my heart. I love him. I'm fifty-two years old and, until now, I've never said those words to any man. Only to a boy of eighteen, and I was sixteen at the time. A girl, not a woman.

Now…after all these years.

It's as if a part of my soul that I've locked away too long has finally been freed. I'm laughing and crying and kissing him, and I can't stop; I don't want to stop.

Warren laughs, too. "Marry me, Ally," he says between kisses.

Oh, God. Bev's psychic. "Warren—"

"I've been waiting a long time."

"Not so long." Only nine months since the first time he asked. Then again three months later. After that, he quit trying.

"It *feels* like forever. We shouldn't just live together, we should make it official. I want the world to know you love me." He places his hands at either side of my face, slides his fingers into my hair, pushing it back. "This sexy, smart, fantastic woman *loves* me. And I love her." Our foreheads touch. "So much. I love you so much, Ally."

His lips taste salty from my tears. Salty and tender and oh, so sweet.

"Will you marry me?" he asks in a voice as quiet and warm as the May night outside my bedroom window.

A *yes* wavers at the tip of my tongue. I'm still terrified, but I know it's the right answer. The only answer. I was crazy to believe we could ever do anything else. "Yes," I say quietly, then laugh and shout, "*Yes!*"

He pulls me into his arms.

"When?" I ask. "Where?"

"This weekend. I don't want to wait and give you a chance to change your mind. We'll fly to Vegas tomorrow afternoon. Hell, we'll fly to Hawaii, if you want, and say our vows barefoot in the sand."

Scooting off the bed, I stand and press my fingers to my mouth, unable to believe this is happening or how excited and crazy young I feel. Like I'm starting over. Like anything's possible. Like everything that's happened in my life was for a reason. To lead me to this place where I belong, to this man, and now I can put the past behind me.

I decide to call Teena and ask her to handle things at the café, then remember I'm catering a bridesmaid luncheon on Sunday afternoon. "Oh, no, honey, I'm sorry." I wince at him. "I can't leave this weekend. We have something going on at the Pea on Sunday. I can't get out of it."

"Can't Teena and Joleen handle things? They won't mind when you tell them you'll be on your honeymoon."

I start pacing. "It's for the mayor's daughter. Her bridesmaid luncheon. I've never left Teena and Joleen and Guy alone to do something so big. This might not be the best event to start with." I bite my lip. "I don't know."

When I pass by him, Warren grabs my hand and tugs me

back onto the bed. "Let me convince you." The doorbell rings. He nibbles my neck. "Ignore it."

I wrap my arms around him.

The doorbell rings again. And again.

"Damn," he mutters.

Letting go of him, I lean back. The bell rings a fourth time. "I'll get rid of them."

"Hurry."

I refasten my bra and start to work on the buttons of my blouse as I head through the bedroom and into the living room. The hardwood floors are cool beneath my bare feet. In the entry hall, I flip on the porch light then look through the front-door peephole.

A boy wearing a sweat-stained backward ball cap stands on the other side of the door, staring down at his shoes. I guess his age to be fifteen, sixteen at the most. Here to sell me something for a school fundraiser, most likely. I hope it's that and not one of those poor dropouts who come around peddling magazine subscriptions. I hate seeing kids in that situation, hate turning them away when they look like they're on their last dime. Inevitably, I end up with more subscriptions to add to my ever-growing pile of magazines I'll never have time to read.

I unlock the door and open it just wide enough to peer out. "Hello."

He has a tiny gold loop earring in his left ear. The shaggy tufts of hair curling out beneath the bottom of his cap are light brown.

"Miss Cole?"

Something about the shade and shape of his restless green eyes is familiar. Hauntingly so. "Yes?"

"Allyson Cole?"

I nod. "Can I help you?"

His eyes change, become as hard and cold as emeralds, sending a tiny shock of alarm straight through me. That's when I notice the large duffel bag at his feet. Lifting it, he steps closer to the door and shoots me a cocky grin. "Hello, Grandma," he says. "I'm Nick. Nicholas Pearson."

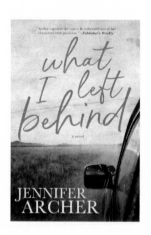

Get Your Copy of "What I Left Behind on Amazon"

ALSO BY JENNIFER ARCHER

WOMEN'S FICTION

Sandwiched

Off Her Rocker

YOUNG ADULT FICTION

Through Her Eyes

The Shadow Girl

CHILDREN'S PICTURE BOOK

A Zack Attack: The Shenanigans of a Picky Eater

NON-FICTION

Happiness Rehab: 8 Creative Steps to a More Joyful Life

ROMANTIC COMEDY

Make A Little Magic Series

Spark A Little Flame (Book 1)

Dream A Little Dream (Book 2)

CONNECT WITH JENNIFER ON AMAZON

Kindle Readers: Sign up to follow me on Amazon to be notified of new releases as they become available. Once you arrive on my Amazon Author page, just click the yellow "Follow" button below my picture.

GET A FREE NOVELLA - SUBSCRIBE TO MY NEWSLETTER

*N*ever miss a new release by signing up for my newsletter at http://www.jenniferarcher.com/newsletter/. When you do, I'll send you a link to download my novella, "Take a Little Risk."

I'll never spam you and will only reach out when there is important information to share or a new release.

I can't wait to connect with you!

ABOUT THE AUTHOR

Jennifer Archer is the author of numerous fiction and non-fiction works. Her novels have been nominated for Romance Writers of America's prestigious Rita Award and Romantic Times Bookclub's Reviewer's Choice Award. In 2013, the Texas Library Association selected her debut young adult novel, Through Her Eyes, for their first spirit of Texas Reading Program – Middle School, and for the TAYSHAS High School reading list. Jennifer enjoys teaching creativity and creative writing workshops. She also writes and edits for clients through her business, Archer Editing & Writing Services (archereditingandwriting.com). She lives in Texas with her husband and three dogs.

If you want to read more about Jennifer or if you're curious about when her next book will come out, please visit her website at: http://www.jenniferarcher.com, where you can sign up to receive email notifications about new releases.

Connect with Jennifer on social media, visit her website, or email her.

facebook.com/Jennifer-Archer-159335414094711

twitter.com/jenniferarcher1

instagram.com/jenniferarcher01

bookbub.com/authors/jennifer-archer

Made in United States
North Haven, CT
20 May 2023

36770133R00186